BONE
DEEP

BONE DEEP

DEBRA WEBB

"Debra Webb is a master storyteller."
-Allison Brennan, New York Times Bestseller

"Debra Webb's name says it all."
-Karen Rose, New York Times Bestseller

PINK
HOUSE
PRESS

Copyright 2013 Debra Webb, Pink House Press, Webbworks, LLC

ISBN: 0692250115
ISBN 13: 9780692250112

This book is dedicated to my daughter, Erica Green. Thank you for helping bring this story to life. May you have a long and successful career following in my footsteps as a storyteller.

PROLOGUE

Sunday, July 10, 9 p.m.

Blood…so much blood.

She peered down at her hands, marveling at the thick, warm fluid that seeped between her fingers, slipped along her arms. Her heart slammed mercilessly against her ribcage, sending her own blood gushing through her veins.

She blinked, tried to focus.

He was dead.

She stared at the motionless body on the floor. A pool of crimson encircled the still torso.

Dead.

She inclined her head and stared at the knife buried deep in his chest.

She'd killed him.

CHAPTER ONE

Jillian Ellington watched an elderly couple stroll along the sidewalk on the east side of the historic town square. Why their slow, steady pace mesmerized her so defied logic. At Pritchard's Pharmacy, the man held the door and smiled as the woman entered the store ahead of him.

It was the same wherever she looked. Life went on as if nothing had changed. It felt wrong to her that the rest of the world hadn't paused for more than a second or two to observe the tragic, life-shattering event that had turned hers upside down. Mothers walked hand-in-hand with their children on the sidewalks. Traffic continued to flow. Shoppers shopped. Unreasonably, she resented and, at the same time, envied their innocence to the horror that had invaded her existence.

This was a mistake.

Disgusted, she powered up the windows and started the engine once more. Hot air blasted from the vents. It wasn't even noon and already the temperature was a sweltering ninety degrees. She'd been sitting in her car, parked across the street from city hall, for more than an hour. Her frustration level had maxed out.

He was late. The big deal investigator who was supposed to be exactly the advantage she needed to prove her twin sister hadn't murdered her husband, and maybe her three-year-old son, was thirty-two minutes late. Jill closed her eyes and rode out the wave of dread and apprehension that threatened. Her sister was in a coma and her three-year-old nephew was missing. And the so-called miracle worker who was supposed to help was a no show.

God, she was tired. Most of last night was spent on the internet doing research on the guy. After what she'd discovered she shouldn't be surprised that he hadn't shown but this was what desperation did to the most rational human. She waited, clinging to an unraveling thread of hope that a stranger, a profoundly damaged one by all reports, would actually turn out to be the miracle she needed.

Deep breath. *Didn't help.* First thing this morning she should have called Richard Lawton, her old friend and law professor, and told him to cancel this meeting. What had he been thinking recommending this guy? Admittedly, Richard had gotten her on the calendar with an excellent attorney. Cullen Marks was the best criminal attorney in the state. His Nashville firm had a reputation for always winning. A quick call from Richard and Marks was ready to accept her sister's case. But, Richard had insisted Jill needed more than a topnotch attorney. She needed an investigator who would look beyond the official investigation.

Problem was the one he recommended seemed so far off what she had expected that she'd almost called Richard back in the middle of the night to demand an explanation. All that prevented her from picking up the phone and doing just that right now was the irrefutable fact that Richard had never steered her wrong. Not once.

Jill sagged against the headrest and let the cool air wash over her. Their relationship had started as one of diligent law professor and eager student, but had quickly developed into more. Regret trickled through her. No one had been to blame, not really. It simply happened. Her father had died and she'd needed someone to fill that void—one that had started expanding well before his death.

Though she'd left home practically before the ink dried on her high school diploma, Jill could still remember the look of stark disappointment on her father's face. He hadn't agreed with her decision and they had scarcely spoken after that. His death had hit her hard.

She forced herself to breathe. Blinked back the emotions that crowded in on her even now when she thought of her father.

The relationship with her mother was an entirely different story. She and Jill had never been close. That position had belonged to her sister, Kate. Another old, familiar ache swelled inside Jill.

"Jesus." Why was she rehashing ancient history? Her nephew was missing. Her sister was in serious trouble on more than one level. And Jill wasn't sure she could fix any of it.

As an attorney she was aware of the pitfalls of emotional involvement in a case, yet, with every fiber of her being she needed to do something. To be out there searching for her nephew. Her chest ached. To be at her sister's bedside trying to reach her. Kate would never have harmed her child. The entire concept was utterly ridiculous.

The ache in her chest twisted deeper. How could Cody have simply vanished? Surely someone had seen or heard something.

The real question was why hadn't *she* been here?

No matter how logically Jill considered the situation, it felt exactly as if it was her fault. She should have been here. Tears burned her eyes. Why hadn't she come home two months ago when her sister called and practically begged her to visit? Jill had sensed Kate's urgency even then. But she'd been too busy with work to worry about her sister, the stay at home mother and wife. The perfect daughter.

Jill had opted not to worry. Kate had their mother, who hovered over her like a secret service team monitoring the president. What did she need with Jill? In her defense, the caseload just kept getting in the way in spite of her best intentions. On the rare occasions when she managed time for a visit to Paradise all those old feelings of inadequacy and failure resurrected. She never measured up. Felt unwanted, like an outsider.

So she avoided coming more often than not.

A decades old hurt tightened around her chest, making it hard to breathe. As children, she and her sister had been inseparable. The Appalachian Mountains that bordered their little town held a kind of magic about them. A mystique that went beyond the clouds that hugged their craggy peaks and the greenery that draped their sloping shoulders. She and Kate had played like little faeries, flitting from one secret place in the woods and meadows to another. Jill had gone over every one of those secret places with the chief of police. There was no sign of her nephew at any of those locations.

How could one little boy be so hard to find in such a small town—a place where everyone knew everyone else?

Each hour that Cody remained missing lessened the likelihood of his being found unharmed. Along with most of Paradise's police force, three teams of local citizens were out looking for him. An Amber Alert had been issued. Cody's picture had run on the area news channels along with a plea for help in finding him. The chief had assured her there was nothing else to be done—except pray and she'd done plenty of that.

An older model Land Rover that had once been white parked at the curb behind Jill's Lexus. She drew her thoughts away from the hurt and focused on her rear-view mirror. It was *him*. About damned time. According to Richard, Dr. Paul Phillips could be the answer to her prayers. As much as she wanted to believe her old friend was right, she'd read too much last night to be encouraged.

Richard hadn't exaggerated Phillips' reputation, at least not from the early years of his career as a forensic psychologist with the FBI. His list of solved cases from a decade ago was incredible. Countless families and their hometown law enforcement spokespersons had chalked solving the unsolvable up to Dr. Paul Phillips, the man with the sixth sense. Some had called him a phenomenon. He, apparently, could see and feel beyond the obvious. Richard had called him special and gifted.

That was where the good news ended. Around five years ago, at the very height of his rise into celebrity status, he'd had some sort of breakdown and fallen off the radar, only to resurface as a sort of psychic advisor for hire in Memphis. He took few cases, charged exuberant prices and failed a whopping forty percent of the time. Hit after hit about his being inebriated at a reading or failing to show had infuriated her. Her fingers tightened on the steering wheel. How could Richard do this to her when she needed his help the most?

Jill watched in her side mirror as Phillips emerged from the SUV. *Deep, deep breath.* Out of respect for her friend, she would give Phillips an hour. Whatever Richard had paid him to come here, she would gladly reimburse.

Phillips stopped at her door. Asking for ID wasn't necessary. Richard had given her the make of his vehicle and pictures of him had been splattered all over the web. This was definitely the man…the *freak*, as some had called him.

Dismissing all else, Jill powered down her window and met his hooded gaze. "I'm Jillian Ellington. Why don't you join me, Dr. Phillips, and we'll talk?" She hit the unlock button.

He gave her a negligible nod before starting around the hood. Her heart sank. Even her low expectations had been a little high. The doctor wore jeans that had seen better days and a wrinkled shirt along with a sports jacket likely leftover from his heyday. He hadn't shaved in a couple of days and though he'd barely made eye contact, Jill had seen enough hung-over witnesses to know a man suffering from long term alcohol abuse.

Oh God. This was such a mistake and yet it was the only option she had at the moment.

He dropped into the passenger seat. When he'd closed the door, he stared forward rather than looking at her as if anticipating a lecture for some wrongdoing.

Oh yeah. He was just sober enough this morning to feel guilty for being late or maybe for existing. Great.

Just get this done.

"I appreciate your coming all this way." Since he hadn't bothered so much as a glance at her, she settled her attention on the row of shops that lined the street opposite city hall. Phillips would certainly demand his full fee whether he was here five minutes or all day. There was no reason for her to regret the four-hour drive from Memphis he'd made at what he no doubt considered an ungodly hour. "I apologize for meeting like this but things are…" What was the proper term for a place that was ones childhood home but where one felt like an uninvited stranger? "Things are tense at my mother's."

"No problem."

His words rumbled through her, made her suddenly uneasy sitting here alone with him in the close confines of the car. Or maybe it was the idea that he seemed unable to muster enough wherewithal to summon a professional response.

As if sensing her dismay, he tacked on, "Your *friend* explained the situation when he called."

There was no mistaking the hint of sarcasm and accusation in his tone. Irritation inched its way up her spine. *Her friend?* "Dr. Lawton is a good friend." She turned and stared at his profile. "I have a great deal of respect for his opinion." The Lawton name was a powerful one in the field of law. Just now *she* needed to bear that in mind.

Phillips hesitated then met her gaze. It was the first time she'd actually gotten a good look at his face. Tension coiled more tightly. The photos on the internet failed to convey the raw edges and hard angles revealed by an up close encounter in the bright light of day. His dark eyes were guarded. His mouth remained set in a grim line, yet his face was attractive in a way that promised carnal acts.

She blinked, cleared the static from her mind and got to the point. "I won't waste your time, Dr. Phillips. Every squandered moment could mean the difference between finding my nephew alive and" she swallowed in hopes of loosening her throat, "the alternative. Do you believe you can help me or not?"

Whatever his internal reaction to her blunt approach, he kept it carefully checked. Those dark eyes remained unreadable. "They have the murder weapon? Prints?" His tone was hard, impatient.

The urge to cry came swiftly, unbidden, and from a place too deep inside her to touch or restrain. Was he trying to alienate her? "I'm certain you know the answers to those questions the same as I do."

"Whatever you think you know," he stared forward once more, "in most cases, it *is* one of the parents who harms the child. The sooner you face that strong probability, the better off you'll be."

Logically she knew he was correct, but with every fiber of her being she believed he was wrong. Her determination rallied. "My sister did not do this. I *know* she didn't. At the moment my first priority is finding my nephew. Are you here to help me or not?" Despite the shot of fortitude, the words came out too vulnerable, too brittle.

He turned to her again, stared at her for a stretch of time that felt far too much like forever. Maybe it was the mix of emotions churning inside her or the sheer insanity of the situation but the scent of soap…of well-worn cotton and a hint of tobacco suddenly overtook her, stole her breath.

"I *know* what you and people like you think of me, Miss Ellington." He lifted one shoulder in a listless shrug. "You're entitled to your opinion. But don't expect me to sugarcoat the obvious."

As if the band around her chest had suddenly sprung loose, she sucked in a breath. Before she could assimilate a coherent response, he went on, "Just so we understand each other, I don't take cases like this anymore." He shifted his attention back to the street. "But I'm here. I'll have a look and give you my assessment. Then I'm gone." His gaze fixed on hers once more, jolting her as surely as if he'd touched her. "Does that work for you?"

Frustration beat against her sternum. For a few seconds she had to hold her tongue to prevent telling him to get the hell out of her car. But Richard had sent this guy and, if there was any chance whatsoever that he could help, she needed him. "That is…acceptable."

At least the messy part was out of the way.

Paul had hoped she would tell him to get screwed and he could get the hell out of here. No such luck. The sooner he took a look at what the local cops had the sooner he was out of here. Couldn't happen fast enough to suit him.

After this he and Lawton were done. The old bastard had called in his marker and Paul was here.

Five minutes in her presence and already he understood this was going to be bad.

Mostly for him.

The woman said something he didn't catch, probably just as well, then she got out of the car. He did the same. Get this over with and get on the road. First stop was a chat with the chief of police. It wouldn't take him long to see what he needed to see.

All he had to do was make himself look.

He barely restrained a laugh at the idea of how easy that sounded.

Get your shit together, man.

Jillian Ellington had done her research and she didn't like what she'd found on the net about him. It wasn't necessary to ask if she'd read all that crap. The answer was right there in the arrogant tilt of her chin. Well, he'd checked her out too. Graduated at the top of her class from Ole Miss Law School and was immediately recruited by Carlisle, Jacobs, and Teller, the most prestigious law firm in Mississippi. They rarely recruited right out of law School, preferring wisdom gained from experience over knowledge gleaned from textbooks. The offer spoke highly of the uptight lady.

Never been married. On the other hand, the sister, Katherine, had completed her education right here in Paradise at Kessler University, a private school whose national academic standing rivaled its much larger Ivy League counterparts. The sister had stayed in Paradise, accepting a position at MedTech, a huge medical research conglomerate. Four years ago she'd married the CEO, Karl Manning. Together they had a son, Cody.

Claire Ellington, the mother, still lived in the family home. Parker, the father and a long time, highly respected county judge, had died seven years ago. That was the extent of the information available on the Ellingtons. The dead husband, Karl Manning, had grown up in Boston. He'd attended Harvard and after graduation had joined an uncle who was the founder of MedTech. The research facility had garnered a renowned reputation in the area of stem cell research. It was all good. Tidy and forthright.

A quiet little Tennessee town where bad things never happened and peopled with fine, upstanding folks. Yet one had committed murder. And the other—the one in the blue dress that fit like a glove and the high heels that made her almost tall enough to look him square in the eye and with whom he kept pace—appeared to be estranged from her family as well as her hometown. Being here made it difficult for her to breathe. He could feel the anxiety tightening around her. There was something bad hanging over this family.

What the hell was he doing here?

Lawton was way too smart to have called in his marker for a case as blatantly cut and dried as this one. There had to be more. Paul glanced at the woman at his side. She was more than an old friend and student. Paul didn't need a hit on Google to tell him the old man had a soft spot for the lady any more than he needed a news flash to inform him what her first impression of him amounted to. She distrusted and disliked him. Her conclusions about him radiated from her as thick and oppressive as the heat rising from the asphalt.

Good. No worry that she would beg him to stay.

"Is your chief going to give us any trouble?" Might as well get down to business. A glance at the ME's report and maybe the crime scene investigator's report would be useful.

"I'm certain he'll be cooperative."

In Paul's experience most small town cops didn't like outsiders horning in on their investigations, especially ones that involved high profile citizens. Maybe this one would be the exception. Whatever. All his deal with Lawton required of him was to take a look. Nothing more.

"I'll want to see everything they've got in the way of reports or evidence. Photos. The body."

Her breath hitched. She tried concealing the reaction by clearing her throat. She wasn't quite as tough as she wanted him to believe. "I'm sure all that can all be arranged."

Sounded like the lady wasn't worried. Maybe her little town would live up to its reputation and prove him wrong. He'd done some research on Paradise too. *Southern Living* magazine had dubbed it the epitome of southern small town charm. Most of the residents were affluent with deep roots in the community, which was, from all reports, close knit. Though the city was certainly no tourist mecca, the magazine espoused Paradise's genteel way of life as generating an immediate sense of security and serenity.

Denial burgeoned in his chest, sharp and demanding. He rolled his neck side to side, to relieve some of the sudden tension. Stretched his back... but the heavy feeling in his chest wouldn't abate. A sense of foreboding made it difficult to draw in a reasonable breath.

It had started.

He gritted his teeth and worked at keeping the crushing sensations at bay.

Just before he entered Paradise proper he'd caught a glimpse of an old abandoned warehouse set back from the main road. The dilapidated structure loomed in the distance, looking like a strong wind would topple it. Despite its fragility, something about it felt potent. The feeling was so gripping he had slowed to look more closely.

There was a story behind that place, one intrinsically tied to this town.

"There's an abandoned mill or factory just outside town," he said, drawing Ellington to a stop as she reached the entrance to city hall.

"The old Benford Plant. I don't know why they don't tear it down. At one time most of the residents of Paradise depended on that plant for a living. But it shut down more than thirty years ago." Her eyebrows drew together. "Why do you ask?"

"Curious." He rubbed the back of his neck, warned himself to keep the darkness at bay until absolutely necessary. "It seemed out of place." From all appearances, Paradise lived up to its name in spite of whatever setbacks it had suffered in the past.

"That must've been a real blow to the economy at the time."

"MedTech, a medical research corporation, and the LifeCycle Center, a state of the art fertility clinic, moved in shortly after that," she explained, "providing even more and better jobs. Paradise has thrived since."

MedTech he knew about since Karl Manning had been the CEO. LifeCycle he'd missed. A looming granite structure that reigned over the town housed the MedTech facility. They were proud of the position and power they held in the town.

That uneasy feeling in his chest spread lower, twisting his gut. The air was fresh, cleaner and cooler than in Memphis. The streets were tree-lined, with lots of attractive landscaping and splashes of color from blooming flowers and plants. Very little crime was reported. The Manning murder had likely shaken the town to its foundation. Maybe he was picking up on that uneasiness. A town chockfull of anxiety and burdened by a truckload of uncharacteristic suspicions.

"The chief is waiting."

When she spoke Paul realized he had stalled at the door. He shook off the feeling of dread that had curled around him the second he entered the city limits. Whatever was nagging at him remained too murky to make sense of just yet.

Inside city hall a sign welcomed visitors with the motto: *We're all family in Paradise.* He wondered if they would consider him family after he told them what he wanted to see. He rolled his shoulders again to release his cramped muscles. He purposely kept his gaze away from Ellington. Not that looking at her was a hardship. Silky blond hair and pale blue eyes. There was something about her, besides a damned hot body, that undermined his control on a level he couldn't quite label. That was a major issue. He could not exist without absolute control. Some aspect of this case…or maybe her…was already splintering his ability to focus.

No matter what she said or what she thought of him, she badly needed him to solve this mystery, find her nephew and absolve her sister of wrongdoing. He might solve the mystery, but he couldn't absolve her sister. And he damned sure wouldn't find the kid. He'd helped find the last dead child he ever intended to. Statistics were not on her side where the kid was concerned. He was probably dead, whether by the mother's hand or the father's.

Paul wouldn't go there. Not ever again.

Inside, Ellington greeted the receptionist in the main lobby, then headed down the wide corridor to the right. Paul followed a couple of steps behind. The uneasiness climbed another notch. The warning—too distant to comprehend just yet—started echoing in his brain.

Ellington walked directly to the chief of police's suite without hesitating or waiting for Paul to catch up. "Good morning, Lucy. Has there been any word on my nephew?" Ellington managed a tight smile for the secretary, but her true emotions telegraphed loudly. She was scared. Scared and alone…those were the vibes he got from her.

It was way too soon to have a potential client get to him like this. He shouldn't be here. His hands shook. He curled his fingers into his palms and ordered the sensation away.

Lucy's wide, practiced smile dimmed momentarily. "No, I'm sorry, Miss Jill. But don't you worry, they're not going to give up. They'll find him." Her expression brightened once more as she looked past Jill to Paul, expecting an introduction.

"The chief is expecting me," Ellington said, drawing the woman's attention back to her but choosing not to make any intros.

"He sure is." She flashed a wide smile for Paul. "You and your friend just go right on back. I'll let the chief know you're here."

Paul gifted Lucy with a smile, the one he reserved for making himself memorable in the event he might need future cooperation. In this instance it was a waste of energy since he wouldn't be staying. A tic snapped into a steady cadence next to his left eye, keeping time with the pulsing tension in his gut.

The corridor was lined with doors on either side. His guide slowed about midway. She took a breath and gestured to the open door farther down. "How should I introduce you?"

He suspected asshole was at the top of her list. "Just get the conversation started and I'll jump in."

She nodded, those blue eyes shimmering with the emotions he had sensed her hiding beneath that calm, well groomed exterior. The lady was on the edge. It was tough to watch anyone fall over that ledge, particularly someone like her. She worked hard to ensure no one saw her vulnerable side but she was losing this battle.

He hated this part...the desperation...the neediness on the part of the victim's families. They wanted something he couldn't give. The only thing he did these days was play the part. For the money. Even that he did only on his terms. Damn Lawton for putting him in this position.

Play the part. Just play the part.

As they entered the chief's office the man behind the cluttered desk stood. "Miss Jill, I sure wish I had some news for you but," he spared a glance in Paul's direction, "unfortunately, we're still coming up empty-handed in our search for little Cody."

"I appreciate your diligence, chief." Ellington gestured toward Paul. "Chief Dotson, this is—"

"Dr. Paul Phillips," he interrupted. He extended his hand across the desk. "It's a pleasure to meet you, chief."

The older man gave Paul's hand a hearty pump. "Are you the specialist Miss Jill ordered from Nashville?" He gestured to the chairs flanking his desk. "Please, have a seat, both of you."

Ellington perched on the edge of her seat, her back rigid. Paul settled into his chair and mentally braced. The climate in the room was about to change. "Actually I'm an advisor associated with the Federal Bureau of Investigation. I'm here to speak with you regarding the Manning case." Five years ago his claim wouldn't have been an outright lie.

The chief's complexion lost a little color. He blinked rapidly to cover his surprise. "Why would the FBI want to talk to me?" He turned to Ellington. "Miss Jill, is there something you haven't shared with me?"

Though visibly startled by his announcement, she recovered quickly. "Absolutely not, chief. I'm—"

"I contacted Miss Ellington," Paul interjected, taking her off the hook. "I'd like to review your reports from the Medical Examiner, if available, and those from the crime scene. I'll be happy to provide you with my insights which are usually very helpful in these situations." He inclined his head and offered a sympathetic expression. "I know you'd like to get this ugly business tidied up as quickly as possible."

Chief Dotson bobbed his head up and down, then seemed to catch himself. "That's the God's truth. This tragedy is turning our Paradise into purgatory." He hesitated a moment, the uncertainty and confusion gaining new ground. "But I'm not sure we can honor your request, Dr. Phillips. After all, this is an ongoing investigation and I haven't seen any sort of official request from the FBI or anyone else."

"My point exactly, chief." Paul gave a succinct nod. "We don't want to wait until jurisdiction comes into question and subpoenas are issued. MedTech is a sensitive situation. Medical research is no longer simply a tax write off, it's a huge money making industry. If there is any possibility that economic espionage is involved, we want all your ducks in a row." With the CEO of a major medical research corporation murdered, it was certainly within the realm of possibility to speculate that the Feds could get involved at some point.

A flush crept up from the collar of the chief's crisply starched uniform and spread across his face as the potential for complications settled in. "Whatever you need, Dr. Phillips. I am more than happy to cooperate. That's the way we do things here in Paradise."

CHAPTER TWO

To Jill's astonishment, when they exited the police department, Phillips carried a file containing copies of all pertinent reports and crime scene photos. The chief had agreed to meet them at the hospital and accompany him to view the body.

Jill restrained the full impact of her disbelief until they were in the SUV, seat belts locked in place. Phillips had insisted on taking his vehicle which seemed somehow prudent now. She was too stunned to focus on driving. "How did you do that?" As much as she hated to admit it, she was impressed. The chief hadn't even shared all that with her.

Phillips checked his rear-view mirror then pulled out onto the street. "Lots of practice."

A frown needled its way across her brow. She resisted the urge to rub at it. "Are you really still involved with the Bureau?" From what she'd read, he'd only worked with the Bureau once or twice since the breakdown or whatever.

He braked for a traffic light. "Does it matter?"

She shrugged and relaxed a little for the first time in more than twenty-four hours. Part of her wanted to be outraged that he had obviously lied to the chief, but she had to remember that Richard had faith in him. And she was up against the wall here. The least she could do was see this through. Doing something was better than doing nothing. "Guess not. I'm probably better off not knowing any more than necessary."

"Good answer."

A shiver raced over her skin at the sound of his voice. Deep and husky, a little rough from the hangover. She wished she could chalk up her uncharacteristic reaction to fear or anxiety, but she'd only be kidding herself. It was him. He made her edgy. That he prompted any sort of reaction in her other than frustration was maddening and clearly a mistake. The kind of mistake Kate would never make.

Jill squeezed her eyes shut and shoved the thoughts away. She had to get a better handle on her emotions. No one else was going to step up to the plate. Certainly not her mother. This case was already closed in the chief's opinion. Finding the truth was up to her and her alone.

As Phillips drove, he reached into an interior jacket pocket and pulled out a pack of Marlboros. She started to protest but somehow got caught up just watching him. He shook out a cigarette and tucked it in one corner of his mouth, then dug around in another pocket for a lighter. With one flick he lit it, her nose wrinkled in disgust. Thankfully, he lowered the window on his side of the vehicle to draw out the smoke.

So this was why he'd insisted on taking his own vehicle. He caught her looking at him and she quickly turned away.

"You might not like it," he commented dryly, "but I don't think you could tolerate my company otherwise."

There was a lot she could say to that. Instead, she said nothing. Whatever he had to offer on her sister's case, she wanted it. That decision had been confirmed as soon as she'd witnessed his interaction with the chief.

"I don't mind." A flat out lie.

He smoked his cigarette without bothering to respond. She watched the landscape, providing the necessary directions when required for reaching their destination. He parked next to the chief's cruiser in the hospital parking lot and they followed him inside. The chief prattled on about the weather and some movie involving the FBI he'd seen recently. He asked Phillips if the FBI really did things like that. Jill only half listened. She thought of her sister on the fourth floor, locked away in the psychiatric ward. Jill wondered if she had awakened. The doctor called Kate's condition a complete psychotic break. Whatever happened in Kate's home on Sunday evening, she had mentally checked out.

Jill allowed another painful reality to surface. There had been a time when she felt what her sister felt, could practically read her mind. Not so unusual for twins. The connection had been strong. But no more. Her efforts to set herself apart—to be unique—had worked a little too well. If only she'd known how much she would need that connection now. But hindsight was twenty-twenty. After Jill left Paradise, she hadn't looked back period.

Inside the hospital they took the elevator to the basement. The chief avoided the stairs. Bad on his knees. Had to save them for his golf game, he'd added with a chuckle.

The basement corridor reminded Jill of one she'd experienced in nightmares as a kid. Her palms were sweating. She swiped them on her dress as she moved down the long passageway with its shiny tile floors and pipes of varying sizes snaking their way overhead. She hated the way it smelled, and the eerie fluorescent lighting that wasn't quite as bright as it should be. The whole atmosphere gave her the creeps.

They paused at the morgue door and the chief knocked.

"I think I'll just…" Jill tried to think of a reasonable excuse, but nothing came. Her heart pounded against her ribcage like a boxer's fist slamming his glove into his opponent's face. She couldn't go in there. Not again. She'd identified the body, like everyone in town didn't know Karl Manning. She had no desire to see him again. "I'll just wait out here."

"Good idea, Miss Jill," the chief offered kindly. "You've been through this once already."

Paul silently agreed with the chief. For different reasons, of course. He operated best without an audience. Her presence would only slow him down.

When the morgue door opened a young man wearing a white lab coat greeted them with a look of surprise. He had an iPod in his shirt pocket and ear buds hanging around his neck.

"Hey, chief, what's up?"

"Randy, we're here to see Karl," the chief explained.

Randy waved his arm in welcome and stepped back. "Mr. Manning's a popular guy."

"Those TBI fellows again?"

Randy nodded. "They're coming tomorrow to transport him to Nashville for the autopsy."

The chief made a disparaging sound. "A waste of time if you asked me." The door closed behind them. "Like we don't know what killed him. I guess the Tennessee Bureau of Investigation needs to show its worth something."

The smell of chilled flesh and death hit Paul's nostrils with the force of a physical blow. He'd never gotten used to it. He doubted he ever would. A fresh wave of tension rolled over him, balled his fists. Blackness swelled inside him...he wrestled it back. His heart rate climbed higher, affecting his respiration and his ability to focus. He systematically reclaimed control of his reactions, first the too rapid breathing, then the hammering of his heart.

Latex gloves were thrust at him. "You gotta wear these, man, if you want to touch him. You, too, chief."

The chief declined. His movements stilted, Paul accepted the gloves and stretched them over his hands. Somewhere deep in his gut nausea prepared to roil. The frigid temperature of the primitive morgue cooled his sweat-dampened skin. He swallowed back the lingering hesitation, the looming blackness, steeled himself and moved purposely toward the small refrigeration unit at the back of the room. Randy swung the door open and gestured for Paul to go on in.

A single gurney stood a few feet away. Voices, images tried to intrude as he took those last few steps. He methodically ignored the unbidden perceptions, first the images, then the voices. He stared at the body bag for a moment before opening it. Paul's first impression was of evil...something dark and menacing, but he pushed it away. Reclaimed his objectivity.

Karl had been a tall man with an athletic build. His skin was gray now and veined like marble. The flesh around the stab wound gaped, leaving a purplish border. The lethal injury was slightly to the left of the sternum. Judging by the location, the knife probably slid between the second and third rib and pierced the wall of the heart. Manning would have bled out in mere minutes.

Paul focused on the body, searching for telltale signs of whatever events occurred in the final moments of life. According to Lawton the victim's wife had been badly beaten. Manning's hands were unmarked. No tissue beneath the nails. No other obvious trauma. The face was ashen, the mouth partially open as if he'd died mid-utterance.

Heart rate accelerating in tandem with the anxiety mounting inside him, Paul's hands started to shake. He curled his fingers into fists and steeled himself for the next step. He had to do that one last thing and that was the part he hated.

Gritting his teeth he looked directly into Karl Manning's sightless blue eyes. Eyes so pale they appeared almost colorless. Everything inside Paul stilled, grew silent as if he'd fallen deep into a well, as he looked— really—looked. Even his elevated heart rate seemed to slow completely as he allowed himself to see.

That dark foreboding he'd been fighting expanded in his chest. Light slashed in his brain with an intensity that made him flinch. Anger, fierce and hot surged through him, obliterating all else. *You will never see him again!* Male voice. Tears scalded the woman's cheeks as she begged the man to listen. He refused. The knife came out of nowhere... he couldn't react quickly enough. His body tensed. The hiss of metal sliding deep into his flesh reverberated through him. *Not good.* He would die before help could arrive.

Paul blinked, shattering the trance, drawing back emotionally. The darkness receded...the pain in his head subsided. Strength drained out of him, leaving him weak and unsteady. Nausea boiled up into his throat. He shook violently once, twice, before he grabbed back control. He sucked in a breath and glanced beyond the open door to the chief and the attendant, who, thankfully, were still engaged in conversation.

Paul squeezed his eyes shut and struggled to regain his equilibrium. He forced his body to obey and stepped back from the gurney. Randy noticed and moved toward him.

"All done, sir?"

Paul dredged up a tight smile. "Yeah, thanks."

Every step…every breath was accomplished by sheer force of will. His mind was attempting to shut down. The overload circuitry had long ago burned out and shutting down was the only way to find relief.

If he could just make it back to the Land Rover…

"I'll look forward to your observations, Dr. Phillips," the chief was saying as they rejoined Ellington in the corridor. Curious or just plain nosey, the morgue attendant followed.

"I'll keep you informed," Paul offered, his voice strained, but it was the best he could do.

"Well, then." The chief nodded to him and then to Ellington. "Miss Jill, I'm keeping close contact with your momma. I'm hoping we'll have news about the boy soon."

Ellington thanked Dotson while Paul started forward. He had to get the hell out of here. Couldn't wait. The pressure was building, closing in around him.

She caught up, walked quietly beside him while the chief's exchange with the attendant about the TBI's visit faded.

"Are you okay?"

Of course he wasn't okay. He was totally screwed— burned up, burned out…a has-been who did a dance for those hopeless enough to want to watch.

He moved forward, slowly, unsteadily, which was about the extent of his physical ability at the moment. All he had to do was get to the elevator and then out to the parking lot. A blast of blinding light struck him and he stopped. Fighting the tremors, he kept his eyes closed tightly while he grappled for control. He would not look. He ordered the images away. He didn't want to see or feel any more. Not now. He had to pull it back together before he looked again.

"Dr. Phillips, are you all right?"

She was touching him…shaking him.

His lids fluttered open and pain pierced his skull. "I'm fine." He started forward again, leaving her no choice but to step aside. The only thing he needed was out of here.

A water fountain hung on the wall near the elevator. Paul walked straight to it and took a small sip of water. The cool liquid provided a glimmer of relief. After another sip, he splashed some onto his face. *Shake it off.*

He sensed her tension, even a little genuine concern. That she didn't throw out any more questions was good because it took every ounce of willpower he possessed to board the elevator and then to cross the parking lot under his own steam.

He paused near the hood of his Land Rover and tossed her the keys. "I think maybe you'd better drive."

CHAPTER THREE

Jill divided her attention between driving and watching the man in the passenger seat. Was this part of his act? A mix of frustration and uncertainty twisted inside her. If he was acting, he deserved an academy award.

Though he'd discarded the jacket and turned the SUV's air conditioning to high, perspiration still lined his grim face. He looked unnaturally pale and drawn. She'd noticed his hands shaking when he'd fastened his seat belt. Jill moistened her lips and focused on navigating through the noon day traffic. What happened in that morgue? Had the chief said something Phillips intended to keep from her? Had the chief figured out the man was a fake?

Dammit! "You're sure you're all right?"

"Just drive."

Frustration won out over the uncertainty. Who was she kidding? Most likely his hangover was catching up to him. What the hell was she supposed to do now? The only place she could think to take him was her childhood home. Her mother wouldn't like it. Like the rest of the town, she would resent an outsider's intrusion. At least that gave Jill and Phillips something in common.

She stole another glance at her passenger. His eyes were closed but his breathing had calmed. If this wasn't an act, did she really want to know what happened back there?

Neither the chief nor Randy had behaved as if anything unexpected or untoward had taken place. The terms *burnout* and *breakdown* kept echoing through her head. Clearly Phillips waged serious internal battles. Just further proof that this was a total waste of time. Her lips trembled with a jolt of outrage. She was not a stupid person. Why the hell couldn't she do this right? All she had to do was find her nephew and prove her sister's innocence.

Before her emotions could get the better of her, she forced her attention back to the street. With a right turn onto Washington, she put forth an extra effort to regain her composure. Giving her mother a glimpse of weakness would only make bad matters worse.

Jill braced for the inevitable feelings of in-adequacy.

The Ellington house reigned over prestigious Washington Street like a regal matriarch. None of the other homes on this historic street stood quite as grand or meticulously maintained as her child-hood home. Brick painted a pristine bride white was accented by classic black shutters. Massive fluted col-umns supported the sprawling two-story verandah.

The need for freedom and with ambition burn-ing like hot coals in her belly had sent Jill running from this place, no matter how grand, a decade ago. She'd wanted to become who *she* was. Not just Kate's twin. Or the Judge's daughter. She'd needed to make her own way as Jillian Ellington, the student, the woman, and now the attorney at law.

Though she'd accomplished her goal, her actions had driven a wedge between her and this place. Another memory surfaced past the barrier she used to keep the less pleasant parts of her past at bay. She and her father arguing. Jill banished the images. Some things were too painful to remember. And too late to amend. Those were the regrets she would take to her grave.

The past was done. Now was her chance to prove she was just as good and as selfless as Kate. That she could be a good daughter and fix this horrific tragedy.

Truth was, she'd been doing that her entire adult life…trying to measure up to Kate. The admission made her stomach clench with emotion.

Just stop. Feeling sorry for herself was childish. She tightened her grip on the steering wheel and parked in front of the house. Cody and Kate needed her and nothing else mattered at the moment. Her sister had never been the enemy. All who'd lived through Jill's formative years would say that she had been her own worst enemy. Maybe, after all these years, she could admit some truth in that accusation. Just not today.

Her mother would be waiting for news and some sort of strategy as to how Jill intended to straighten out this misunderstanding. It was nothing more than an unthinkable mistake. That was Claire Ellington's way of dealing with the situation. Somehow Jill had to make her see the circumstances they were facing for what they were: real life and Claire didn't get to make the rules.

Jill shut off the engine and turned to Phillips. Some of his color was back. That was a good sign. "We can discuss your thoughts over lunch." She couldn't recall the last time she'd eaten and she doubted he could either.

"There's no hotel?" he asked without looking at her.

Why did he need a hotel? Was he staying? Did he really believe he could help? Hope dared to make an appearance. Another mistake. Anger nudged her. However special and gifted Richard thought this man to be, Jill had witnessed no indication of either.

She had an appointment with Cullen Marks, the attorney from Nashville, a little later. Right now, she wanted to lay her cards on the table with Phillips. Hear his thoughts and move on. She had no intention of wasting time with him. Her mother would simply have to be content with her chosen course of action or she could make arrangements of her own. Jill was sick to death of waiting on everyone else to decide what to do next.

"There's no need for a hotel, Dr. Phillips. Let's not make this any more complicated than it has to be." She didn't wait for a reaction. She got out of his SUV and slammed the door.

He'd seen the body. He had the files. He should be ready to discuss this case—unless he had nothing to say. All those nasty reports she'd read last night haunted her. What kind of person took advantage of another's despair? And why the hell couldn't she make up her mind what she wanted to believe?

Shaking her head, Jill marched toward the verandah. Her mother would be waiting.

A self-professed agoraphobic, Claire Ellington never, under any circumstances left the house. Not since the death of her husband. Life *period* in the Ellington home had not been the same since his untimely passing. Just another reason Jill rarely came home any more.

But that was no excuse. Her stomach churned with remorse. She had allowed the resentment to widen the emotional gap between her and her family. Her selfish attitude had been wrong. Rectifying that misstep might just prove impossible but she had to try just the same. She had no power to change the past. What was done was done. She hadn't been here. Not for her father before he died. And not for her sister before this horrible thing happened.

But she was here now.

Exiling what she couldn't change to the back of her mind, she trudged up the six steps to the verandah. Phillips followed. The least she could do was feed him before she heard what he had to say and sent him on his way.

Jill didn't have to fumble for a key. No one in Paradise ever locked their doors. There was nothing to be afraid of…at least until now.

"Hello," she called out in the empty foyer. The silence sent a shiver up Jill's spine. When she and Kate were kids there had always been happy sounds in this house. Their mother humming as she baked. Their father enjoying a cigar and evening drink with a colleague. Never disquieting silence like this.

Uncertainty wound tight inside her. Knowing Claire, she had handled the problem as she had all her problems since the Judge died, she'd hidden away to wait it out.

Jill turned to Phillips who appeared genuinely interested in these new surroundings. He moved about the entry hall, studying artwork and pictures that told the story of the Ellingtons and their prominence in Paradise over the last one hundred years. He picked up a small silver-framed photograph of her and Kate at the rambunctious age of ten. A tiny smile tugged at Jill's lips. She remembered that day vividly. Matching pink ruffled dresses and white patent leather shoes and enough ringlets to make Goldilocks envious.

"Jill, thank Heavens you're home."

Paul carefully replaced the framed photograph and looked up at the woman who'd spoken from the second story landing. Though the worst had passed, he was still a little shaky. He hadn't had this much trouble maintaining control in a long time. It was this place, he was sure of it. There was something, but he couldn't get a handle on it. Something ugly lurking beneath the Norman Rockwell facade.

"I thought you were resting," the younger Ellington offered, an apology in her tone, as her mother slowly descended the staircase. "I hope we didn't disturb you."

Paul glanced at Jillian, surprised at the sudden about face. Her expression, even her posture had changed noticeably. Up to now she'd been cool and all business. Barely kept her derision of him in check. But this was Jillian, the daughter, not the attorney. His attention returned to the woman descending the stairs. She was an older version of the daughter, medium height, slender, same delicate facial features. Still attractive. Her hair was more silver now than blond, but the eyes were the same clear sky blue. Blue and watchful, overly cautious. Also like her daughter, she dressed impeccably.

"Mother, this is Dr. Paul Phillips," Jill said, drawing Claire's full attention to him. "He's advising on Kate's case. We're going to have lunch, would you like to join us?"

Mrs. Ellington descended the final step. With her left hand still on the newel post, she offered her right. "Claire Ellington, Dr. Phillips." Her voice was softer than Jill's, the diction perfect, not even a hint of a southern vernacular. According to Jill, her mother and father had both grown up in Paradise.

He clasped the hand she offered, felt her tension and frustration. This lady was every bit as suspicious of him as her daughter. "The pleasure is mine, Mrs. Ellington."

"Are you a neurologist?" she asked, obviously wondering how this stranger might help her daughter. She was as easy to read as a cheery birthday card to a point, a very shallow point. Beyond that was a firm wall of resistance. Strange.

"No, ma'am. I'm a forensic psychologist. I'm here to review your daughter's case and suggest a proper course of action for unraveling the events of the past forty-eight hours."

Claire nodded uncertainly. "Isn't that what the police are doing?" She looked from Paul to Jill. "I'm sure the chief is doing everything possible to find my grandson and to catch Karl's killer. He calls me every few hours with an update. I don't see how you could expect any more from the man, Jillian."

"My presence," Paul offered, "is no reflection on local law enforcement, Mrs. Ellington. I'm here to assist." At least the lady was honest. He had to give her points for that.

"Mother," Jillian scolded, "the chief thinks he's already found the killer and he's made no headway in finding Cody. I'd say he needs all the help he can get."

That she made the statement despite her misgivings about him surprised Paul. The lady lawyer had a serious case of needing to prove herself to mother.

Claire looked indignant. "Don't be silly, Jillian. The chief knows Katherine would never harm anyone. He's simply doing his job."

Paul watched, fascinated, as the daughter steeled herself for battle, summoned the attorney in her that had moments ago fled for parts unknown. Claire reacted in kind, but it was much more subtle. A tightening along the line of her cheek, the flattening of her lips. Something stood between these two…something hurtful, but he couldn't see it. Both did a hell of a cover-up job. Or maybe he was still subconsciously blocking.

"Her prints are on the murder weapon," Jillian said coolly. "*Only* her prints."

Claire shook her head, a new flush flagging her cheeks. This one motivated by anger. "I will have no such talk in this house, young lady. You'd like nothing better than to see your sister suffer just to prove a point. I called you here to help her, not accuse her of murder."

Paul waited for the offensive, but it never came.

"I'm certain Kate is innocent," Jillian said softly, her tone, her expression bordered on pleading. The abrupt change surprised him all over again. "I'm doing everything I can to prove it. I won't let you or Kate down, Mother."

Claire managed a stiff nod. "I'm sorry, dear." She dabbed at her watery eyes. "I've worried so that I'm not thinking rationally. Of course you'll do what's best." Another startling about face. "Thank you for coming, Dr. Phillips. We appreciate any and all efforts to find the truth."

Paul gave an acknowledging nod and Claire Ellington retraced her steps and disappeared upstairs with all the dignity of British royalty.

"Would you like a drink, Dr. Phillips?"

If he'd been confused by the lady before, he was genuinely startled now. Her every vibe since introducing herself had suggested she had no tolerance for the idea that alcohol could be a man's best friend. He, on the other hand, preferred lunch in a glass any day.

"I'll have whatever you're having, Miss Ellington."

Her posture rigid and her expression unyielding, she turned and strode through the double doors of the room to his left. Ever the glutton for punishment, he tagged along.

More pictures of dead relatives adorned the rich paneled walls of the room. He had almost no history and even fewer photographs of his family. His parents had died in a house fire when he was in high school. He'd been alone for so long, he rarely thought of them anymore.

Who was better off, he wondered, him or Jillian Ellington?

A leather tufted chair sat behind a massive mahogany desk. The paneled walls not weighted with photographs and paintings were lined with shelves filled with ancient looking leather-bound volumes. He picked up on the vague scents of cherry flavored tobacco and Old Spice.

"The Judge's private chambers," she proclaimed as she closed the double doors behind them. "Mother keeps it closed up so the essence of my father won't fade completely." She inhaled deeply. "It still smells just like him." She turned slowly in the middle of the room and indicated the endless array of reading material. "His law books." She sighed, the sound wistful. "Ancient tomes that personify wisdom and justice."

A stern but affectionate voice echoed those same words in Paul's head. *The Judge.* She'd heard her father say those words time and again. He surveyed the cherished room. Courage and strength resonated within these walls. Confusion pulled at him. Courage and strength and something else... another element much less pure. Less good but obscured by numerous concealing layers. All those sensations were underscored by a simmering desperation.

"Your father longed for you to follow in his footsteps." The words were out of his mouth before he could stop them.

She faced him. "What?"

He swallowed tightly, searching for something amid the Judge's worldly possessions that lent logic to such a knowing call. This was the precise reason he didn't get personally involved with his cases. His control always slipped. It was a constant battle, one much easier won when he was alone with reports and photos. His gaze landed on the painting on the wall behind the ornate desk.

The Judge seated in a throne-like chair, the sister, Katherine, sat in her father's lap, but Jillian stood at his side. He gestured to the painting. "You're standing beside him...an equal. He knew you were the strongest."

Jill didn't bother looking at the portrait, only at him. He tensed…he'd made another misstep. Said too much. Those clear blue eyes searched his so closely he barely restrained the need to look away.

"How do you know it's me standing beside him?" Her voice was eerily calm. "It could be Kate. We're identical twins. No one has ever been able to tell us apart."

Damn. "It's you." No point in attempting to evade the inevitable bullet of her suspicion. "How old were you when you decided to go to law school?"

That piercing gaze shifted from him to the portrait. "I was nine." She moved to the cabinet where liquor decanters waited and poured two drinks, both bourbon, both neat. "I ditched school and sneaked into the courtroom where the Judge was presiding that day."

His mouth watered as she handed one glass to him. "Did you get caught?" Every molecule of strength he possessed was required to prevent downing the bourbon.

She leaned against the corner of her father's desk. "Of course, but he didn't tell. Father took me into his chambers and spent the afternoon telling me all about his work. I've been in love ever since."

But that wasn't how the story ended. Sadness enveloped her. He could feel the hurt. He looked away. Surrendered to the thirst and took a long swallow. Relief surged through his body. But this one polite drink would never be enough.

"The framed photos are Kate's." She gestured with her glass to the array of small framed photographs on one shelf. "She's as avid about photography as I am about the law." Jillian smiled. "She always had a camera swinging around her neck."

That smile tugged at him, made him want to look more closely. He downed another swallow of Bourbon and hoped it would dull his senses. It was all he could do to keep the voices and images at bay.

"I have an appointment with an attorney in an hour." She knocked back a hefty slug of her drink, grimaced at the burn. "Before I go, I want this settled." She looked directly at him. "As much as I respect Richard, I have to tell you, Dr. Phillips, I don't see the point in pretending. I don't see how you can help."

A rather polite way of saying she had concluded he was a charlatan and not worthy of her time. His fingers tightened around the glass in his hand. Didn't matter. He wasn't staying. "I'll review the reports, give you my conclusions and then I'll be out of your way." He finished off his drink. He'd done as Lawton asked. There was nothing else required of him here.

She shook her head, set her glass aside. "How do you live with yourself and do this?"

As hard as he tried to hold back the anger, he failed. He had nothing to prove to this woman. To anyone. "I don't go to them, they come to me." If he could have successfully stopped the hordes who begged him to help he would have done that long ago. Just like this one. He didn't want to be here.

Indignation flared in her eyes. "I guess you're just lucky the forty percent of the time you get it right."

Damn he needed another drink. "I'll be done here today. Three or four hours tops."

She made a breathy sound that wasn't quite a laugh. "Just leave your report on my father's desk. As far as I'm concerned you and I are done now."

CHAPTER FOUR

"You're suggesting an insanity plea?" Jill could scarcely believe she'd heard him right. The meeting with the attorney had turned into a late lunch, but she'd lost her appetite well before they were served.

How could she eat when her nephew was still missing? She couldn't help thinking he was out there, scared and hungry. The advice she'd just gotten regarding her sister's case only added to her anxiety.

Cullen Marks leaned back in his chair. "I believe that's the only avenue we have available at this time. I'm familiar with the neurologist and psychiatrist reviewing the case and both men are excellent."

Jill felt stunned. The great attorney Richard had highly recommended wanted to take the easy way out. Beneath that thousand dollar suit and store bought tan, the man who'd first impressed her as a mover and a shaker with his brilliant smile and distinguished looks, was nothing but a slacker. A well-polished actor who played at being a high stakes attorney.

He knew the law well enough. He could quote the landmark cases that would absolve Kate of responsibility…but not of guilt. He wanted to plea bargain to prevent having to go to trial. He wanted to win without the race, which in Jill's book amounted to not winning at all. Especially since her sister would be the ultimate loser.

And, the worst transgression of all, he wanted to assume the child was dead.

This was exactly why she hadn't gone with anyone from her firm. Malcolm Teller was a damned good lawyer but he took the easy way out far too often.

Was that the new malady among her peers? Or worse, the new standard for the top legal eagles?

First Phillips, now Marks. Had Richard wanted her to fail? That just didn't make sense…he was her friend. She'd known him for nearly a decade.

Jill took a moment to gather her composure. She plucked her linen napkin from her lap and squeezed it in her hands to blot her damp palms, then laid it carefully on the table next to her untouched meal. "Mr. Marks—"

"Cullen, please," he insisted in that refined, oily tone which was even less sincere than his high voltage smile. "We're a team. I'm aware of your association with Malcolm Teller. I'm sure your expertise will be a bonus to this team."

Jill glanced at the assistant seated to her left. The man spared no attention from his bone china plate.

His boss had everything under control. Though she hated to judge him solely on his performance at a lunch table, if he represented the kind of team players Cullen employed, then she was out before they even started.

"It's my goal to prove my sister didn't commit the crime," she clarified just in case he hadn't gotten it the first two times she'd stated her intent, and obviously he hadn't. She knew the law too, but she wanted this case to go all the way to trial if necessary. Yes, she readily admitted that her goal had an emotional base, but putting that aside she *knew* her sister was not guilty of murder.

"That's an honorable goal, Jillian." Cullen sipped his wine, swirled it in his stemmed glass, then set it aside. "But I'm not sure your family is prepared for the price of achieving that unlikely outcome."

She lifted a skeptical eyebrow. "There's no question. I'm prepared to go the distance in and out of the courtroom." Was this guy full of himself or what?

Cullen sighed and considered her statement. "What about your mother?" His direct gaze sliced into hers. "Is *she* prepared to see her daughter's name splashed across half the newspapers in northeastern Tennessee? You know the DA's office will drudge up more dirty business than you can stir with a stick. The fact that a major research corporation, which is already making its own kind of headlines, is involved will only bait the press hounds. It won't be pretty. Nor will it accomplish your goal of proving a third party was involved if we don't discover at least some substantiating evidence." He leaned forward, speaking more quietly now, but with the same intensity. "I've reviewed the reports, Jillian, the case against your sister is concrete."

Jill shook her head. She knew all that. "There's no motive."

He made a disparaging sound in his throat. "They'll find one. Hell, they'll find three just to be safe."

She lifted her chin and met his steady gaze with the sternest one she could muster. She knew that too, but she wasn't about to back down. "And what about the bruises? There had to be a third party."

He nodded solemnly. "It's from those very injuries, my dear, that they'll produce the strongest motive. Think about it, and you'll know I'm right. This is already labeled a domestic dispute that turned deadly. Did your sister have an illicit lover?" He stopped her with an uplifted palm when she would have raised an objection. "A man who, perhaps, had grown tired of her promises to leave her husband? A man who beat her when she refused his final ultimatum, then left her to face the wrath of her husband when she could no longer hide the truth?"

Shock quaked through Jill. What he proposed was preposterous. But a part of her, the analytical side, knew he was right. It was the DA's job to come up with a motive, an affair on her sister's part was the perfect solution. An angry lover, a jealous husband...a desperate wife.

God. That just couldn't be the truth.

But any DA with even half the usual measure of ambition would make it the truth in the eyes of the jury. She knew it and Cullen Marks, damn him, knew it as well.

She sighed, defeated, weary of the struggle already and it had barely begun. "I'll need to think about this."

He nodded, his expression carefully composed, devoid of any signs of triumph and infused with sympathy. "I understand. Give me a call in a couple of days. The chief doesn't expect the DA to pursue an arraignment until after the autopsy results are back. That'll take a week at best."

For the first time since their introduction, the assistant looked up and smiled. He was tall and thin, far from handsome with a high forehead and a narrow face that lacked a chin to speak of, but he was just as well groomed as his superior. "We'll take care of everything, Miss Ellington," he said knowingly. "We're very good at what we do."

Cullen Marks summoned the waitress and settled the bill, insisting that the meal was on the firm. Which meant that ultimately it would be added to the Ellington tab. They exchanged cell phone numbers and good-byes in the vestibule. Jill lingered, still a little stunned. She stared at the attorney's gold embossed business card for a time after he'd gone.

Everything he'd said was right. There would be no way to turn this thing around. Unless Phillips found something everyone else had missed. How likely was that? He was probably gone already. He hadn't said a word as he'd driven her back to her car so she could come to this ill-fated meeting. She should have kept her conclusions about him to herself until he'd put his assessments in writing. A forty percent probability rate of success looked far more appealing after this meeting. That familiar ache of failure, of not getting the job done where her family was concerned, coiled inside her.

There had to be something they were missing. Just because she couldn't see it or Cullen couldn't see it didn't mean it didn't exist. There was far more to her brother-in-law's death than met the eye. Every instinct warned that she couldn't give up.

"Jill? Is that you?"

She paused before reaching for the door and looked back to see who'd called her name. A short brunette, eyes bright with recognition, bounced in her direction. *Connie Neil.*

"I can't believe it's really you," Connie enthused before throwing her arms around Jill.

Jill hugged her tightly, then drew back and looked at her old friend. "My God, you haven't changed a bit." And it was the truth. Connie still looked terrific and incredibly vivacious, like the cheerleader she'd been back in high school. She and Jill had been best friends all through those tumultuous years. After going their separate ways to college, they'd eventually lost touch. The realization added another layer of sadness to this already emotional homecoming.

"When did you get home?" Connie swiped at the tears in her eyes. "It's so good to see you." Her exuberant expression wilted. "Oh, God. Kate." She shook her head sadly. "I'd almost succeeded in putting that out of my mind. It's unbelievable."

Jill nodded, the catch in her throat prevented speech. She hugged her old friend again and swallowed the lump of raw emotion. "It's good to see a friendly face." She fiddled with her purse a moment. "I feel like a stranger here now."

"Oh, sweetie," Connie placated. "You'll never be a stranger here. This is home." She patted Jill on the shoulder. "As soon as your head's above water, let's have a sleep over just like we used to and catch up on the last decade of gossip."

The idea went a long way in soothing Jill's frazzled nerves. "That would be really nice. I fear, though, that this investigation is going to take some time."

Connie blinked. "Investigation? You mean finding Cody?"

Jill nodded. "That and I'm working on clearing my sister's name. You know she couldn't have killed Karl."

"Oh." Connie's expression grew distant.

When the silence dragged on, Jill asked slowly, "Is everything all right?"

Connie's lips stretched into an unnatural smile as she gave a resolute nod and fished around in her bag. "Ah…yeah…call me." She jotted something on a piece of paper. "Here's my number. We'll have lunch."

"Sure." Jill watched as her friend hurried away. Connie's abrupt change in demeanor completely baffled her. Any headway she'd gained in feeling more at home vanished.

She was still the outsider.

* * *

PARADISE GENERAL

Paul scanned the papers spread across the dash and passenger seat of his Land Rover once more. Something was way off. He reread the ER report on Kate Manning. Multiple contusions. Scratches on her right arm and shoulder. An inordinate number of bruises. A green stick fracture on her left wrist. Complete disorientation upon examination. Yet her respiration and heart rate were low, as if she had been completely relaxed. He tossed that report aside and studied the crime scene photos for the fourth time.

The Manning kitchen was large with all the amenities one would expect in the home of a corporate CEO. Directly in front of the kitchen sink was Karl Manning's body. A large pool of blood had coagulated on the tile floor around him.

But it didn't add up. Paul shuffled through the pictures. The kitchen was clean, neat...perfect. Not the first item was out of place. No indication of a struggle. But a man lay dead on the floor. His wife, the supposed killer, was marred by what could only be called a beating nothing short of brutal. Even more confusing were the victim's hands. No indication whatsoever that he'd lifted a finger to harm his wife. Had he worn gloves there would still have been some indication somewhere on his body that his wife had fought back. A single scratch. An abrasion. Something. But there wasn't a mark on the dead man. When complete, the autopsy report would surely confirm Paul's conclusion.

Karl Manning had not touched his wife.

Paul stared at the photos of Katherine Ellington and thought about the portrait of her with Jillian, and then the ones of her with her attractive family, scattered around the Ellington home. Unbidden, the image of the child intruded and blocked out all else. The boy, blond haired and blue eyed like his parents, had been missing for almost forty-eight hours now. Odds were against his being alive…but something deep inside Paul resisted that conclusion. He blinked away the image and focused on Kate.

She was the key somehow. She'd been beaten and then delivered to her home to face her husband's wrath. Maybe for whatever she'd gotten herself into. Or whatever he'd gotten her into, Paul countered, playing out the scene in his head. The child wasn't around. He was…away. Paul cautiously lowered his defenses…concentrated hard…tried to see.

It was the right thing to do.

The words reverberated inside him, around him, jerking his head up. The voice was too distorted to know if it was male or female…but the words were clear. *It was the right thing to do.*

Paul stared at the photograph of a bruised and battered Kate. He wondered why Jillian didn't talk about the fact that she and her sister were twins. Only that once when he'd recognized her in the portrait with her father. Twins, especially identical ones, had a deep connection. Was that why Jillian was so certain her sister hadn't killed her husband? Then again, he'd picked up on her serious need to be her own person. She'd left home and scarcely returned. To blot out that deep connection? Did she know more now than she realized? Had she convinced herself that if she pretended it didn't exist, it wouldn't?

But it did. The link was written in her DNA.

Paul had learned at a very young age that he was different. He sensed things…heard things others didn't. He could read feelings as easily as breathing, could pick up on the last presence in an empty room. His parents had urged him to keep quiet about what they called *the gift* and he had. But when he'd begun his career there was no hiding his innate ability to know certain details. When his superiors had learned of his ability, they'd pushed him relentlessly to solve more and more cases. They'd pushed him until he snapped.

He closed his eyes and forced thoughts of his past away. He had to concentrate on the here and now. There was something rotten in this sweet little town. He should have left when he had the chance but he couldn't. Jillian Ellington had unknowingly struck a chord deep inside him. He had to do this part. Give her something to go on and then get the hell out of here before he got dragged into this abyss.

His gaze settled on Kate's image once more. What was she hiding? What was so unspeakable that she would withdraw into herself and play dead?

A sense of urgency poked Paul.

Everything depended upon Kate.

He glanced at the time on the dash. Three thirty.

What the hell was he thinking? He should just go. Now.

The vacant blue eyes in the photograph haunted him. Someone had to bring Kate Manning back to the land of the living before the state institutionalized her and steady medications reduced to about zero percent the possibility of her ever coming back. She was the only one who could save herself...and her son.

Ten minutes later Paul was striding up to the hospital's main entrance. He had the file the chief had provided tucked under his arm in an official manner. He'd donned his sports jacket, even finger combed his hair. He looked professional enough.

Inside the lobby he scanned the register and located the psychiatric ward. Fourth floor. Since Kate Manning had not been officially charged there would be no guard assigned to her room. The hospital staff he could handle.

The elevator whisked him upward with scarcely a sound of complaint. The doors opened with a whoosh and he stepped out into the quiet corridor.

The smell of pharmaceuticals and fear—not his own this time—assaulted him.

Two nurses were busy behind the station outside the lock down area. This was where Kate Manning would be. He didn't have to ask. She would be under close observation since fleeing or suicide was often contemplated by those involved with or suspected of heinous crimes.

Paul stopped at the nurse's station and flashed the credentials that identified him as a psychologist. "Good afternoon, ladies." He smiled, pumping up the wattage until he garnered an answering smile from both.

"May I help you, sir?" the older of the two, Nurse Mathis according to her nametag, asked, wariness dimming her smile.

"I'm Dr. Phillips from Memphis. Miss Ellington retained my services for evaluating her sister, Katherine Manning. Since the evaluation is needed as soon as possible I'd like to see her now if convenient. I was supposed to be here earlier today," he added wearily as if he'd had the day from hell just like the two of them.

The nurses exchanged glances. Bennett, the one who appeared in charge, eyed him speculatively. "We have no record of hospital approval for you to see the patient. I'm—"

"There must be some delay in the paperwork," Paul interrupted smoothly before she could say the deadly five-letter word. In his experience once *sorry* was on the table, few took it back. "I'm sure I was scheduled for today," he insisted, his gaze traveling from her eyes to her mouth and back with blatant approval. "I'm later than I'd expected to be." He adopted a harried look, much like hers. This was something else he'd learned long ago, consummate lying. Tell people what they wanted to hear and life went a whole lot smoother.

Nurse Bennett glanced at the clock. "I should verify—"

"My evaluation won't take long," he urged. "Chief Dotson will be very disappointed if I don't have my conclusions to him tonight."

She caved. The change in her posture told the tale before she spoke. "Well, what can it hurt? There's no point in you having driven all this way just to have me hold you up." She pulled Kate's chart. "Come on, I'll show you the way."

"I sincerely appreciate your assistance," he said as they moved away from the station.

Nurse Bennett used her ID key card to unlock the door at the transition point. Paul followed her down a long corridor where she paused at room 415. She passed her key card through the reader and opened the door.

"Buzz me when you're finished. She's all yours."

Paul flashed her another smile. "Thank you, Nurse Bennett."

She passed him the patient chart and scurried back to the station.

He moved to the foot of the bed and scanned the chart for a time before focusing his attention on the woman, mostly to brace himself. She hadn't spoken since they found her hovering over her husband's body. She showed no emotion and ate only if fed.

Placing the chart and the file he'd brought with him on the portable serving tray, he moved to the bedside. The swelling was diminishing, the bruises fading from purple to yellow. She looked vulnerable and helpless. Restraints prevented her from getting up without assistance.

Katherine Ellington Manning was a bright woman, educated as a research analyst. She had an excellent work record with MedTech according to the chief's report. She was cited as a loving wife and mother by all who knew her. And Paul sensed, without having read it, that she was not a violent person. Unlike her rebellious sister, Kate was quiet, submissive, always obedient.

Yes, mother. Yes, father.

His heart beat faster as the sensations toppled one over the other inside him. The voices whispered to him. Kate would never harm anyone, much less her child or her husband. Jillian knew this without reservation. She felt it. The connection was there, despite being buried beneath years of sibling rivalry and bitter disappointment.

But she loved her sister. She wanted to save her.

Kate's eyes abruptly flew open. "They're coming for us."

Paul jerked back a step. He inhaled sharply, blinked repeatedly and stared down at the unconscious woman. "Jesus Christ."

He squeezed his eyes shut and shattered the image seemingly burned onto his irises. Kate hadn't moved a muscle. What he'd seen and heard had come from inside his own head. Maybe. The warning, wherever it came from, was real. The only question was, did the *us* in her warning apply to Kate and her sister, or to Kate and her son?

He scrubbed a hand over his face. Slow, deep breaths. No panic. Turn it off.

But he couldn't...not just yet.

He took her hand in his and closed his eyes. This was the part he hated most of all. He focused intently on Kate Manning. The pictures he'd viewed from the crime scene...the family photos. Her snapshots as a photography buff. But nothing came. A brick wall met his continued attempts. She wouldn't let him back in. Or maybe he held back on a subconscious level.

Why warn him, then hold back? Didn't make sense. He picked up the chart and the file, buzzed the nurse and walked to the door. He had to get out of here before the next phase hit. The routine was always the same. He had maybe a minute.

As if to defy him, pain split through his head, followed by a bright flash of light. He groaned, pushed it away. He didn't want to go there now. He steeled himself and focused on the door. He needed out of this place. Just turn it off. Don't think.

The panic reared its ugly head, a creeping, swelling fear that rose in his throat inhibiting his ability to breathe. It burgeoned in his chest, pressing against his thudding heart. Sweat broke out across his skin. The urge to run raced through his veins.

Where was that nurse?

They mustn't find him…

He'll never be safe if they find him…Save us!

He had to get out of here.

"Is everything all right, Dr. Phillips?"

Nurse Bennett's voice jerked him from the trance…the panic. She held the door open, waiting, looking up at him with mounting concern.

He nodded. "Everything's fine. Thank you."

He couldn't get out of the hospital fast enough.

He burst through exit and gulped in breath after breath. Didn't help. The voices…the haunting images followed him. He couldn't make them go away. The darkness edged in…threatening his control…dragging him back to that place where he'd lost himself completely.

He forced the images away. Breathed more deeply.

He wasn't going back there…not for anyone.

Not for Kate or her son…not for Jillian.

* * *

Jill dropped her purse onto the hall table and checked the answering machine for messages. The day was almost over and there was still no news about Cody. Her apprehension was mounting fast now. He'd been unaccounted for since Sunday morning. A neighbor had seen Kate and Cody getting into her car, presumably to go to church. But no one saw them at church. The urge to join the search was very nearly overwhelming. But how could she do that and all this?

Jill frowned, suddenly too aware of the silence. *He was gone.*

But then that was what she'd wanted, wasn't it?

After what Cullen Marks had to say, she understood more than ever that she absolutely needed some kind of miracle that would save her nephew and sister.

Even if it meant believing in someone like Paul Phillips.

Dear God, she was losing her mind. Jill closed eyes and struggled to hold onto her composure. How could she fix this?

First things first. She would check her father's study to see if Phillips had left a report.

Insistent knocking echoed around her. The possibility it was the chief with an update had her hurrying to the door, praying there was good news. She yanked it open and Paul Phillips filled the doorway as if her desperation had somehow summoned him. Whatever foolish relief she felt was short lived.

He was ready to bolt. He didn't have to say a word. She could see it in his eyes, in the dark, tense angles of his face.

"Can I come in?"

"Of course." She stepped back, opened the door wider. He came inside just far enough for her to close the door. Again she wondered about the demons that haunted him. He was unquestionably a tortured man. This looked like far more than burn-out…deeper than a breakdown. When he stared at some point beyond her and said nothing, she asked, "Have you learned something about my sister's case?"

"You said you didn't want me to waste your time so I won't." He looked directly at her then. "There's nothing I can do for you."

He was right. She had said that. Some random brain cell screamed at her not to let him go. She was all alone in this and she needed someone.

"You found nothing that might help." Her voice sounded as hollow as she felt. There had to be something.

He reached for the door. She didn't miss the fine tremor in his hands. "The police will figure it out. They can't be that blind."

Adrenaline fired through her. He had found something. *Stay calm.* "You're probably right." *Don't challenge him. Lead him.* "They aren't blind. I'm just not sure they're going to look."

In a few days they would call off the primary phase of the search for Cody. It was the only logical thing to do. She knew the routine. A bigger story would come along and the press would lose interest, search volunteers would return to their lives and jobs. Then it would be over for Cody. But every fiber of her being cried out for them to continue. He was out there. She knew he was. And he was alive.

"I can't control what the local authorities do," Phillips argued. "I can only tell you the three things

I know." The haunted look in his eyes—this man she had deep down hoped would be her miracle—spoke of uncertainty and fear. Emotions every bit as strong as her own.

There was something. Jill's heart rose in her throat. "Please, tell me."

"First," he said tightly, "any fool can see the beating your sister suffered didn't take place in her home. It happened somewhere else, at the hands of someone besides her husband. Whoever did this to her, she feared for her safety. Make them look harder."

"There is more to this." It wasn't a question, she'd known it all along. But to have it substantiated, even by someone she had every reason not to trust had victory soaring inside her. This was no love triangle. Her sister hadn't been involved with another man.

Phillips held up a hand for her to listen. "Second, your sister, in my estimation, most likely did kill her husband. I can't give you motive for her actions or even for my conclusions," he went on before she could interrupt, "it's just something I know."

Jill's hopes wilted. She still resisted accepting that her sister could do such a thing. How could he know with such certainty? He couldn't. More of that frustration she'd been battling swooped in on her. How could he give her such hope only to knock her down again?

She wanted to rail at him that he couldn't be certain but one more look into those fierce, dark eyes and she had to admit that, somehow, he was. Defeat settled heavily onto her shoulders.

"Third," he continued, his voice low and tight, tension spiking. "The boy" he paused, looked away. "The boy's alive...somewhere."

Jill's heart leapt in her chest, her hands went to her mouth to hold back the sob that shook her. Thank God. Oh, thank God. She'd known Kate couldn't hurt her son. She'd known it with all her heart.

"We have to find him." No matter what she thought she knew about this man, he believed her. She couldn't let him go.

"Don't." He held up his hands, his face grim. "This is all I can give you. Don't ask me to stay." He shook his head, the movement scarcely visible. "I can't."

As frustrated and confused as she felt, she understood that whatever had happened to this man, the pain and fear he suffered was very real. He was rigid with the weight of it, distant, untouchable. The articles she'd read about him...the horrors he had investigated and evaluated...the breakdown...all of it zoomed into vivid focus like scenes from the latest bestseller by Stephen King.

He'd said he didn't do this anymore. Coming was a favor to Richard. In that moment Jill suddenly realized the heavy price it had cost Paul Phillips to come here.

As much as she needed him, basic human compassion wouldn't allow her to beg him to stay. This battle was going to consume her life, perhaps even tear it apart. How could she ask him, a man who had no personal ties to the crime or the people involved, to set himself on a course for self-destruction again? She couldn't.

"I understand." The words were hers, but the voice was alien to her ears.

He nodded, the movement stilted, his gaze shifting away.

She extended her hand. "Thank you."

He stared at her hand. For a long moment she wasn't sure he was going to touch her. Then he wrapped those long fingers around hers. He flinched, startled or pained. Her own body reacted to a flutter of awareness.

"At least I have something to go on. Thank you for that. I will find my nephew."

He drew his hand from hers. All signs of pain or fear or the other emotions he battled disappeared. "Wherever he is," he warned, the change in his tone chilling her to the bone, "he's safe from the threat." He looked around the room as if searching for the right words, then his gaze zeroed in on hers "Whatever this is, don't go looking for it, Jillian. It's already looking for you."

CHAPTER FIVE

His lungs would not fill completely with air, no matter how deep the breath he took, no matter that his driver's side window was open and allowing the wind to whip against his face.

Paul drove faster, wanted this damned town as far behind him as possible. He wanted images of Jill, Kate, and her son out of his head.

But they wouldn't go.

Save us.

He couldn't save them. He was way beyond saving anyone. Didn't they know that? He couldn't even save himself.

The urgency wouldn't go away. Those needy tentacles reached out to him, urged him to go back. He couldn't go back. *Not and survive.* Right now survival was all he had left.

His panic grew, expanded, crowding out all rational thought. He had to get back in control.

Breathe.

Don't think.

Just breathe and drive faster. Get the hell out of here.

A sign inviting him to *Please Come Again* mocked him. The idyllic garden scene depicted behind the name Paradise made his gut clench with the urge to heave. But the symbolism was more accurate than anyone knew. Paradise was the perfect small southern town, all right. Just like the Garden of Eden to Adam and Eve. Perfect, serene, offering all that their simple lives required.

But they hadn't been alone…something bad had been in that perfect garden with them. That same kind of evil was in Paradise.

He hoped Jill would watch her back. Saving her sister and nephew might just prove the last thing she ever did.

Sweat bloomed on his skin. Not the clean kind you earned with hard physical labor. But the tainted kind, soured by the essence of pure terror.

His terror.

He couldn't risk getting sucked into that kind of darkness. He'd gotten lost there too many times… until he'd broken. Now he could never go back… not and walk away with his sanity, such as it was.

The deepest of the darkness had been waiting for him in Paradise. Like a cancer that lay dormant until just the right moment and then it awakened, consuming all in its path. He had worked for five long years to keep that abyss at bay.

Still they came to him, begging for his help. He told them what they wanted to hear and took their money. He'd hoped that with enough failures they would stop coming.

But a single success out of dozens of failures gave all the others hope. And they kept coming. Wanting answers he couldn't give without wading into the darkness.

He couldn't do it.

A cat darted in front of him. He slammed on the brakes. Tires squealed. The odor of burning rubber filled the air.

The Land Rover skidded and rocked to a stop.

For long minutes he couldn't move. Just sat there on that deserted road and tried to regain some semblance of control. Inside, where no one could see, he was shaking with a fear that refused to be conquered.

A fear that wasn't about Jill or Kate or the missing kid.

It was about Paul Phillips.

A secret fear that had been growing, becoming stronger every day as long as he could remember.

His work had only exacerbated it. No matter how hard he focused on something else it was always there. Waiting. It had taken over completely that once…in that dark, dank cave where a little girl had died just because he had been a coward.

The threat of it hadn't left him since. It hummed just behind his every waking thought, never really quieting. Never really going away. His only escape was sleep and even then he dreamed. Dreamed of staring at himself…hearing his own voice, tasting his own fear and knowing somehow that he was already dead. The only time that perpetual awareness had slowed, at times ceasing altogether, was when he drowned it with enough alcohol. Didn't matter what kind. The stronger, the better.

Not even the loving parents he remembered so well could protect him from the fear of that darkness. They had loved him, had protected him as best they could. But he'd always felt separate from them. An emotional distance he couldn't quite identify. He could replay every birthday, every Christmas, every vacation they'd shared, but it was as if seeing it from some detached place. Pictures in a book. His book, but one that held nothing except impersonal landmarks of his early life which stirred no distinctive reaction.

That emptiness and the perpetual undercurrent of fear marked him as flawed, seriously screwed up.

He let go a shaky breath and almost laughed. This was why he never got close to anyone. Never allowed another human being to touch him. His whole life was superficial…skin deep.

Somehow Jill Ellington was in a similar place. Detached yet eyeball deep in the muck. She couldn't do this alone. Her ability to deny what she felt was far too strong.

She needed help.

He shook his head. He wasn't supposed to get involved.

Yet he wanted to go back. Needed to help her for some reason that eluded him.

He was a fool.

More of that panic exploded in his chest.

He shoved the door open and half stumbled out of the Land Rover. He reached back onto the dash for his cigarettes. His hands shook so badly it took three attempts to light one. He inhaled deeply, waiting for relief that wouldn't come. He closed his eyes and exhaled. The silence was deafening, broken only by the hiss of smoke as he released it from his lungs.

He'd lost complete control once and it had cost him everything. It had taken him nearly a year to pull himself together again. Two months of that year were spent in a psychiatric hospital. Oh the Feds had sprung for a ritzy joint. They'd wanted the best for their top dog-and-pony show. The doctors had filled him full of powerful meds unknowingly sending him deeper into the black abyss.

He'd barely survived.

He took another deep drag from the cigarette. He couldn't go back there.

The hero the world had once deemed him to be had died in that darkness a long time ago. There wasn't a force on earth that could resurrect the dead.

He dropped the cigarette butt onto the pavement and squashed it with the heel of his shoe.

Besides, Jill Ellington didn't need a hero. She needed a miracle. He'd stopped believing in miracles about ten years ago.

CHAPTER SIX

Kate suffered a grand mal seizure during the night. Her condition had been touch and go for a time, but she eventually stabilized. The doctor was performing tests this morning to determine the cause of the seizure and any possible damage incurred during the episode.

Jill sat at Kate's bedside, not bothering to restrain the tears that trekked down her cheeks. Her sister was asleep, had been since Jill's arrival. She had prayed over and over this latest turn of events wouldn't make things any worse for Kate. And if her sister suddenly awoke, how would Jill tell her that Cody remained missing? The chief had warned her this morning that hope of finding him alive was waning fast. There had been no hits on the Amber Alert. No one had seen him...no one had come forward with any sort of knowledge about him or about Kate.

Richard called to see how things were going. Jill couldn't bring herself to tell him Phillips had gone.

Instead, she discussed Cullen Marks' recommendation with Richard. To her surprise, he agreed. If no supporting evidence could be found, her options were sorely limited. She had to face that reality. When Richard asked what Phillips thought, she'd at first considered not telling him. It would only make him all the more certain of her only recourse. In the end, she'd told him that Phillips felt confident Kate had killed her husband. What else was there to say?

Jill barely slept last night. Those last few minutes with Phillips kept playing over and over in her head. His fear had been palpable. At first she'd been angry that he'd just walked away. Despite the glaring fact she'd wanted him to go from the beginning. But some part of her wouldn't let go of the idea that he knew something. Sensed something more than he'd shared.

He made several valid points.

If only she could get the police to look more thoroughly into why Kate had been beaten and where it happened. What, if anything, did the beating have to do with Karl's murder? Those were answers she urgently needed but no one wanted to bother finding them. They had their murderer, who was clearly not competent to stand trial. End of discussion. Kate's motives would only sully the family name. Jill should let it be. That was the general consensus. The chief was only dragging his feet with formal charges because it was unnecessary until all the facts were in. But it was only a matter of time before charges were made.

But Jill wanted answers, whatever it did to the family name. She wanted Cody found. Hope bloomed anew as she replayed Phillips' certainty about her nephew being alive. Why she foolishly clung to that hope was beyond her.

Jill exhaled a heavy breath, her gaze settling on her twin's battered face. Why would Kate hide her son? What if he'd been kidnapped by whoever beat her? Jill stilled. She hadn't considered that scenario. Had the chief? What if someone had taken him and that's what this was all about?

Maybe Karl had been the one to inadvertently allow it to happen and in her grief and despair, Kate killed him. Jill frowned. That didn't feel fully plausible. Karl wouldn't have done such a thing on purpose. If a scenario like that had taken place, surely he would have called the police. But, as a criminal attorney, she'd seen and heard a lot that appeared far less plausible. The human psyche was a strange and delicate thing. Maybe some external trouble, such as the loss of her child, had disrupted the delicate balance of Kate's.

But why wouldn't she and Karl have contacted the police?

Who had beaten her so badly?

Jill chewed her bottom lip. What if this was solely about the child or money or both?

Phillips was so certain that Kate had killed her husband, but what if he was wrong? He couldn't be absolutely certain. It wasn't like he'd been there. His success rate was only about forty percent.

Funny how she tossed those percentage points around to best suit the scenario she preferred.

One thing was certain, she would never know what happened if she didn't get out there and find out for herself. No one else was going to do the job. Renewed enthusiasm revved inside her. If she could find Cody, this mystery would unravel itself. Kate would want her to find the truth. She placed a gentle kiss on Kate's forehead and pressed the buzzer to let the nurse know she was ready to leave. Jill intended to start her own investigation. She didn't need the police or Paul Phillips.

Movement beneath the bed sheet jerked Jill's gaze downward. She drew the cover back and watched, startled, as Kate's right leg trembled for ten or fifteen seconds before growing still once more. Kate slept through the episode, her respiration and heart rate remaining the same according to the monitors.

"You ready to go, Miss Ellington?" the nurse asked from the door.

Jill looked from her sister to the nurse in confusion and no small amount of fear. "Kate's right leg suddenly started shaking. Has that happened before?"

Sympathy shadowed the nurse's expression. "I'm afraid so, Miss Ellington. It happened several times last night. The doctor is running tests to try and determine if the episodes have anything to do with the seizure."

Jill nodded slowly, defeat tugging at her. What was happening to her sister? She smoothed the sheet back over Kate and pressed another kiss to her forehead. Somehow she would find the answers... she wouldn't let Kate down.

* * *

Twenty minutes later, Jill parked in front of Kate's High Point mansion. She emerged from her car, unable to take her eyes off the yellow crime scene tape that marked her sister's home as a place where tragedy had occurred. The tape fluttered in the on again, off again breeze, running a chill over her skin despite the suffocating heat. High Point was an exclusive housing development on a ridge overlooking Paradise. Most of the homeowners were local professionals either at MedTech or the thriving fertility clinic, LifeCycle.

Karl Manning had been a wealthy man. His family would certainly be a ripe target for kidnapping. The theory was definitely worth looking into. Why the hell hadn't the chief investigated this avenue? She supposed he may have but he certainly hadn't mentioned it. Jill studied the homes of the surrounding neighbors on the cul-de-sac as she formed her plan of action. Why not start right here?

She moved up the paved walk of the house to the right of Kate's. Though the residents of Paradise had always been considerably more affluent than their counterparts in other small Tennessee towns, this, she studied the sprawling home, was not old money whose roots went back more than a hundred years. This was new money, the kind earned in recent decades.

People like Karl Manning built their houses high above those he wanted to impress. He and his new money could look down on those who had struggled for generations to pass along their dwindling wealth to their heirs. Karl resented having to earn his standing in the community despite the fortune he'd amassed. That was one of many things Jill hadn't liked about him.

She pushed her personal feelings aside and pressed the doorbell. The door opened immediately, as if someone had watched her approach. A young woman with Asian features and holding a squirming toddler in her arms stood on the other side of the threshold.

Dark eyes widened. "Kate?" She gasped. "I didn't know you'd been released!"

"I'm sorry," Jill hastened to explain. "I'm her sister, Jillian."

The young woman's expression immediately turned guarded. "Oh, sorry. May I help you?" Her tone had dropped somewhere in the vicinity of the Arctic.

"Are you the lady of the house?" Jill pushed a pleasant smile into place.

"No. Mrs. Radcliff is at the clinic. Would you like to leave a message for her?" She swayed when a boy of about four crashed into her legs. "Roman, stop that," she scolded.

"Are you the nanny?" The woman looked entirely too young to be the mother of two.

She shifted the toddler to her other hip. "Yes." She frowned then. "I don't mean to be rude, but I'm very busy right now."

Jill tacked her sagging smile back into place. "I apologize for the intrusion." She extended her hand. "As I said, I'm Kate's sister and I wanted to ask you a few questions that might help her."

The woman's expression froze, as did her hand, just shy of reaching Jill's. "I'm afraid I can't tell you anything about the Mannings." She drew her hand back and lifted her chin into a more wary tilt. "You'll have to excuse me, I have the children to attend to."

Neighbors had always been close in Paradise. Jill didn't understand this reaction. She flattened her palm against the door and held it open a moment longer. She needed answers. "What about the children? Did Roman ever play with Cody?"

Uncertainty flashed in those dark eyes. She hadn't anticipated that question. Or Jill's persistence. "No. Never."

Jill scoffed. "You're telling me that two rambunctious little boys living this close together never managed to share the same outdoor playtime."

She shook her head. "Cody attended the MedTech Child Development Program. He was never home." She seemed relieved that she'd come up with what sounded like an irrefutable answer.

"I see. Well, thank you anyway."

Jill knew fear when she saw it and this woman was scared. Once she'd recovered from the initial surprise of seeing Kate's identical twin, she'd done okay until Jill asked that one unexpected question. Why would anyone tell her not to answer questions about Kate? That was exactly how it felt. And it didn't make sense.

"One more thing." Jill turned back, once more preventing the nanny from closing the door. "Did my sister and her husband quarrel frequently?" The question came out of nowhere, surprising Jill almost as much as it did the other woman.

She shrugged. "I…ah. I wouldn't know."

Jill nodded. "Thank you again."

This time it was the younger woman's voice that stalled her departure. "Miss Ellington?"

Jill hesitated, her heart racing at the prospect of gleaning some tidbit after all.

"Don't bother going across the street. No one's home. And they don't have any children." She glanced around the yard as if fearful someone would overhear her. "You shouldn't waste your time here. The police have already talked to everyone. No one here knows anything."

The door promptly closed.

Despite the woman's warning, Jill spent the rest of the day going from door to door. When she'd been to every house in High Point, she dropped by Kate's medical doctor's office. Then the library. Kate loved to read. She'd told Jill about taking Cody to the library even as an infant. After that, Jill hit the market and shops where she knew Kate most likely shopped. She had shocked most of the citizens before the day was through. They all thought she was Kate. Apparently the whole town had forgotten all about Jill. Of course, the moment she'd made the correction there was a new set of questions to be answered. *When did you get back into town? How's your law practice? Are you married yet?*

In the end, the story of the Manning family was always the same. Kate was a wonderful mother. Cody a lovely child, obedient and so intelligent. And Karl, he was a perfect father and husband. The Mannings were touted as a storybook family. No one could think of a thing negative to say. And no one had seen Cody since that fateful day. It was such a tragedy. Not one of the people she interviewed could believe it happened.

By the time Jill parked in front of the garage behind her mother's house, it was almost dark and she was ready to cry with defeat and exhaustion.

Her mother was waiting for her at the back door. "Where have you been?"

Jill was taken aback by the question and her tone. "I've been following leads. Has something happened?" Her heart fluttered.

Claire stepped aside so that her daughter could enter through the kitchen door. "I want to know exactly what you've been doing all day."

Jill tossed her purse onto the oak breakfast table and dropped into one of the Windsor back chairs. She kicked her shoes off. Her feet were killing her.

"I told you. I've been running down leads on Kate's case."

"You've been talking to people," her mother accused. Her chin jutted out at a defiant angle, her slender shoulders rigid with outrage.

Jill couldn't fathom what this was all about. "Yes. I have." She massaged one foot. "Why are you so upset?"

"Would you like a glass of iced tea?"

Talk about split personality. "Sure. I'd love one." It hit her then that she hadn't eaten all day and she was suddenly starved. As soon as she caught her breath she'd make herself a sandwich. But first, she had to figure out what was going on with her mother.

Claire busied herself with preparing two glasses of iced tea, carefully placing a wedge of lemon on the rim of each. When she'd completed her task, she joined Jill at the kitchen table that had served Ellingtons for more than a century.

"Chief Dotson called me," Claire announced after tasting her tea.

Jill almost choked on her first sip. "Have they found Cody?" Anticipation pounded in her chest. Why hadn't her mother said something right at the start?

Claire shook her head. "It wasn't about my grandson. It was about *you*."

The anticipation drained away, leaving a deeper sense of exhaustion. "Me? Why did he call about me?"

Claire folded her hands primly on the table and studied them, anything to avoid meeting Jill's gaze. "He said you'd spent the entire day going all over town asking questions about your sister and her marriage."

Dumbfounded, Jill could only shake her head in confusion. She worked hard at keeping a respectful tone with her mother. Sometimes, like now, it was difficult. Jill had always tended to speak her mind, Kate was the more discreet one. What she'd done today shouldn't surprise anyone, least of all her mother.

"That's true." No need to lie. "I hope to find some lead on what happened to Cody and why Karl is dead. I would think you'd be interested in that as well."

Claire cut her a sharp glance. "Of course I'm interested in the welfare of my grandson. And certainly I would like this whole business solved. Put to rest once and for all. It's you who's creating trouble."

Trouble? "What on earth are you talking about?" All thoughts of food or fatigue evaporated.

"How much more humiliation do you think this family can withstand? The chief is attempting to find some way to work this out for the best. Can't you see that?"

Stunned, shocked, neither of those things were an adequate description of how Jill felt at the moment. "Aren't you the one who demanded I come home and fix this problem?"

"That was before that man showed up."

That man? Anger rippled through Jill. "Why don't we get to the heart of the matter, Mother?" Jill suggested with cold calculation. "There is only one adult member in this family besides me and Kate. So if I'm not humiliated by my actions, and, God knows, Kate isn't, then it must be you. Would that be an accurate deduction?"

"Don't use your lawyer talk on me, young lady," she snapped. "I will not have you coming here and working against what's right. The Judge would turn over in his grave if he could see you now."

Jill shoved her feet back into her shoes and stood, the legs of her chair scraping across the floor. She didn't need her mother to remind her that her father had been disappointed in her more often than not. "Well, the Judge is dead, Mother, he can't see anything. However, you're very much alive. I wonder why it is that you can't see what's right in front of you? Don't you want Cody found and Kate cleared of guilt?"

Claire Ellington's cheeks flushed with anger, but her voice was calm when she spoke. "Of course I want those things! I love you, Jill, and I love your sister and my grandson. All of you are gifts straight from God. But I won't allow you to drag this family's good name through the dirt while you try and prove some pointless theory. I asked you to come here and see that your sister was properly cared for and that the situation was resolved appropriately. If you can't do that, then you should at least have enough respect for what your father stood for to admit defeat and suffer through this as I am."

Jill stormed out of the room before she said something she would regret later. Her mother was unbelievable. Another blast of fury thundered through her at the idea that the chief was watching her. What the hell was wrong with these people? Didn't they realize that a child was missing and a man was dead and something had to be done about how and why it happened? Did they think they could sweep it under the rug and it would simply go away? That life in Paradise would go back to business as usual as if a murder had never happened?

She considered locking herself away in her room to cry it out, but thought better of it. She needed a walk to burn off some of this adrenaline. Her feet were already aching but she couldn't trust herself under the same roof with her mother at the moment. Jill wanted to shake her. But it would change nothing. Claire Ellington had been born and raised to consider the family name first and foremost over all else. Even her own daughters and grandson.

Jill immediately regretted the thought. Her mother meant well. Claire had known and trusted Chief Dotson her whole life. She had no idea how the law could be manipulated to suit one's own purposes.

Just more proof that Jill was alone in this. She jerked the front door open and took an immediate step back.

Paul Phillips stood on the opposite side of the threshold, one fist poised to knock.

For several seconds Jill couldn't speak. At first she was afraid she'd somehow conjured up his image and that if she blinked he'd disappear. She reached out and touched him. He flinched. A cyclone of emotions whirled through her. He was real all right. His eyes were a little red around the rims and a lot blood shot as if he hadn't slept much or had gotten rip roaring drunk last night. Five o'clock shadow darkened his lean jaw. As usual the jeans were faded, the shirt worn comfortable, and he'd opted for that one concession to the establishment, a sports jacket, a lightweight one in deference to the heat.

Jill's knees went traitorously weak with relief. She'd never been so glad to see anyone in her life. "Did you forget something, Dr. Phillips?"

He shrugged one wide shoulder. "If you still want my help, I'm available."

Anger flared hot and fast. He'd left her here to do this on her own, forcing her to almost admit defeat. Gratitude at the idea of having him back vaporized that emotion in an instant. Whatever his past, he was on her side. Maybe he was a charlatan but at least she wouldn't be in this alone.

"Are you sure about that?" She worked at collecting the composure that had scattered far and wide this day. God, she was tired.

He glanced about the verandah as if looking for a new topic to discuss. "Yeah. Unfortunately, indecision is one of my many vices."

"You'll help me find the answers I'm looking for before you take off again?" She held her breath, praying that he planned to see this thing all the way through. As many doubts as she had about him, after today she was one hundred percent certain she couldn't do this alone.

He shrugged again. "Why not? I've tortured myself before and lived to talk about it."

Relief, so profound that she almost wept, washed over her. "I'm glad you're back."

"We should talk." He looked beyond her shoulder for a moment. "Privately."

Her nerves frayed a little more but she held onto the hope his presence provided, foolish as that might prove. "You're timing is perfect, Dr. Phillips. I was just going out to dinner. We'll get a quiet table somewhere."

* * *

Jill chose the same restaurant where she'd met with Cullen Marks. It wasn't that Quinton's was the classiest place in town, it was the ambiance. Quiet, tasteful, and spacious. Tables weren't too close together and if she asked for one in the back, she and Phillips would have plenty of privacy.

When the valet had driven away in his Land Rover, Phillips hesitated before going inside. "Did something happen today that you're not telling me about?"

That he'd picked up on her agitation so quickly surprised her. "It's a long story."

"I've got all night."

The restaurant's double doors opened and Mayor Austin Hammersly exited along with one of Paradise's other esteemed residents, Senator Kenneth Wade. The senator was far taller than the mayor and considerably more charming.

"Good evening Mayor, Senator." Jill hadn't seen either man in years. The senator had attended Vanderbilt with her father.

Both men looked straight at Phillips, then at Jill. She tensed. After the chief's call to her mother, everyone who was anyone in Paradise likely had heard about *the man* she'd invited to town. The chief didn't make a move in this town without the mayor's input. She wasn't so sure that dance extended to the senator.

"Jillian," the mayor said coolly.

Oh, yes. He was aware of her poking around in the investigation and he was not pleased.

"Why, Jillian Ellington," the senator enthused, "it's good to see you." He took her by the shoulders and dropped a fleeting kiss on her cheek. "I certainly wish it were under more pleasant circumstances."

"That makes two of us," she agreed. Then she pretended to remember her manners, when in actuality she'd hoped it wouldn't come to this. "This is Dr. Paul Phillips. He's here to help me with Kate's situation."

"Ken Wade," the senator said, grasping Phillips' hand and pumping it twice. "Let me introduce you to Mayor Austin Hammersly."

His face beet red, the mayor's gesture was noticeably brief, a mere grazing of palms. "I wish I could say it's a pleasure."

Jill braced for the inevitable.

The mayor's hell fire and brimstone expression flew in her direction. "How could you come back here, young lady, and bring in an outsider to check up on us? Why, the chief is appalled. Have you no respect for the man? He's had folks calling all day, demanding to know about the deceptions to which you're alluding."

"Mayor, there's been a misunderstanding. I wasn't—"

"I know what you're doing," he blurted. "You're behaving just as you did back in your melodramatic teenage years. Grow up, Jillian. Stop trying to turn this tragic event into some sort of spotlight for yourself. Have some respect for your sister and her poor dead husband!"

And what about her son? She should have been angry at his accusations. She should have winced at the injustice of it. Instead, all she could think was why hadn't he mentioned the child. Didn't it matter that he was missing? Presumed dead?

"Austin, good heavens, man!" the senator implored. "Jillian isn't trying to cause trouble. She's only trying to understand this unspeakable tragedy. Give her some grace!"

She found her voice. "I'm sorry if my actions caused any trouble, Mayor. But the Senator's right. I need to understand how this happened."

The mayor glowered at her without sympathy, but refrained from further comment.

"Rest assured, Jillian." Senator Wade dragged her attention back to him. "I won't rest until this matter is cleared to both our satisfactions."

She dredged up a smile. Whether it was his heartfelt desire or simply the politician in him, she appreciated the sentiment. Her negativity tolerance had already far exceeded its daily limit.

"I look forward to meeting you again, Dr. Phillips," the senator said in parting. "I hope you'll work with Chief Dotson and help us right this terrible wrong."

Phillips nodded and watched the two men walk away before reaching for the door. He sent an assessing glance in Jill's direction. "How about we order a drink before I ask what that was about?"

She nodded, too physically and emotionally drained to speak.

Things just couldn't get any worse.

Strike that, things could get a lot worse. Cody was still missing.

CHAPTER SEVEN

Jill stared at her salad, fork clasped in her hand as if she was weighing the pros and cons of taking that first bite.

"You should eat," Paul suggested.

When she'd opened that door and found him standing on her mother's verandah, she'd looked ready to collapse in surrender. Her expression had brightened as if he was the answer to her prayers. That was asking a hell of a lot from a burned out has been like him. Considering he was on pretty shaky ground in more ways than one, maybe it was crazy to even hope. Despite the cold, hard truth, for the first time in a long time, for reasons he couldn't fully fathom, he wanted to get this right.

He was a fool. But it wasn't the first time and he doubted it would be the last as long as he was still breathing.

"I'm not sure I can," she murmured, then propped her chin in her free hand. "Everything has gone wrong."

He watched her eyes grow moist with tears and the urge to reach out to her was almost more than he could resist. He had to be very careful here. Tread slowly and cautiously. He was purposely putting himself at risk...for her. Control was all that kept him sane. As risky as this decision was, he knew with every fiber of his being that Jillian Ellington was in danger and he had to discern the source before it was too late.

Maybe for both of them.

"It's easy," he said, scooting those troubling thoughts to the side. "Take a forkful into your mouth, chew, swallow. Repeat."

Those blues eyes darted up to look at him. "There's more than mechanics involved, Phillips."

He gestured to the stemmed glass at her right. "That'll make it easier."

"Are you speaking from experience?" A skeptical arch of one golden eyebrow punctuated the pointed question.

He pushed his own, empty salad plate away and relaxed more fully into the chair. "I thought you were glad to see me."

Contrition instantly replaced the skepticism. "I'm very glad. I apologize for being a...well, a bitch." She straightened and stared down at her salad once more. "Like I said, it's been a really bad day."

"Eat," he ordered. "I won't discuss the case with you until then."

She shot him another look across the table. "Blackmail?"

"Trust me, I've been known to stoop lower than that."

This lady didn't like being bossed around, but she acquiesced because the end would justify the means. So she ate, slowly, daintily. Nothing like the way he wolfed down a meal. He often went for a day, two even, without remembering to eat, then he was like a ravenous animal. The way a person ate spoke volumes about them. Were they shy? Confident? Eager? Reluctant?

Confident and reserved. That was Jillian Ellington. She, more than the case, was why he had come back. There was a strange connection between them. For the first time in a long time he wanted— no he needed—to protect someone.

Cutting himself some slack, he had driven all the way back to Memphis, drank himself into oblivion, and then awakened at noon with a hellacious hangover and fear knotting in his gut. The fear had been different this time. He'd faced his reflection in his dreams, as always, and had known somehow that looking at that image was like staring at his own death. But this time the fear hadn't been for him. It had been for her. He felt the danger all around her. Knew if he didn't stay close something bad would happen to her. Soon.

He had to come back.

For once since his life turned into this waking nightmare, he wanted to do the right thing regardless of the consequences.

He wanted to stop running from the fear. To face his demons. He wanted some kind of life back. Hell of a decision to make in less than forty-eight hours. Or maybe irrational decisions were a new level to his ongoing nightmare.

Time would tell just how badly he'd screwed up this time.

"That's the best I can do," she said of the half-eaten salad. "Satisfied?"

He studied her for a moment or two before giving her what she wanted. "Tell me what happened today."

"The hospital called early this morning. Kate had a grand mal seizure late last night and things were shaky for a while. The doctor hopes to know more about what caused the episode in a day or two. He's running tests."

Paul was familiar with the drugs used to medicate Kate. He'd reviewed her chart. If she had been medicated last night, and according to her chart that happened at eight each night, she should have been out for the duration. If she didn't have a history of epilepsy, there could be an underlying cause, drug interaction, or even something related to her psychotic break. The timing just seemed a little off, a little late for a drug interaction since she'd been taking the same ones for two days with no adverse reaction, and a little early for the drugs to have worn off sufficiently to facilitate conditions for a seizure. He opted to keep that to himself until he could review her chart again.

"After spending some time with her," Jill went on, "I decided to start interviewing her neighbors and the people she associated with frequently to see if anyone remembered seeing Cody Sunday afternoon or evening. I asked if they'd noticed anything odd in hers or Karl's behavior lately." She shrugged. "I spent the whole day going from door to door, shop to shop."

The waiter came, cleared the salad plates from their table, then deposited the steaming entrees before them. The steak and baked potato Paul had ordered had his mouth watering. He glanced at Jill's selection, linguini with white clam sauce and steamed vegetables. Only a woman would order something that delicate and insubstantial, in his opinion, when she hadn't eaten all day. But then, the starch-laden carbs would serve as a good energy booster.

"And what did you learn?" he asked as he sliced into the medium well New York strip.

"Nothing."

The defeat in her voice brought his head up. "Nothing?"

"They were the perfect couple. The perfect family. No one can believe it happened. No arguments, no strange behavior, no money woes. Nothing. Well, except for their neighbor's nanny. She seemed a little nervous. But if she knows anything, she isn't telling." Jill sighed. "Bottom line, everyone I spoke to said the same thing."

If she'd told him that a close family friend, or even two, had insisted all was perfect in the Manning household, he wouldn't be surprised. People only saw what they wanted to. But *everyone*?

"How many people are we talking about?"

Her brow lined in concentration. "Thirty, maybe thirty-five."

His instincts kicked into overdrive. "Start at the beginning. Who, exactly, did you interview?"

"I stopped at every house in High Point, the housing development where she lives. The baker, the grocer, the librarian, several shop owners, and even the postmaster. They all said exactly the same thing."

His gaze narrowed, alarm bells going off in his head.

She leaned forward slightly as if she wanted to be absolutely certain that no one else heard the next part. "Then when I got home, my mother cross examined me." Her eyes widened with disbelief. "My mother, for Christ's sake! She demanded to know what I'd been doing. When things escalated she admitted that the chief had called and wanted to know what I was doing asking questions and making accusations!"

"Were you making accusations?"

She made a sound of frustration. "Of course not. If anyone really said that, it was only because they came to that conclusion on their own."

"You did learn something," he said. Her expression argued his assertion. "You learned that no one here wants to see the truth. They prefer to pretend bad things don't happen in Paradise."

"That's it." She laughed, a dry, weary sound. "It felt like I was in Stepford, Connecticut. You know, the movie about the perfect wives."

"I know the one." He nodded to her plate. "Eat." Paul took a bite of his steak. Eventually, Jill surrendered. She swirled the linguini around her fork and then lifted it to her lips. She had nice lips.

He waited before saying anymore. He wanted her to focus on the meal. For a while they ate, allowing the hum of other conversations to fill the void. Eventually she placed her fork on the table and turned her attention to her wine. He did the same.

"The chief knows who I am." He should have foreseen this problem and used an alias. With only a few calls the chief had likely determined they had an ex-profiler who specialized in missing persons and in getting into the minds of the perpetrators as well as the victims. He'd no doubt also perused the less flattering stories available on the internet. But then, he hadn't intended to stay.

"I hadn't thought of that," she murmured distractedly. "But my mother did seem inordinately annoyed that I'd brought you here. Makes sense that the chief said something."

"The chief has told people to be careful what they say to you. That you're trouble." Paul considered the hurtful words the mayor had flung at her tonight. "What's the deal with you and the mayor?"

Jill stared at her plate again. He suspected it wasn't because she wanted to admire the remnants of her dinner or that she didn't understand the question. She just didn't want to face the question. The subject was painful. He could feel her hurt.

She leveled her gaze on his, those blue eyes open, honest. "From the time I was fourteen I had a problem being a twin." She sipped her wine and considered the stemmed glass before continuing. "I hated being a twin. I wanted to be *me*. So I did everything different from Kate. I wouldn't dress anything like her, wouldn't wear my hair the same way." She sighed. "Got into trouble at school. Refused to obey my parents on more occasions than I care to admit. The whole shooting match. While Kate continued to be the perfect student and perfect daughter."

There was more. He opted to let her have her say in her own time.

"Don't get me wrong," she continued, "my father loved us both. And so did—does my mother." Jill frowned, remembering. "She was different back then. You know, normal."

Jill was a fighter. She'd been fighting for what she believed in for a long time.

"I dated the boys my parents would have preferred I avoid. I ran with the wild crowd." She laughed softly. "At least the wildest crowd we had here in Paradise."

"While Kate focused on her studies and probably dated the same nice guy all through high school," he suggested.

"Exactly." Jill studied the gold liquid in her glass as if it was a crystal ball. "I never stopped loving them, I just refused to be what they wanted me to be."

Paul watched the woman seated across from him as she relived the regrets. She was tough. She still hadn't given up. Even in her career. Malcolm Teller had a reputation as a pompous ass who just happened to be a fantastic attorney. That Jill could hold on her own with sharks like him spoke volumes about her strong will. It also explained why Teller wasn't representing her sister's case. Professional tolerance only went so far. He doubted Jill had any intention of putting up with his crap outside work.

"How did you end up at Ole Miss?" Paul had his own ideas about how that happened, but he wanted to be sure.

"Pigheadedness, what else? They wanted Kate and me to stay close to home and attend Kessler, but I secretly applied to Ole Miss."

He had to smile. "I bet mom and dad were surprised."

The silence that followed was telling.

"Surprised is an understatement. They refused to allow me to go," she admitted. "I went anyway, but I had to do it on my own. Loans, scholarships, and I worked every minute I wasn't in class."

That's where the rift lay in the seemingly perfect Ellington family. A wide, painful gap that could never be completely healed.

"I walked away and never looked back." She emptied her glass. "Oh, I came back for the occasional visit, but nothing more. I couldn't bear to see the disappointment in my father's eyes. So I stayed away as much as possible."

And then he died, sealing her fate. Paul knew the rest. And daddy's little girl had been trying to

make it up to him ever since. That's what the obsession with helping her sister was about. She loved her
sister and wanted to help, but ultimately she had to
do it to redeem herself in her own eyes if not her
parent's.

Paul refused to admit that his being here fell
along those lines as well. But the truth was he
needed redeeming too. He just wasn't sure this was
the place…or the woman to do it despite this bizarre
connection to her he felt. If he failed in some way,
which was likely if control continued to be as big a
problem as he anticipated, his weakness might just
prove a devastating mistake for them both.

He didn't ask any more questions. She looked
exhausted. They both needed a good night's
sleep. He resisted the impulse to laugh at that one.
He couldn't recall the last time he'd had a good
night's sleep, at least not without the aid of alcohol.
Attempting to start now without his preferred sleep
aid would be biting off a hell of a lot more than he
was prepared to chew.

As they left the restaurant, she asked, "Do you
mind stopping at a convenience store? It's on the
way. I need to pick up a quart of milk. We're out and
Mother will do without before she'll call the market
and schedule a delivery more than once a week."

"Mrs. Ellington doesn't leave the house?"

"She goes into the yard to tend her flowers. But
she never goes more than a few feet from the closest door. She claims she's agoraphobic. After my
father died, she just stopped leaving home. As far as

I know she hasn't left the house since the day of his funeral."

Something else to mull over. "Has she sought treatment?" Agoraphobia typically came with panic disorder. There were treatments, counseling and medication.

"She refuses to discuss it. That's the way we do things here in Paradise." She glanced at him. "If something is too close to the bone we don't talk about it."

It was uncanny how much they had in common. "I can understand that motto." There were some things no one needed to know.

At the convenience store, Paul waited in the Land Rover as Jill went inside. The storefront was glass, allowing him to follow her movements through the store. Uneasiness stirred in the pit of his stomach, something more than the general bad feeling he had about being back in Paradise.

Jill selected a carton of milk from the refrigerated case and made her way to the counter. A brunette woman, petite and confident, judging by her energetic stride, entered the store. Jill turned to see the new arrival. Paul watched the automatic smile slide across her face. She knew the woman, was pleased to see her. The other woman went wide around her and hurried toward the other side of the store. Jill's smile faded. The brunette's movements turned hasty, uncoordinated, completely different body language from only moments before...before she had noticed Jill at the checkout counter.

When Jill climbed back into the passenger seat, her purchase in her arms, she looked puzzled, even a little hurt.

Paul waited for her to mention the other woman.

"That was so odd," she said almost to herself. "I ran into Connie Neil. She was my best friend back in high school." She fastened her seat belt as he backed out of the slot. "She was an accessory to a number of my infamous exploits."

Paul offered the smile he knew she expected.

"I haven't seen her in years. Yesterday I ran into her at the restaurant. She saw me and gushed about how happy she was I was home and how she couldn't wait for us to get together." Annoyance vibrated in her tone. "I mean, there was something a little off, but mainly she acted glad to see me."

"So what's the problem?"

"Tonight—just now in the market—she gave me the brush off. Couldn't get away fast enough."

That was the way Paul saw it. The woman hadn't wanted to face Jill.

"You don't suppose the chief warned her off, too."

No need to answer that one. She knew already.

"Jesus, why is he doing this? Just because I'm taking a different view of the case?"

"There's always the possibility he sees your actions as a personal affront." Paul didn't believe that to be the case but if it made her feel better no harm done. "Your questions might lead the people in *his* town to think *he* hasn't done his job."

"Maybe."

She didn't sound any more convinced than he was. There was a lot more going on here than met the eye, that was for damned sure.

"I think I'll just ask him." She folded her arms over her chest in a defiant gesture. "I have the right to know why I'm being black-balled."

That fighting instinct again. "You should get a good night's sleep before you confront the chief."

Silence hung between them for a few blocks.

"Thank you for coming back."

For such a fighter her voice sounded small and scared.

He stopped at the intersection of Washington Street, dared to meet her gaze. "Don't thank me yet."

* * *

Once Phillips was settled in a guestroom, Jill went in search of her mother. She didn't look forward to this confrontation any more than she did the one with the chief, but the air had to be cleared. Paul Phillips would be staying in this house, though he had resisted the invitation, until this was over.

Jill found Claire in the family room watching television. Many happy memories had been made in this room. Christmases, birthdays. When had all the happiness drained out of this family?

Deep breath. She battled back the tears. "Did I have any calls?" Jill checked the answering machine when she arrived and there were no messages.

"No," her mother said succinctly, her attention fixed on the television screen.

Jill sat down on the sofa next to her and reached for the remote to turn down the volume.

Claire looked annoyed but said nothing.

"Mother, I need you to understand what I'm doing."

"I want no part of it." She sliced her hands through the air, then refolded them in her lap. "Basic human compassion won't permit me to throw out your friend, but I am not in agreement with your actions."

Jill grabbed her mother's hand, held it tight when she resisted. "It doesn't work that way. I'm your daughter, Kate is your daughter. Cody is your grandson. You're in this whether you want to be or not."

Claire stared at her, agony and disbelief in her eyes. "You think I don't know that? My God, I've got a husband in the ground, a grandson missing, and one daughter in a psychiatric ward while another is running around making wild accusations." She snapped her mouth shut as if there was more, but good sense had prevailed.

Jill held her tongue to the count of ten. "Let me explain as best I can the reasons I'm doing the things I'm doing."

Her mother pulled loose from Jill's hold and crossed her arms over her chest. Thankfully she made no move to leave the room. At least that was something.

"There are a number of inconsistencies in this case." Jill took another deep breath and focused on remaining calm. "First, Kate was beaten badly, yet Karl had no marks on his hands, indicating that he wasn't the one who hurt her. Judging by the crime scene photos, the struggle didn't even take place in the room where Karl's body was found. The chief seems to think this is all irrelevant."

"I don't want to hear any of this." Claire's chin trembled. Tears brimmed on her lashes.

Jill couldn't stop there. Her mother had to hear the rest. "There is no motive. Everyone insists that Kate and her family were happy, no money problems, nothing. Yet the chief would have us believe that perhaps there's some unsavory something we don't need to know about the beating. Something best kept quiet. How is that possible if Kate and Karl were so happy?"

"It's true," Claire protested. "They had no problems at all. They were happy." She said the last with a bit less conviction.

Holding back the questions she wanted to fire at her mother, Jill went on, "If they had no problems, then Karl shouldn't be dead by his wife's hand. Likewise, our chief of police should be very concerned how and why one of his citizens was brutally beaten by someone other than her husband."

Claire paled, her breath caught. "Kate could not have killed him."

"Mother," Jill stopped, steadied her emotions, "her prints are the only ones on the murder weapon."

"I don't care, there must be a mistake."

Finally. "My point exactly." Jill savored the mini triumph. "There has been a mistake and we must find the truth."

Confusion claimed her mother's expression. She blinked, obviously seeing for the first time the dilemma confronting Jill. Or maybe simply growing weary of pretending she didn't see.

"And then there's Cody," Jill pressed on. "Where is he? We both know Kate wouldn't hurt her son. And he didn't just disappear."

Claire looked away again.

Jill ignored the rebuke. That part was more than her mother simply not wanting to hear. She didn't want to discuss her grandson period. There was something not right about that. "I'm thinking he might have been kidnapped and that the whole thing revolves around Karl's work at MedTech."

A gasp escaped the grim line of Claire's lips. "Kidnapping? That's absurd. Where do you get these foolish notions?"

Her mother wasn't this dense or this naïve. "Mother, it happens all the time. As CEO of MedTech, Karl was a wealthy man in the public eye. He and Kate may have been trying to deal with this without involving the police."

Claire shook her head. "You're wrong. I would have known. Karl…"

Jill waited for her to continue, but she didn't. "What about Karl?"

"Nothing."

"Mother, what is it you're not telling me?"

"I will not speak ill of the dead."

Jill rolled her eyes and prayed for patience. "Fine, as long as it's not pertinent to the case."

Her mother looked her dead in the eye. "You mustn't involve yourself with Karl or MedTech. Do you understand me, Jillian? I mean it. Stay out of that."

What did MedTech have to do with anything other than being the source of Karl's income?

Oh, Jesus.

MedTech was one of the largest medical research corporations in the country. What if they were working on some new drug or healing technique that... what if Phillips had been right when he'd alluded to espionage? Dear God...

"Mother, is there something about MedTech you're not telling me?" Jill demanded, the whole concept gaining momentum. There was no way to disguise the agitation or the accusation in her voice. She didn't bother trying.

Claire blinked, looked away quickly. "I don't know what you're talking about." She stood abruptly. "You need to get some sleep, Jill. I think the past couple of days are catching up with you. You're overtired, overwrought. The police will find Cody. They'll find the truth. We'll all be fine."

Jill shot to her feet and took her mother by the shoulders but didn't shake her as she wanted to. Her heart thumped hard. She was on to something. "Tell me, Mother. Is there something you know about MedTech that is relevant to Kate's situation?"

Her mother's gaze didn't waiver this time, she looked at Jill with more ferocity than she'd thought her capable. "Leave it alone, Jill, or we'll both be sorry."

She shrugged off Jill's hands and walked out of the room. Jill watched, too stunned to say anything or to go after her. She wilted onto the sofa and tried to rationalize what had just happened. Her mother knew something. That was the only logical explanation. She knew something that frightened her enough to keep her quiet.

No one in this town, not even her own mother, wanted Jill to get to the bottom of this murder. Even the chief was working against her. Then again, could everyone be wrong except her? That kind of thinking reeked of paranoia. At least she had Phillips on her side. When Jill considered his unstable emotional condition, that wasn't comforting in this particular instance.

But he was all she had.

She climbed the stairs, feeling more and more defeated. She hesitated outside the guestroom door. It was quiet on the other side. Maybe he'd already called it a night. She glanced at the grandfather clock at the end of the hall, nine forty-six. It was still early.

Taking a deep breath for courage, she knocked on the door. A few seconds later it opened.

"Is something wrong?" He looked her up and down.

Jill almost laughed. She should just say yes but that would be a vast understatement. "The real question is, is anything right?" she admitted with a pathetic shake of her head. More hysterical laughter bubbled up in her throat. "My sister killed her husband. My nephew is missing. And I think my mother has gone around the bend."

One of those rare smiles tugged at his lips. He opened the door wider and stepped back. "I hope you can afford me, I'm very expensive and I warn you I don't have a couch."

Tamping down the bout of hysteria, Jill stepped into the room, immediately noting the reports and photos spread over the bed. Knowing what the photos were was more than enough to dissolve any laughter left inside her. She suddenly felt more tired than she could ever remember feeling before.

Out of the blue, she remembered that he smoked. "Do you need an ashtray or anything?"

He shook his head. "It's an on again, off again habit."

"Oh." Well, that explained everything. A kind of disorientation swirled inside her. His unopened bag lay on the floor at the foot of the bed. A laptop case right next to it. "Mother doesn't have WiFi but there is Internet access in my father's study. Feel free to use the study. Just—"

"Keep the door closed," he finished for her.

She nodded. "Yes."

Silence stood between them for a few seconds.

"There was something you needed?" His expression remained impassive, as did his tone. He was being very careful. One of them had to be. All the stress made her yearn for escape, however temporary.

Where in the world had that come from? She hadn't come in here for that kind of escape. Had she? Jill shivered in spite of herself. Her mother was right, she was being foolish.

"You know," she admitted as much to herself as to him, "we can talk about it tomorrow." She was losing her mind. Totally losing it. She turned to go.

He stopped her with a hand on her arm. The contact sent a shiver through her. "I'll be here. I'm not going anywhere."

She didn't look at him, just nodded. She was so desperate at that moment if she'd looked into his eyes she might have lost all semblance of control, and ended up spending the night in his arms—assuming he was willing—seeking the kind of distraction that came with far too many problems of its own.

So she did the only thing she could, she escaped to her own room. Ran from the uncertainty…from the danger.

She sagged against her closed door and shut her weary eyes. And why not run?

Like mother, like daughter.

CHAPTER EIGHT

THURSDAY, JULY 14

Paul took no offense at Claire's blatant rebuff as they'd had coffee that morning. She didn't want him in her house. On the way to the hospital to see Kate, Jill told him about her mother's outburst last night. Aspects of Claire's reactions were common for the family of a victim. And Kate Manning was a victim regardless of the fact that she had most likely killed her husband.

Jill was still reluctant to grasp that part. Murder was an act gentle people like her sister didn't commit. Until all the pieces of the puzzle were in place and she could see the motive, Jill would continue to deny what she couldn't rationalize in her own mind. Another common reaction.

The elevator doors slid open and Paul followed Jill into the main corridor on the fourth floor of Paradise General. They hoped to catch Kate in the least medicated state. The night's meds would have hopefully worn off to a large degree and the morning dose wasn't scheduled until nine.

"Good morning, Dr. Phillips," Nurse Bennett beamed from behind the nurse's station. "It's nice to see you back."

Obviously the chief hadn't spoken to everyone in town. "Nurse Bennett," Paul acknowledged. Nice wasn't a word he would use to describe being back here. What little sleep he'd gotten last night had been riddled with voices and images. He'd finally admitted defeat and drowned the voices with the fifth of bourbon he'd stashed in his bag.

His head was clear enough this morning. Clear enough to know he had to tread damned carefully where Jill was concerned. If she'd looked back just once before leaving his room last night, he wouldn't have been able to let her go.

That couldn't happen again. Those kinds of emotions threatened his control. And complete control was the only way he'd get through this.

"How is she this morning?" Jill asked.

"Still sleeping last time I checked." The nurse skirted the station. "We'll go see if she's awake. It's past time she had her breakfast."

Bennett led the way, unlocking doors as she went, smiling at Paul every chance she got. Jill followed without making any more small talk. Paul wondered if she'd gotten any sleep herself. She still looked exhausted. Dark circles underscored those blue eyes, enhancing the paleness of her fair skin. She'd dressed more comfortably today with navy slacks, a matching sleeveless pullover and practical flats. He would have been happier if the outfit hadn't fit so nicely to those subtle curves of hers.

That's right, dumbass, go ahead and play with the fire.

"Let me know if you need anything," Bennett offered before leaving the room.

Jill stood at her sister's bedside, staring down at her sleeping form, torturing her bottom lip with her teeth.

Paul moved to the foot of the bed. The discoloration on Kate's face was fading into that ugly yellow and purple. The external wounds would heal long before the internal ones.

Those might never heal, for Kate or for Jill.

This was the first time he'd seen the sisters together. Even with the bruises, the resemblance between the two was startling. Perfect mirror images.

Without warning or preamble, Kate's eyes opened and she looked straight at Paul. "You're back."

Paul blinked, looked from Kate to Jill. Her hand went to her throat as her startled gaze flicked to his. For a second there he'd thought maybe he was the only one who'd seen and heard that one.

"Kate, how are you feeling this morning?" Jill took her sister's hand in hers and cradled it lovingly.

Kate looked at Jill with more curiosity than recognition. "I'm fine. How are you?"

New color bloomed on Jill's pale skin. The color of hope. Kate hadn't spoken a word, except in Paul's head, since the police discovered her and her husband's body. This could be the start of a major breakthrough. And some answers.

Jill sat on the edge of the bed and stroked her hair. "I'm fine now." The emotion in her voice almost undid him. "Do you know who I am?" The words quaked with renewed optimism and its underlying anxiety.

"No," Kate said. She spoke in a monotone, her words mechanical. "Would you help me?"

The hair on the back of Paul's neck stood at attention, his heart rate accelerated. He moved closer, watching Kate's expressionless face for even the subtlest change.

"Of course, I'll help you," Jill said softly. "Tell me what you need."

The expression, the monotone never changed. It was eerie to watch. Like a robot. Paul couldn't shake the idea. Not real...not quite human. Like Jill said last night...*Stepford Wives.*

He listened intently, his profiler's instincts on point.

"I first saw him in Lynchburg. At Hattie's," Kate rambled on with no inflection in her tone. "That's when it began."

And just like that, she was gone.

Her jaw fell slack and distance replaced the gleam in her eyes. She lay in the bed, her gaze glued to the ceiling as if some fascinating movie that only she could see was showing there. Complete withdrawal.

"Kate, what do you mean you saw him?" Jill gently shook her sister's shoulder.

Paul didn't stop her. She needed to see for herself that her sister had drifted back to Oz. He wondered again about her medications. He'd noted the kind and dosage the first time he visited. If he were the physician assigned to the case, he'd drop the meds completely and see what happened. Something was keeping her in this state of limbo.

Save us.

The words struck like a bullet to the brain. He watched Kate a moment or two longer and then he knew what he had to do. Whatever she'd seen in Lynchburg they needed to see it too. She'd even given them the place to begin.

"Let's go."

Jill looked startled by his voice. Tears had left a salty path down her cheeks. "I don't understand what she meant." She shook her head. "Maybe it didn't mean anything." She stared at her sister. "How can I help her if I don't understand?"

Paul gently prodded Jill from her sister's side and pressed the buzzer for the nurse. "Let's go. We'll talk about this on the way."

Reluctantly, she allowed him to steer her to the door. She kept looking back, hoping her sister would speak again. But that wasn't going to happen.

* * *

As Phillips drove away from the hospital Jill sat in the Land Rover, depressed and heartsick. Was her sister never going to be well again? She squeezed her eyes shut and banished images of little Cody. She'd called the chief's secretary and asked if there was any news. Even Lucy had given Jill the cold shoulder, informing her in a brisk, exceptionally unfriendly tone that the chief would call *Claire* Ellington if he had news. Though she and Lucy had never been anything other than acquaintances, the accusation in her tone was hard to take.

Jill gritted her teeth and silently cursed the tears that would not abate. Dammit. She was sick to death of crying. She wanted to do something. To find some answers.

"How do we get to Lynchburg?"

The question startled her. Her head came up and she stared at Paul. "What?"

His dark gaze rested heavily on hers. "I want to go to Lynchburg. That's where it started. At Hattie's."

Jill slowly let out the air she'd held in her lungs. As an attorney she knew that a good investigator followed up on every possible lead, no matter how seemingly insignificant. But this went far beyond insignificance. This was a wild goose chase without the goose.

"But we don't know what she saw or even if her statement is anything more than her imagination talking. Shouldn't we just stop all this and focus on finding my nephew?" There had to be a way to help somehow! Her heart squeezed with worry. She'd come here to help and no one was cooperating. Her own mother was off in some freaked out zone Jill couldn't reach. What the hell did she do now?

Her new partner said nothing.

Why should he? Jill dropped her head against the seat and groaned. His point was valid. Doing anything was better than doing nothing and this lead was the only one they had. She needed to calm down and think rationally.

Besides, wasn't she supposed to trust Paul's instincts now that they were working together? Hadn't she made that decision at some point last night?

"You're right," he said patiently, another unexpected facet to the enigma of Paul Phillips. "We don't know what it means or if it'll lead us to your nephew, but it's worth a look."

The man was right. It wasn't like she was getting anywhere here.

"We have to dissect the pieces of your sister's life to find the truth."

She turned to study him. He was on to something. She could feel the ionic change in the air around him.

"Each piece, no matter how small, means something," he went on, "bridges one part to another. Like a puzzle or a map." He flashed her a smile. "We're going to follow the map and see where it takes us."

A new surge of anticipation had her daring to hope. "It's a small town about two hours from here. Less if we hurry."

This one was no different than the cases she worked all the time—except for the emotion. Emotion had kept her so focused on the big picture that she forgot the bigger picture was nothing more than hundreds of smaller pieces.

It was almost always the smallest, most unexpected piece or detail that closed the case.

* * *

One hour and forty-nine minutes after pulling out of the hospital parking lot they rolled into downtown Lynchburg.

Hardly more than a speed zone on a long, lonely stretch of highway, Lynchburg was nestled in a valley amid lush green hills. The small town consisted of a few shops, a post office, grocery store, and not much else. The people were friendly and the main source of employment was the Jack Daniels Distillery. Jill had been here more than a few times growing up.

"Where would you like to start?" She'd wrestled with conflicting emotions for the first half of the drive. Finally, she'd landed on cautiously optimistic. Seemed safe enough.

Maybe that was her mother's problem and she too had found the only place that didn't hurt. *Denial.* Pretend the problem didn't exist and it went away.

Jill feared this one was not going to just go away. If they didn't find Cody soon—she couldn't think about that. Perhaps that was her boundary before reaching the denial stage. Everyone had a limit.

Phillips braked at an intersection. "We'll park and take a stroll. Hattie's is our destination."

Her sister's words echoed as Jill climbed out of the SUV and fell into step with Phillips. What could she have seen in this little out of the way town? Well, actually, the question was who. She'd said, she saw *him. That's when it began.* What began? Better yet, saw who?

A dozen possibilities filtered through Jill's mind. Had she seen Karl with another woman? Had she met another man here? Cullen Marks' suggestion that the DA would try and insinuate an affair scenario on Kate's part zoomed into the midst of Jill's muddled thoughts. She dismissed that idea. Kate simply wasn't the kind of woman who dabbled in affairs. But, as a defense attorney, Jill knew that overlooking that possibility, however unlikely, was a risk she shouldn't take. Somehow she had to set aside her emotions and find some answers.

Beside her, Phillips remained silent. Quietly absorbing all that he saw and heard, she imagined. There was a stillness about him that made her want to peel back the layers concealing his whole story. Power emanated from him so subtly, that you really had to pay attention to feel it. His strength was like a sleeping lion, peaceful and nonthreatening, but instilling urgency and fear with a single low growl when disturbed. Two days ago she had him pegged for a conman. But she realized now the go-to-hell persona was just that, a façade to keep the world at a safe distance. What kind of demons drove a man so well educated and skilled to withdraw so completely? What made her yearn so to trust him? To know him…better?

More importantly, what made her want to know all those intimate details?

"You keep looking at me that way and I'm bound to get the wrong idea."

That deep voice startled her back to attention. She'd been staring and he'd caught her.

"Sorry. I was just thinking."

"About whether or not you can trust me?" He stopped, faced her and looked directly into her eyes.

She blinked, forced all emotion from her expression. "In a sense," she hedged. Telling him that she wanted to know him better might not be a brilliant move.

His gaze fell to her mouth. Heat rushed through her veins.

"I know what you're thinking," he said, his voice quiet and low. "Trust me on this." He cranked up the intensity in that dark gaze. "You don't want to go there."

The heat that had surged through her, now pooled in her cheeks. "Is mind reading a part of your vast repertoire as well?"

"It doesn't take a mind reader to see what you think you want."

Resisting the urge to retreat, she managed to stand her ground. "Fine," she confessed, the single word shakier than she would have liked. "I'm human. I feel," she dragged in a ragged breath, "alone in all this and you're the only one…standing here with me." She cleared her throat, refusing to feel as foolish as she sounded. "Forgive me for committing such a grievous error." She glared at him, forcing steel into her voice and fire into her eyes. "I suppose the idea hasn't even crossed your mind?"

Why the hell were they having this conversation?

"Do you want the truth or do you want me to tell you a pretty little lie?"

"The truth." Her answer startled him. Clearly he'd expected her to drop it the moment his darker side surfaced. But she'd be damned if she would. "I've never cared much for lies."

"I've thought about it. But then, I have a reputation for bad decisions." He turned and started forward once more, leaving her to follow. "Anything else you want to know?" he called back to her.

Fury snapping along her nerve endings, Jill trailed after him, reminding herself to breathe. "I think that covers it."

* * *

Four hours later, with lunch behind them, Jill wasn't the only one losing patience with this lead. Paul's instincts couldn't have failed him this badly. The impression that they would find something here had been strong, still was. But, so far, the effort was a bust.

As an attorney, Jill needed tangible evidence to keep her motivated. She worked on instinct, to a degree, just as Paul did. But he looked for that intangible, almost imperceptible something that made his instincts sit up and take notice. Like when Kate had spoken directly to him. *You're back.* She recognized his presence although they had not spoken on his previous visit, they hadn't even made eye contact, except for his little flash of insight. Still, the connection was there. Kate instinctively knew he was there to help. Those instincts had propelled a sense of urgency and another piece of the puzzle had bobbed to the surface of the lake of nothingness that was her existence just now.

There was something or someone in Lynchburg relevant to the case.

Hattie's had turned out to be a simple craft shop that specialized in unique toys for children. Chances were, Kate had shopped there. The owner didn't remember her and had no idea when she'd last been in her shop. She didn't accept checks or credit cards, cash only.

Dead end.

They'd flashed both Kate's and Cody's pictures around the small town. No hits.

"Oh, my God," Jill breathed. She froze next to him. "It's Cody."

Paul tensed. A too familiar sense of uneasiness erupted inside him. "Where?"

She pointed across the supermarket parking lot. "There! With that woman. The blue van. It's him! It's my nephew."

The next few minutes were a blur of activity. The young woman forgot her groceries, leaving them to defrost in the cart, and snatched up the child when Jill reached for him, calling him Cody. If the child wasn't Cody Manning, he could have been his identical twin. Silky blond hair and blue eyes. Paul had seen recent pictures of Jill's nephew. This child was either him or an exact double.

"Lady, I don't know who you are, but you're crazy," the young woman cried, fear in her voice. "This is my son."

The child whined and clung to the woman.

Paul's tension escalated. This was wrong.

Jill reached for the boy again, drawn by the sound of his distress.

The woman jerked away. "I'm gonna call the cops if you don't leave us alone."

Paul reached in the side pocket of Jill's bag and produced her cell phone since he didn't carry one himself. Hadn't bothered with one since he'd stopped carrying a gun five years ago. Who needed a gun or a cell phone when they didn't get involved? Well, he was involved now. He punched in nine-one-one. "That's a good idea. We'll let the police sort this out."

Jill and the other woman watched in a kind of shocked horror as he made the call, neither speaking, both looking like cornered animals. The internal nudge that this was way, way wrong somehow came again. He couldn't shake the feeling.

No one moved or spoke until the police arrived. Then everyone started talking at once.

Officer Dunn, Paul noted the name tag above his shirt pocket, held up a hand. "One at a time."

The woman, being the local, got first chance at telling her side of the story. "They're crazy! Ellis, you know me and my boy. Tell'em they've made a mistake."

Officer Dunn, Ellis, looked from the woman, who had identified herself as Sarah Long, to Jill and then to Paul. "I don't know what you two've been smoking, but this is her son. Any other questions?"

"I'm telling *you*," Jill pressed, fury blazing in her eyes, "he is my nephew. I can prove it. I have pictures." She jerked her bag around and fished for the photograph she carried.

Officer Dunn shook his head. "Lady, I sympathize with whatever's going on with your nephew. But I know the Longs, this is their boy."

"See." Jill produced the photograph of Cody.

Paul wanted to drag her away from here. To save her from this pain and to make her heart see what her brain likely already knew.

This child was not her nephew. The resemblance was uncanny, no question. He had a theory or two about how that happened, either way the situation warranted further investigation.

One thing was certain, Kate had seen this child. *That's when it began.*

"That's not my boy," Mrs. Long denied, shaking her head at the photo. "I never had a picture like that taken. I don't know who you are, but that's not my kid. This" she held her son more tightly "is my boy."

"Ma'am," Officer Dunn implored, passing the picture back to Jill, "I can understand the reason you're upset. But even if I didn't know these folks and believed for a second that this boy was your nephew, how do you explain the fact that he won't even look at you?"

Jill's defiant posture wilted, tears welled in her eyes. "I...I haven't been to visit for a long time. He..."

Her pained words trailed off. Paul couldn't take anymore. "Officer Dunn, if we can't resolve this to the satisfaction of both Miss Ellington and Mrs. Long, we'll need to call in the FBI. There's an Amber Alert for Cody Manning," he reminded the officer. This was getting them nowhere. Whatever was going on here, Jill needed satisfactory answers. Mostly, he just couldn't watch her suffer any more of this uncertainty.

Mrs. Long's eyes widened in fear. Her son squirmed in her arms. "Ellis, what's he talking about?"

Officer Dunn looked a little flustered and a lot irritated. He held up his hands stop sign fashion. "There's no need to call the feds. How about we follow Mrs. Long home and the two of you look at her family photo albums. She's probably got pictures all the way back to the day she brought that child home from the hospital." He glanced at the other woman for approval, then looked proud of himself for coming up with such an easy solution. "Will that clear up this mix-up for you?"

"Sounds reasonable," Paul agreed. Jill said nothing.

Tension thickened between them during the brief ride from the market to Sarah Long's modest frame home. When he parked at the curb and shut off the engine, he turned to Jill. "I don't understand this anymore than you do, but we both know this child is not your nephew."

She shook her head, fear and uncertainty making the move jerky. "He isn't my nephew, I realize that. But somehow he's connected to why Cody is missing. This has to be what Kate meant."

Paul relaxed. He'd known she would find her way to the logical explanation. "Let's play this out. See what we can learn."

Photo album after photo album of little Brady Long's life history from birth to present, proved beyond a shadow of a doubt that Sarah Long had brought this child home from the hospital with her.

The father, Jill noticed from the photos, had the same dark hair and eyes as his wife. Sarah Long insisted her son got his coloring from one of his grandmother's. It wasn't like the occurrence was genetically impossible. Recessive genes did occasionally pop up in the least expected situations. But there had to be a connection to Cody. There was no pretending otherwise, and still she did for the sake of this worried mother.

"I'm so sorry," Jill offered. "It's just that, he looks so much like my nephew."

The heart-wrenching details about Cody's disappearance had brought tears to Sarah's eyes. "I can't imagine what y'all are going through," she said with an understanding nod. "I would've done the same thing." She patted her son's head as he raced past, a plastic airplane held high, the sound of its engine rumbling from his active imagination. "I'd surely remember if I'd ever met your sister and her boy."

"Thank you for understanding." Jill looked to Phillips for her cue. Her head was still spinning. Forming a logical thought much less the next step was out of the question. Officer Dunn stood by as if he'd feared the need to intervene if Jill grew unreasonable again.

God, she was so tired. She'd checked her phone a dozen times. No calls from her mother. Certainly nothing from the chief.

"Would you mind answering a couple of personal questions?" Phillips asked. "Any information could potentially be helpful in our search for Cody."

Sarah looked from him to Dunn and back. "Guess not." She shrugged. "Anything I can do to help."

Jill felt herself leaning forward in anticipation of what he intended to ask.

"Is there any chance that you and Cody's mother, Kate, may have run into each other at the same doctor's office or clinic?"

Sarah frowned. "Can I see her picture again?"

Jill dug for Kate's photo and passed it to her.

Taking her time, Sarah studied it carefully before shaking her head. "I don't remember ever seeing her."

"You and your husband had your son without any assistance from tests or fertility medications?" Phillips flared his hands. "Any invitro procedures?"

"Nothing like that." Sarah shook her head. "Never been to the doctor for anything related to having babies before I got pregnant with Brady. Except my yearly check-ups."

Phillips pushed to his feet. "We appreciate your help, Mrs. Long."

Air rushed into Jill's lungs. She hadn't realized she'd been holding her breath until he stood. She joined him, feeling bone tired. "Thank you. It was most generous of you to go through this with us."

Another wave of emotion hit her and Jill could not wait to get out of this house. She couldn't bear to look at that sweet child another second.

"Miss Ellington?"

Heart aching, Jill hesitated at the door and turned back. "Yes."

"When you find your nephew, bring him to see my boy." Sarah's smile was a little shaky. "I'd like to see him for myself."

Jill nodded stiffly.

No matter that it was at least ninety-five degrees outside, Jill felt as cold as ice.

Officer Dunn walked them to the Land Rover.

"I hope you find your nephew safe and sound real soon," he said, shaking his head sadly. "There's nothing more heartbreaking than a missing child."

Jill couldn't respond to that. She climbed into the passenger seat. How could any of this be real? Her sister was gone, for all intents and purposes. Her brother-in-law was lying on a slab and Cody was missing. And now this! A child, a carbon copy of Cody, who was somehow connected to how this all began.

She closed her eyes, vaguely aware of Phillips thanking the officer for his assistance.

"There's just one thing," the cop said.

Whether it was the sound of his voice or some internal instinct, Jill opened her eyes and listened up. Thankfully she hadn't closed the door yet.

Dunn scratched his head. "While y'all were talking to Sarah, I checked in with dispatch. Funny thing is," he said, thinking for a second or two before he went on, "she couldn't locate an Amber Alert on your boy. Doesn't make much sense that your chief of police would fall down on the job like that."

Strangely, it made a great deal of sense to Jill.

CHAPTER NINE

The moment Jill walked through the door of her mother's house she found the most recent picture of Cody on display. Pictures Kate had taken herself. Jill stared at the photograph and shook her head slowly from side to side. "This just isn't possible."

Phillips came up behind her and looked over her shoulder. He hadn't said much on the trip back to Paradise. Jill assumed he was processing. She certainly had been. The only question about the Long child that remained in her mind was how he came to be since his mother insisted she had not been involved in any fertility procedures.

"We need to discuss this with your mother."

Jill plunked the brass frame onto the table. "Oh, that'll just be the perfect finale for this day, Phillips. Shall we pay a visit to the chief as well?" She continued to use his surname for distance. As weak and unsteady as she felt as this point, she didn't trust herself to be familiar with him in any shape, form or fashion. If last night hadn't been blatant enough, today had certainly done the deed. She was the typical desperate female in need of a man's strong arms.

Dear God, what was happening to her?

"I have a theory."

She did need to check in with the chief for the good it would do. Particularly when she demanded to know what happened with the Amber Alert. How the hell had that happened? She rubbed her tried eyes, needed to erase the images of Brady Long from her head. "If your theory involves my mother I'm not sure I want to hear it."

"We need to find out if your sister experienced any fertility issues."

Jill was on that same page though she doubted she would get any answers from her mother. She hadn't so far. Images of that little boy in Lynchburg plowed their way back into her thoughts. What had her sister discovered?

New outrage kindled deep in her belly. What was her mother hiding? "Mother!" Jill stormed through the house. Phillips was right—as usual. They needed answers and it was way past time Claire Ellington broke her silence. "Mother!"

"In here, Jillian," she called from the kitchen.

When Jill entered the kitchen, Claire Ellington was fussing over the stove. Taken aback, a moment or two passed before Jill could comprehend that the heavenly smell she'd just encountered was coming from whatever her mother was cooking. Her mother never cooked anymore unless she counted the microwave meals.

"Is there any news about Cody?"

Claire glanced at Jill, then beyond her to Phillips, not bothering to hide her distaste before shifting her attention back to the stovetop. "Nothing new. Arvel—the chief—assured me they're not giving up."

What was with her tone? She answered the question as if she'd just relayed the day's weather forecast. The idea of *Stepford Wives* flitted through Jill's head again. "I have a question about Kate?"

"The doctor said she's doing better. He called not an hour ago." Claire turned off the oven and peeked inside. "Dinner will be ready shortly."

Jill braced for the backlash. "Did Kate have any problems conceiving?"

The wooden spoon Claire had just picked up clattered to the counter. "What kind of question is that?" she demanded, taking immediate offense. "You know your sister has never been sick a day in her life."

Yes, Jill did know that. Something else Kate was better at. "Be that as it may, did she use LifeCycle or some other fertility clinic when she wanted to get pregnant?"

Claire retrieved the spoon, rinsed it, then started to stir once more. "I don't see what that has to do with anything." She flicked a glance in Phillips' direction. "This is neither the time nor the place to discuss such a personal matter."

Jill's temper ruptured the thin membrane of control she'd managed to retain. "I'm an attorney and Dr. Phillips is a forensics psychologist. This point could be extremely important to Kate's case. So let's not argue about it, just answer the question."

Jill bit her lips together to prevent adding a few dozen expletives. She was so damned tired of the runaround from her mother.

"If it makes you feel better to humiliate your sister in front of a stranger, then fine." She glowered at Jill. "Yes, Kate had trouble conceiving so she used the LifeCycle Center for help."

Another skeleton from the family closet. "Why didn't anyone tell me?" Jill hadn't meant to voice the hurt, but she did. She was always the last one to know anything. This was just another prime example of how the whole family had punished her for leaving in the first place. She was the outsider. The black sheep. But then, that was her fault, wasn't it?

"Would you have cared?" Claire looked away, her lids fluttering rapidly to hold back her tears. "You left here all those years ago to have your own life. What did you expect? We gave you what you wanted." Her gaze settled heavily onto Jill's, it was impossible to miss the pain there. "We let you go." Claire turned her attention back to the stovetop. "I don't want to discuss this any further."

Jill reminded herself that she had asked. Her mother's words were nothing she didn't already know and still they hurt.

"Thank you, Mother." She walked out. Refused to cry again today. Her mother had told the truth. She was right on all counts. Jill had gotten what she asked for.

When she was out of earshot of the kitchen, she turned to the man keeping step with her and demanded, "Now what?"

To his credit, if he felt any pity for her, he kept it to himself. "Since the locals won't let us in on the official investigation, we're going to the library."

"What're we doing at the library?" She snagged her purse from the table in the entry hall where she'd left it only minutes ago. She really didn't care about the what as long as they were out of here.

"Digging for anything we can find on LifeCycle where anyone who cares to look will see us."

She paused at the door. "We want them to know what we're doing."

A rare grin stretched across his face. The impact disrupted the rhythm of her heart. "We do. On the way, why don't you give the chief a call and ask him about the Amber Alert."

"Lucky me." It sucked being second chair.

* * *

Paul rubbed his bleary eyes and glanced at his watch. They'd been here three hours already. According to the posted hours of operation, the library closed at ten. They hadn't found anything to speak of yet and had only half an hour until closing. The librarian had strolled past at least once every half hour, shooting daggers at them, evidently hoping to garner intelligence for the chief. Worked for Paul. He wanted the chief to sweat.

Mostly he wanted him to react.

In the back issues of the local paper there were the usual announcements and headlines about LifeCycle. The ribbon cutting ceremony from just over thirty years ago, employees of the month and the introduction of new doctors being brought onboard. The occasional milestone released to the press, but those were few and far between and didn't pique his interest. The *Paradise Gazette* was the only local newspaper.

Paul wasn't sure what he was looking for. He would know it when he saw it. That's just the way it worked.

More out of curiosity than anything, he went back a couple of years before LifeCycle's arrival in Paradise. MedTech had moved in around the same time as The LifeCycle Center. He recalled Jill saying the primary source of employment before that had been the old Benford plant. He wanted to know more.

Charles Benford Found Murdered.

Paul scrolled back and read the article. Charles Bedford, owner and operator of Benford Chemical of Paradise, had been found murdered in his home. The newspaper was dated February fifth, thirty-three years ago. His instincts starting to vibrate, he scanned the article more closely. There were no suspects in the case. In light of the recent startling discovery that Benford had been allowing pollutants with

Endocrine-disrupting effects to seep into Paradise's ground water a number of theories were rampant.

Anticipation burning through him, Paul went back further, scanning for related articles.

Bingo. Among other things, all of which were legal, Benford Chemical had been producing Dioxins, furans, and PCBs. The grimmest news of all, according to an EPA spokesperson, was that the pollutants had been allowed to contaminate the local ground water. The entire town was up in arms. Two days after the EPA's announcement, Charles Benford was dead.

Murdered.

A knowing chill settled deep in Paul's bones.

Endocrine-disrupting pollutants.

He needed more details.

A few taps of the keys later and he was inside a classified government database, one of many to which he was still allowed access. He typed Dioxin in the search box. Characters, words spilled onto the screen. He read quickly, knowing he would print the material for later, more in-depth perusal.

The next paragraph had him leaning forward. With Endocrine-disrupting organohalogens, the most common adverse side effect in humans was *sterility*.

His heart pounding, Paul printed the article. The Benford murder still nagged at him. He reviewed the *Paradise Gazette* for three years after the murder. The only related article was a brief blurb that mentioned the case and indicated that, as of that date, nearly thirty years ago, the murder was still unsolved.

Vigilantism was Paul's initial impression.

He kicked the idea around in his head until it solidified. Someone had gotten even with Benford for his inhumane activities. Of course, there was always the chance it had to do with money or payoffs of government officials. But every instinct told Paul that it was a lot more personal than that.

It was about as personal as a matter could get.

Like Manning's murder, the law enforcement officials of Paradise had swept it under the rug. No one seemed worried at all that there might be a killer running around their quiet little town. Maybe two, considering Benford's killer could still be alive.

He watched Jill for a moment before he moved close enough to make her aware of his presence. She tucked a handful of hair behind her ear. He'd seen the desire in her eyes today. Nice to know the attraction was mutual. He'd damned sure done some lusting after her.

But clearing the air and putting thought into action were two entirely different things with vastly different consequences. He needed her to be strong because he wasn't sure how much longer he could resist the temptation of working this closely.

The librarian walked past, tapped the watch on her wrist.

Jill looked up. "I'm ready if you are," he let her know.

She stretched and made a soft sound of fatigue. He had to look away. His body just didn't want to follow instructions.

When she'd gathered her purse, he followed her to the door. "Would you hit a drive-thru before we go back to your mother's?"

"Mother cooked." She flashed him a fake smile. "The least we can do is eat."

"Works for me."

Outside the library entrance, Jill stopped abruptly on the sidewalk, causing him to brush up against her.

"Miss Jill, I've been looking for you."

Chief Dotson waited near the Land Rover. His expression openly suspicious.

"Have you found him?" Jill's hands went immediately to her lips. She trembled.

Paul just wasn't strong enough to keep his distance. He rested his hand at the small of her back, offering what comfort he could.

The chief sighed, his face grim. "We can't be certain just yet, but we believe so. We should have confirmation by morning."

"Oh my God." Her knees buckled. Paul pulled her against him.

On the way here Jill had left him a voicemail about the Amber Alert. Paul's instincts warned they'd gotten his attention.

"What's the hold up with identification?" Paul asked. Jill and her mother shouldn't have to wait unnecessarily.

Dotson turned his hands up. "Burned beyond recognition. TBI's gonna pick up the remains tomorrow morning and we'll know more after they've completed their work. We're pretty sure it's him. A good portion of the bear he always wagged around, according to Ms. Claire, was recovered from the scene. She's identified it just a few minutes ago."

Jill turned her face into Paul's chest, sobbing. That feeling of wrongness stabbed through him again. But he couldn't press the chief for details right now, not with Jill falling apart in his arms.

"I'll be around tomorrow to see how her and her momma are faring." He hesitated before walking away. "It's out of our hands now, Dr. Phillips."

Paul didn't bother responding. He helped Jill into the Land Rover, buckled her seat belt and closed her door. When he skirted the hood, he glimpsed the chief climbing into his cruiser. For three beats their gazes met.

And Paul knew the chief was hiding something.

No.

The chief was flat out lying.

* * *

Claire Ellington, holding up surprisingly well, insisted on seeing her daughter to bed without any help from Paul. Feeling more in the way than anything else, he retired to Judge Ellington's study and paced.

He reviewed all that he'd absorbed about this case. The crime scene was all wrong, or staged. There was no motive. The child was missing and now suddenly found. How convenient that the body was burned beyond recognition, with only part of a stuffed toy to use for identification at this point. There were no dental records since the child had never been to a dentist.

That would certainly tidy up the missing child aspect of the case. But what about the murder? How did the chief intend to cleanly resolve that element? Would it simply go unsolved as the Benford murder had?

Paul knew in his gut that something was already in the works. The chief was dirty. The child had never been considered missing, not in the usual sense. No Amber Alert. Bullshit. People went postal when children were missing. Heavy media coverage, especially in a small town like this.

Nothing about this case felt right. Someone with enough power was keeping a tight lid on things. A very tight lid.

Somehow Benford and Manning were small pieces of the same bigger picture. It was a huge leap but his gut told him he was on the right track. He wondered if Jill really wanted to know what lay at the bottom of all this.

He stalled in the middle of the room, his gaze landing on the sideboard and the crystal liquor decanters there. Just one drink. That was all he needed. The stash he'd brought with him was gone. He reached for the bourbon then hesitated. If they pushed this investigation any further, things were going to get dicey. Jill was depending on him. He dropped his hand to his side.

He had to do this right.

Focus on the case. Walk off the temptation. Hands in his pockets, he paced the small room. Kate was the key. She knew all the answers, but they were locked inside some little compartment that was too painful to open. Only time would make that happen. Maybe not even then. There was no way to know what might have been done to ensure she never told the story of what happened the day she murdered her husband.

He thought again of the Benford murder. Of the coincidence that The LifeCycle Center had chosen Paradise as the site for the newest, largest and most aggressive infertility treatment facility to date. How convenient that salvation had appeared only one year after the closing of the chemical plant which had spewed pollutants into the ground water…rendering sterile a large percentage of the humans who came into contact with it over an extended period of time.

"Too damned convenient."

A gasp in the entry hall jerked Paul's attention there. Claire Ellington stood at the bottom of the stairs staring at him, and balancing a glass of milk on a shiny silver tray.

"How's Jill?" He moved to the door of her husband's study.

"She's resting."

"I'll take that to her," he offered.

"I'd prefer to do it myself." She sent a pointed look at the study. "I'd appreciate it if you'd keep the Judge's doors closed."

"Sorry." Paul stepped into the hall, closed the doors behind him. "I'll go up with you."

Claire looked exasperated at his insistence but she said nothing. Instead she climbed the stairs with him trailing a few steps behind.

He wondered for the second time in the last half hour why the woman wasn't all broken up over hearing that her grandson was dead. She was as cool as the proverbial cucumber. Hadn't shed a single tear that he'd seen. Jill, on the other hand, was devastated. Paul wanted to tell her about his suspicions that the boy was still alive...but what if he were wrong this time? He couldn't put her through that without more than his hunch.

It didn't take a film director with an eye for detail to see that something was seriously wrong with this picture.

Jill was curled into the fetal position on the bed. She sat up when they entered the room. Her eyes were red and puffy. He ached to somehow make this right, to comfort her. It had been so long since he'd attempted to comfort anyone, he wasn't sure he remembered how.

"Drink this, dear. It'll make you feel better." Claire placed the glass in Jill's hand. "I warmed it for you."

Jill nodded and took a long drink from the glass of milk. Her mother sat down on the side of the bed, the silver tray held against her chest like a shield.

"I made some decisions tonight after the chief told me about...Cody," she said quietly, then cleared her throat of what Paul presumed was emotion. It would be the first she'd displayed since hearing the news.

He remained at a distance, observing, his gut clenching with growing apprehension. The voice of reason was screaming at him. Wrong…wrong… wrong!

"Karl's friends at MedTech are holding a memorial service for him tomorrow at the church they attended." She paused for a moment, allowing Jill to digest that information. "I think it's a fine idea. There's really no need to wait until the body is released for burial. In fact, I'd like to include Cody in the service. There's no point in dragging this out. You're here. The sooner we get this behind us, the sooner we can pick up the pieces. I'm sure you need to get back to Jackson and your own work there."

Jill said nothing. She simply stared at her mother, the half empty glass of milk clutched in her hand.

"We'll call the doctor in the morning and see if Kate can be released long enough to attend the service. Since official charges haven't been filed, I can't see why they wouldn't allow it." Claire breathed a sigh of finality, as if all was right in the world now that she'd made certain decisions. "Drink up now."

Jill obeyed and Claire took the glass. She pressed a kiss to her daughter's forehead before rising to go. She looked directly at Paul and smiled, it wasn't pleasant. "She needs her rest."

He let the tension dissipate for a few seconds after her departure before he approached Jill. She sat there, staring at nothing at all.

When he eased down onto the side of the bed she looked at him, a high-octane blend of fear, pain, and disbelief in her eyes. "She wants me to leave."

He couldn't argue the point. It certainly sounded that way to him.

"She just wants to pretend it all away." Jill hugged her arms around her middle. "Just like when my father died."

Paul tugged her right hand free and held it in his. Her skin was so soft, her hand so small compared to his. "Is this the way she always reacts to trauma? She's just been told her grandson is probably dead and she hasn't shed the first tear." An atypical response to the death of a family member—a child at that—if Paul had ever seen one.

"My grandparents died when I was really small, so I don't remember." She stared at their hands as if the contrasting tones and textures fascinated her. "No one we were especially close to ever died until my father." Her gaze grew distant, misty. "She just called me and said, 'Jillian, your father is dead, you'll need to come home for the funeral.'" Jill shook her head. "Not once did I see her cry." She looked at Paul in earnest. "But I know she loved him. And I know she loves Cody. Maybe it's just her way. Otherwise I can't explain it."

Maybe. Paul wasn't convinced. "I don't know about exposing Kate to this memorial service. It could set her back."

Her fingers tightened around his. Every part of him tensed. "I can't believe this is happening. It just seems so impossible."

"Look," he said softly, drawing her gaze back to him, "there are some things we need to discuss but we'll do that in the morning." They both needed a good night's sleep.

She nodded, fresh tears blooming on those golden lashes.

He started to get up...but hesitated. One more look into those tortured eyes and he had to touch her. He stroked one finger down her soft cheek, reveling in the feel of her skin. "I'll figure this out. I swear I will."

"Thank you."

He told himself to go but he couldn't make it happen. Slowly, he leaned forward and brushed his lips to hers. Just the barest of touches, but it was enough. For now.

"Good night."

She fisted her fingers in his shirt and pulled him back down to her. "You could stay...with me... tonight."

He smiled. The alien sensation in his chest startled him. "Not tonight. When we spend the night together it won't be about loss and pain."

She moistened those lush pink lips and released him. "You're ruining that bad guy image of yours, you know."

It was all he could do to walk out of her room. But it was the right thing to do.

He closed the door behind him, drawing up short when he came toe to toe with Claire Ellington.

"I want you to stop filling my daughter's head with nonsense," she demanded in a harsh whisper. "You're only making matters worse."

Paul held his tongue out of respect for the woman, though he wasn't sure yet whether she deserved it, but mostly he did so out of respect for Jill.

"Good night, Mrs. Ellington." He moved around her and strode to the far end of the hall, past the staircase, to the guestroom. He didn't look back.

In his room, he studied the article on the Endocrine-disrupting pollutants he'd printed at the library.

This, he suspected, was where it started—whatever the hell it was.

All he had to do was follow the map from there.

By midnight, Paul had yet again reviewed all the reports from Kate's case and all the other material he had gathered. It was like reading a book or watching a movie a second or third time and noticing something missed the first time or even the second. There was a major cover up going on in Paradise.

All he had to do was prove it.

To do that he had to stay alive.

The thought came out of nowhere. But Paul had learned long ago to trust his first instincts. He wasn't about to change his MO now. He wasn't wanted here. Hell, Jill wasn't even wanted here. No one who represented a threat to the perfect balance in Paradise was welcome.

He stripped down to his boxers and slipped under the covers. Tomorrow he intended to check out a couple more things in the old issues of the *Paradise Gazette*. Like the number of births during the two years before and after the dumping of the pollutants was discovered. He also wanted to know if the Benford murder had ever been solved. He had a feeling the answer to that would be resounding no. More than anything, Paul just wanted to see the reaction on the chief's face when he asked about it.

The secrets in Paradise lay in the past. Buried bone deep. But those ugly secrets were rising to the surface now, coming back to haunt this town. Or maybe the ugliness had always been here.

Above all else he feared that at the very center of it was Jill.

CHAPTER TEN

It was late when Jill woke the next morning. Tears rushed, brimming against her lashes, making her chest ache with grief and regret. Grief for the loss of a precious child. Regret that she hadn't spent as much time with him and his mother as she should have. And that she had come home and somehow failed to save him.

Seeing the little boy in Lynchburg had made her think. She wondered if Cody would have recognized her after all these months as anything other than someone who looked like his mother. She shook off the unnerving sensation that accompanied thoughts of the Lynchburg child. The resemblance was just too surreal.

When Kate recovered and understood that her child was dead, she would be devastated. What if the police discovered that Kate was responsible? That just couldn't be true. Jill refused to accept that scenario. She closed her eyes and wondered, considering what she knew now, if maybe it wouldn't be better if her sister stayed in Never-Never Land.

Jill pushed to a sitting position and scrubbed the dampness from her face. She had to pull it together. She owed it to her sister to put on a brave front, to be the closely connected twin she had refused to be for nearly two decades.

She held her head in her hands and struggled with the overpowering need to lie back down. She glanced at the clock again, almost nine. She never slept this late.

Maybe all the stress and exhaustion had finally caught up with her. She felt so...groggy, listless, like she'd overindulged in champagne the night before. Champagne, even a little, always gave her a hangover. Throwing back the covers, she dropped her feet to the floor and stood. The room shifted a bit, then steadied. She licked her dry lips and slowly, one wobbly step at a time, moved toward the door. A shower would wake her up. She paused by the dresser and picked up a note addressed to her. A smile teased her lips as she read the scrawled words. Phillips had gone back to the library and would return as soon as he could. She traced the bold strokes with a fingertip and thanked God again that he was in this with her. She stared at her reflection and for the first time in her life admitted, if only to herself, a deep dark secret. She was so tired of being alone.

After a long, hot shower Jill felt more human. She swabbed her hair and body dry with a thick terry cloth towel that smelled of the same spring-scented laundry detergent her mother had always used. She closed her eyes and allowed herself to go back in time and relive one of her childhood's pleasurable moments. Her mother hanging towels on the clothesline in the backyard. Jill and Kate racing around the yard, the sun reflecting off their blond heads. Her mother's gentle laughter and pleasant voice as she sang 'Ring Around the Rosy.' The sweet smell of the spring air. Her lids fluttered open and she wondered how everything had changed so very much.

"Don't start that." Jill squared her shoulders and reminded the weary woman in the mirror that she had to be strong today. She slung the towel around her and shimmied it back and forth to dry her back. A prick of pain made her wince. She dropped the towel and twisted to try and see the source of the discomfort in the mirror. There was a red mark in the center of her back, right over her spinal cord, high between her shoulder blades.

"What in the world?" Frowning, she fumbled through the drawers until she found a hand-held mirror to take a closer look. The mark was small, circular and angry red. A little puffy.

"Damn," she breathed. Just her luck to get bitten by a spider or something equally repulsive. She shuddered.

Now wasn't the time to worry about her arachnophobia. Apparently all the Ellington women had some sort of phobia. She slipped on her gown and hurried back to the bedroom. She searched the bed and its covers for any signs of a spider. She shivered at the thought of having one of the creepy little buggers crawling around on her bare skin.

Disgusted at not being able to find the multi-legged perpetrator, she smoothed the rumpled covers and considered the worst. If she developed other symptoms she'd drop by the hospital and have it checked. She wondered vaguely if it had anything to do with her earlier grogginess. Just something else she didn't have time to worry about today. She hoped the one black dress she'd brought was suitable. The fabric slid over her skin as she stepped into her heels. A quick mirror check and she was good to go.

She grabbed a clip for her hair and went downstairs. A quick call to her office as well as one to Cullen Marks was necessary and then she had to talk to her mother. Maybe coffee first. She hoped their appearance at this memorial service could be brief, in and out. She had no desire to face all the suspicious looks and cold receptions she would no doubt be exposed to by the people she had known her entire life. It was more than apparent that she was just another outsider to them now. Someone who threatened what they loved most—their perfect way of life.

The realization that it had been her mother's idea to go to the memorial service nudged Jill hard. Was her agoraphobia suddenly cured? Jill shook her head. Just as she'd always suspected. Her mother's phobia was a matter of convenience. She didn't want to face the world either.

Speaking of her mother, where was she this morning? She searched the downstairs then hustled back up the stairs. Two knocks at her mother's bedroom door without an answer had a new kind of worry rushing through her veins. Jill opened the door and found her mother sitting at her dressing table wearing nothing but a slip and staring at her reflection as if she expected a response to some question she'd asked herself.

"Mother, are you all right?"

For several seconds, Claire didn't speak. She seemed lost in thought, or strangely mesmerized by the image in the mirror.

"Mother." Jill moved to her side, crouching down to her eye level. "Please talk to me."

Claire blinked from her trance, then stared down at the fine toiletries arranged neatly on her dressing table, avoiding her daughter's gaze. As children Kate and Jill had loved playing with their mother's perfume bottles and decorative boxes of sweet scented powders.

"It's all falling apart," Claire said quietly, calmly as if she'd just announced it wouldn't rain today after all. "I can't stop it."

Jill eased her weight onto her knees and clasped her mother's hand between hers. "Please, Mom, tell me what that means. Let's face this awful thing together. What can't you stop?"

Claire shifted her gaze to Jill's. Fear, stark and vivid, glittered there. "I lost your father. Now Cody…" She shook her head, tears spilling down her cheeks. "And possibly Kate." Her gaze collided with Jill's once more. "I can't lose you too. I just can't."

She clutched Jill's hand against her chest. "Promise me, Jillian, that you'll be careful. Swear to me that you'll give up this useless investigation! Go back to Jackson today, please."

The intensity in her mother's eyes, the urgency in her voice told Jill in no uncertain terms that Claire was afraid—no, she was terrified.

"You don't have to worry about me. I am not afraid. I will find the truth."

Claire shook her head so adamantly that a pin flew from her neatly coifed French twist. "You don't understand. You have to stop. You have to send that man away and you have to go." A new flood of tears swelled then rolled down her pale cheeks. "Please, Jillian. Do this for me. For your sister. Please. I can't lose anyone else."

* * *

Paul stared at the notepad where he had arranged his research into chronological statistics.

His investigator reflexes had kicked into overdrive and his heart sped up to triple-time as more pieces of the puzzle fell into place. He resisted the urge to rush to Ellington House and physically drag Jill back to Jackson. His instincts were screaming at him, something too awful to imagine much less accept as fact. But it was real…too real.

For two years before and after Benford Chemical was shut down, there was not a single birth in

Paradise. Not one. Then, suddenly, one year after The LifeCycle Center set up shop, there were dozens, including Jill and Kate Ellington.

For the entire thirty years since its closing, not one word had been mentioned in print about Benford Chemical, other than the brief blurb a few years after Charles Benford's murder saying the case was still unsolved. Ironically, the newspaper reporter who had written the brief piece died only one month after its publication. Then nothing. From what he could see, Charles Benford and Benford Chemical never existed as far as Paradise was concerned.

Like it never happened.

Even stranger, when he did a search on Benford, a long list of articles related to the illegal chemical dumping popped up. But not when he searched Paradise. The only connection between Paradise and Benford was in the articles about Benford Chemical. Someone had gone to a great deal of trouble to keep the town out of the limelight during that ugly business.

Since the *Paradise Gazette* was only one issue per week, it didn't take Paul long to scan the last year's editions. The ones Jill had perused last night. But she hadn't known what he was looking for...not really. Hell, he hadn't even known. But he did now.

He hesitated on the front page of a three-month-old edition. *Ribbon Cutting Ceremony for New MedTech Wing*. Karl Manning and Mayor Hammersly had officiated at the landmark event. The ceremony celebrated the opening of an entire new wing for highly advanced medical research, such as cloning. A chill blew through Paul. MedTech, according to the article, was the first research corporation in the United States to be granted limited license to perform animal *and* human cloning studies.

Voices whispered through Paul's head, echoing a warning that was already mushrooming in his chest.

His gaze snagged on something in the background of the article's accompanying photo. The new wing...large, sleek walls of glass and granite. But that wasn't what drew his eye. It was the emblem mounted high on the six-story building. *Gemini*... the astrological sign...twins.

Paul lunged to his feet, sending his chair thudding against an adjacent table. He could hardly think over the fear rushing through his blood... pounding in his chest.

The image of the boy in Lynchburg who looked so much like Cody soared into his consciousness... then Kate and Jill. Cody's body suddenly being found...the crime scene staging in the Manning home photos...the whole town seemingly on the defensive about Jill's questions.

Paul shoved his notes together in a transportable pile and rushed out of the library. He needed help on this one. Information he no longer had the power or, at the moment, the time to access.

After driving outside the city limits to the convenience store he'd stopped at on his way here, he parked and went inside. Every muscle in his body was jumping as he waited for the guy behind the counter to finish waiting on his last customer.

Paul flashed his credentials that looked official but weren't. "I have an emergency and I need to use your phone."

The guy looked him up and down, his expression openly suspect. Paul knew he looked a little rough around the edges this morning. He wore the same clothes he'd worn yesterday and there'd been no time to shave.

"It's official business," he added when the clerk looked ready to say no.

"Okay." The clerk passed him the phone.

Paul stepped away from the counter and punched in the number he still knew by heart. He waited, his pulse tripping, as it rang, once, twice, three times.

"Federal Bureau of Investigation," the pleasant voice greeted.

"Extension two-three-oh." Paul struggled for a deep breath.

"One moment, sir."

Three rings later the voice he needed to hear echoed across the line. "Cuddahy."

"Tom, this is Paul Phillips."

Silence.

"How's it going, buddy?"

Paul heard the concern in the other man's voice. Typically that set him off on a rampage. He didn't need his old friend or anyone else worrying about him. But there was no time. "I'm good," he lied. They hadn't spoken in more than a year. Tom called, but Paul never returned his messages.

"It's been a while."

Paul understood what he was about to ask was a big favor and he sure hadn't earned the right to ask but he did anyway. "I need...a favor."

A pause. "What can I do for you?"

Paul closed his eyes and rode out the wave of relief without embarrassing himself. "I need you to look into a medical research corporation. MedTech. Located in Paradise, Tennessee." He could hear the scratch of Tom's pen. "Also, there's a fertility clinic called The LifeCycle Center. I need to know if these two are somehow connected." The pen abruptly stopped scrawling.

"Should I even bother asking what this is about?" Tom knew Paul too well.

"I can't tell you anything just yet, but you'll be the first to know when I figure this out."

Another pause. "This isn't official business, is it?"

Paul considered whether to respond to that one, but he didn't see the point in lying. Tom would know. "It's personal."

"How do I get in touch with you?"

Since Paul refused to carry a cell phone and he didn't want the call going to the Ellington home, his options were limited. "I'll call you back. How long before you can have some preliminary answers for me."

"Give me a call tomorrow morning and I'll give you an update on what, if anything, I've found."

Tomorrow would be good. "The sooner the better," he pressed. Tom would understand. "I owe you."

"Paul, listen," Tom said, worry vibrating in his voice. "Personal is not good. You know that. Whatever's going on, you need to step back and keep your distance."

"Too late," Paul admitted. Tom was the only real friend he'd ever had and even that relationship had been strained. Mostly because Paul had a problem with close human contact, physical or emotional. "I'll call you tomorrow."

Paul disconnected before his old friend could dig any deeper. He had one last call to make, but he didn't know the number for this one. He called directory assistance and provided the last name and street address, since he didn't have the husband's first name.

"Hello."

"Sarah Long?" Paul hoped he had the right Long.

"This is Sarah, who's this?"

"Mrs. Long, this is Dr. Paul Phillips. We met yesterday."

"Did Ms. Ellington find her nephew?"

Paul opted not to go into that. "He's still missing," he hedged. "I wanted to ask you another personal question. I hope you don't mind."

"I…guess not. Anything I can do to help but I—"

"Did you use a local obstetrician while you were pregnant?" he interrupted before she could talk herself out of answering.

"I used the clinic," she said. "Most folks around here do. It's based on your income and they got real good doctors."

"What clinic is that?" Anticipation spiked again.

"It's over near Tullahoma. It's the Women's Clinic. All the patients are women. You know, for your yearly check-ups and having babies. Stuff like that."

Paul made a mental note of the name and location. "Thanks, Mrs. Long, you've been an immense help."

"This doesn't have anything to do with my boy?" she asked cautiously.

"I just needed to know the facility you used. Thank you." He ended the call before she could ask anything else.

He didn't want to upset the woman, but Paul would bet his life the Women's Clinic was connected to The LifeCycle Center. He would also stake his entire reputation, such as it was, on one conclusion: Cody and the Lynchburg boy were twins. They were too identical to simply be related by merely sharing the same biological father. He'd first thought that maybe Kate and Sarah had used the fertility clinic and there'd been a mix-up, but that wasn't the case. This was no accident. The Gemini emblem flashed through his mind. MedTech and The LifeCycle Center were tampering, experimenting with conception, specifically twins, if his conclusions were correct. Nothing that hadn't been done before. Except, he suspected this was far bigger.

All he had to do now was prove it.

"Thanks." He handed the clerk back his phone and walked out.

The sun was already heating up.

And things were only going to get hotter.

* * *

Paul parked in the Ellington drive, near the house.

His old friend was right, he needed to step back. Getting too close on an emotional level was a dangerous risk. With this investigation he and Jill had enough trouble already.

He found her in her room.

"You're back!" She looked relieved to see him.

"Everything okay?" he asked hesitantly.

She nodded, pulling a brave face. "Mother had a bit of a breakdown this morning. She's worried about losing someone else she loves. She finally cried." Jill chewed her lower lip thoughtfully. "That's the first time I've ever seen my mother cry?"

Paul wanted to pull her into his arms and hold her, but he resisted. He had to keep his distance. He had to think clearly. That he'd gotten through the morning without a shot of bourbon was a miracle. He planned to keep it that way.

"I should bring you up to speed on what I've found so far."

Jill took his hand and tugged him toward the bed. Reluctantly, he sat down next to her. "Tell me," she urged.

He went through the statistics he'd collected. She listened, spellbound. No births for two years before or after the closing of Benford Chemicals. He didn't mention the Gemini thing. There was no point just yet since his thoughts on that were mostly speculation at this point. Nor did he mention calling Sarah Long and Tom Cuddahy.

Jill shook her head. "How could I have grown up here and not known about this?" She massaged her temple and he wondered if her head hurt. "No one ever mentioned there having been any type of chemical disaster in Paradise. Even when we studied local history, there was no mention. It seems impossible that no one would talk about such a life-altering event."

Paul wasn't sure how she would take this next part. "One year after the plant closed The LifeCycle Center set up shop in Paradise."

She frowned, trying to see the connection. "Does that tie in somehow?"

He shrugged. "It looks that way. After four years of no births, LifeCycle comes in and suddenly there are dozens."

"That would have been…"

"Including you and Kate."

Confusion and a hint of fear cluttered her face. "Mother is so upset right now, how can I ask her about this?" She laughed but the sound held no humor. "Hey, Mom, did you and Dad have to resort to test tubes to conceive?"

The realization of what that meant seemed to hit her then. Her expression turned bleak. "If they were sterile, that would mean…" She shook her head. "But we look so much like mother. How could that be?"

Paul couldn't answer that question, but he offered a feasible option. "Maybe only your father was affected. Or maybe neither. The adverse side effects of drugs or chemicals don't affect everyone precisely the same. You and I could take the same type and dose of a certain drug and have very different reactions."

"Oh God." She closed her eyes. "This is too… incredible to contemplate."

This time he had to touch her. He reached for her and the door swung open, jerking their gazes to the intrusion.

Claire Ellington, her eyes red rimmed, looked startled. "Excuse me. I was…Jill, are you ready."

It was obvious, Paul noted immediately, from Claire's manner of dress, all black, that she planned to attend the service.

My mother is agoraphobic.

"I have work to do." Paul rose slowly, studying the nervous woman lingering at the door. He glanced over his shoulder at Jill. "I'll see you downstairs."

Wordlessly, Claire stepped aside for him to pass, she didn't look at him.

She knew he knew.

The feeling was overwhelming, undeniable. It penetrated straight into the center of his being. Hummed just beneath the surface, a sound inside a sound, more like a vibration. But it was, at the same time, crystal clear.

Claire Ellington was part of this mystery.

She was aware, at least to an extent, what was going on in the perfect little southern town of Paradise.

She had known from the start.

Ten minutes passed and Paul was pacing the entry and then the study waiting for Jill to come downstairs. The urge to accompany her to the service was powerful, but he needed to be here. He had every intention of executing an illegal search, and seizure if he came across anything pertinent to the case. Damn, he wanted a drink. Needed a cigarette. But he would not be distracted.

The framed photographs on the Judge's credenza drew his attention. He had looked at them before, but he had a niggling urge to look again. He moved behind the desk and picked up the picture of Jill at age nine and wearing a tee-ball uniform. In the photograph she smiled widely while poised for swinging the bat. He smiled, touched the innocent face there and finally set it aside. He reached for the matching frame, Kate in the same pose, her smile every bit as mischievous as Jill's. That's when it struck him. He looked at each photograph again and the answer was there.

Footsteps on the staircase drew him into the entry hall. Closing the doors behind him, he turned to meet Jill and her mother. Claire managed a tight smile for him when she descended the final step.

"I'll wait in the car, dear," she said to her daughter.

Jill looked beautiful, even in black. The unembellished sheath fit to every sweet curve. "We're going to see Kate after the service. The doctor didn't want her to attend."

If the doctor had allowed it, Paul would have had serious doubts about his credentials.

"If you need me to go…" The offer was out of his mouth before he could stop it. God, she looked good.

She smiled and something inside him shifted. "Thanks. But I think Mother and I need to do this alone. It's the first time in a long time that we've bonded on any level."

Paul didn't mention the supposed agoraphobia. Let Jill have at least this time with her mother without analyzing it to death. As far as he could see, it was about all she'd gotten in the way of closeness with her mother since she'd arrived.

Unable to stop himself, he brushed a kiss across her cheek. He lingered for a moment, wanting more and unwilling to let go of the breath-stealing pull of desire, then he drew back.

"I'll be back soon," she murmured, her eyes not quite meeting his. "Thank you for being here."

She started for the door but Paul stopped her with the question he'd almost forgotten to ask. "Is Kate left-handed or right?"

Jill faced him. "Right-handed, why?"

He nodded once, ignoring her question. "And so are you?" He already knew the answer to that one.

She laughed uncertainly. "Yes. Why do you ask?"

He shook his head. "No real reason. Go on. Your mother's waiting."

A frown still troubling her smooth brow, she did as he instructed. He watched her go, uneasiness ratcheting up inside him in slow, steady increments.

It would come to Jill later, as she sat on that hard, polished pew on the front row of the Paradise Methodist Church that true identical twins were most often mirror images. If she was right-handed, Kate should be left-handed.

* * *

Jill stood on the steps of the church between her mother and the somber minister. The service had been relatively short, but agonizing. Now, as they shook the hands of all who had graciously attended, Jill wished it was over. It was impossible to miss the difference between the way she was addressed as each friend and neighbor passed and the way her mother was. Each outstretched hand barely grazed her palm and the owner allowed only the tightest of smiles.

What had she expected? She had come here prepared for this very reaction. After all, she'd moved away years ago and had hardly visited. Deep down, she understood the shunning had nothing to do with her leaving or her staying gone, it was about the investigation she'd chosen to conduct. The people here didn't want their town or its officials scrutinized. It would serve only one purpose in their eyes, to tarnish the prestigious image of Paradise.

A tear slipped past her steel-like restraint and she quickly swiped it away. She didn't care what these people thought. She wanted to know what had happened to her nephew and her sister. She would not rest until she had some answers. An innocent child was dead, so was his father, and her sister was trapped in a prison of her own making in the eyes of the powers that be. Jill would know the reason why before she was through, regardless of what any of these people thought.

The next hand to touch hers was cold and tense.

Jill's gaze zeroed in on the nearest face in the long line. Connie. Her friend. Her confidant. A girl she'd loved at times more than her own sister.

Connie smiled as tightly as the blur of faces that came before her and would have moved on if Jill had not held her back, clutching her hand with all her might. "Thank you for coming, Connie. You're a good friend."

Eyes wide and brimming with her own tears, Connie rushed down the steps without even acknowledging Jill's mother. Jill had been lying to herself. She did care what a few of these people thought, and Connie was one of them.

At least now she knew where she stood.

She had no friends left in Paradise.

When it was finally over, the trip to the hospital started out in grave, empty silence. Claire surveyed the changes in the town like a child confused and frustrated by the remodeling of her room.

"I didn't realize how much things had changed."

Jill forced a smile. "Paradise is even lovelier than ever."

Oddly, her mother didn't respond. The silence resumed.

Claire didn't speak again until they were in Kate's hospital room. "Jesus in Heaven, how can this be my sweet Kate?" She drew a sharp breath, then let it out slowly as she shook her head in painful resignation.

Jill realized then that her mother hadn't expected it to be quite so bad. Kate lay there, the head of the bed elevated slightly, staring off into space. She didn't acknowledge the presence of company or the sound of their voices. She just lay there, unaware that her son had been pronounced dead, that her husband was currently being dissected like a lab rat. And that most of the community had shown up for a memorial service to honor their passing.

Tears burned the backs of her lids and Jill promised herself she would not cry again. It was enough. She was too tired to expend the necessary energy.

Claire eased down on the side of the bed next to Kate and stroked her cheek. She hummed softly, a tune Jill recognized. Her mother had hummed or sang that sweet song to them whenever they were sick or hurt. She'd hold Jill or Kate, whichever needed her, and rock them gently in her arms, humming that unforgettable melody.

Hush little baby…now don't say a word…

This time Jill didn't bother fighting the tears. She didn't have the strength.

The door cracked open and one of the nurses stuck her head inside. "There's someone here who'd like to speak with you, Ms. Ellington."

Jill knew the nurse was addressing her because she looked directly at her, but she couldn't fathom who needed to speak with her. Everyone in town went out of their way to avoid her. Another stab of pain went through her at the thought of Connie's slight.

"I'll be back, Mother," she said, but Claire didn't look up or stop her soft crooning.

Jill knew it wouldn't be Phillips waiting for her, he would have come into the room.

Before heading back to the desk the nurse offered, "I'll just put this stop under the door so it won't lock on you." She pulled a small rubber stop from her pocket and tucked it under the door to Kate's room, leaving it open a few inches.

"Thank you." When the nurse was on her way, Jill turned to the man waiting in the corridor.

Senator Wade, looking elegant in his expensive suit, smiled sympathetically. He'd spoken to Jill at the service, but there had been so many people his words had been brief, rushed. She hadn't expected to see him here.

She manufactured the expected smile. "Are you here to see Kate?"

He glanced through the window, the same one where Jill had watched her sister that first day back in Paradise as the chief had relayed the unbelievable chain of events that had landed Kate here.

"No, no," Senator Wade said quickly. "I don't want to intrude. I just wanted to tell you again how sorry I am that all this has happened." He shook his head. "I can't imagine the devastation that you and your mother are suffering right now. If the Judge were here, he'd be proud of you both for holding up so well under these tragic circumstances."

Jill forced herself to be cordial considering the chief was doing little to solve the *circumstances* and the senator apparently hadn't noticed. "Thank you. I appreciate your saying so. We're doing the best we can."

His posture changed and he sighed. He'd done his good deed for his grieving constituents. "Remember, Jill, if there is anything I can do, all you have to do is say the word."

A renewed jolt of fury made her reckless. "There is something," she said, assuming the picture of innocence. She had to have the answer to this. Maybe it wasn't the time or place but the question weighed heavily on her mind.

"Anything," he emphasized with a nod of that regal head.

"Why is the Benford Chemical incident a secret in Paradise?"

The flare of surprise in his expression was so subtle she almost missed it, his recovery was nothing short of masterful. "Why do you say it's a secret?"

Ah, good one. Answer a question with a question. The hallmark strategic maneuver of a thoroughbred politician.

"Because I'd never heard of it and no one I knew growing up ever spoke of it. It just seems odd that no one talks about it or the fact that for years Benford seeped chemicals that posed the risk of sterility in humans."

"I don't know why you've never heard of that ugly time in Paradise's history, but I can tell you that the EPA spent a great deal of money cleaning up the mess. I suppose," he offered with seemingly genuine intentions, "that most folks consider something as painful as that is better left in the past. Too close to the bone to speak of in public."

It was close to the bone all right. Jill fumed but she held her tongue until he finished.

"The town council voted to leave the old building standing as a reminder of how very fragile life is and how fiercely we must protect it."

As with most answers given by politicians, she needed clarification. "So you're saying that nothing came of it since the EPA cleaned up the mess."

"That's correct," he said emphatically. "Why, you must have noticed that Paradise's population has never dwindled."

Yes, she had noticed that, but that didn't answer her question. "Except for two years prior to the plant's closing and another two years afterwards. There wasn't a single birth in Paradise during those years. I checked."

He folded one arm over his chest and braced his elbow there, then tapped his lips with his forefinger as he pretended to consider her words. "I can't answer that one for you. But I would imagine that during any town's history there will be a dry spell from time to time. As a matter of fact, I remember a number of us, your father and mother included, had put off starting families until we were more settled career wise." He laughed at his own faux pas. "In fact, it appears that I've put it off indefinitely."

The senator being in his late sixties, the same age as her father if he were still alive, she would have to agree with that particular conclusion. Strange, she decided, he showed not even the slightest uneasiness at her pursuit of the subject.

His smile beamed full force. "Of course I have dedicated myself to the state of Tennessee. I really haven't had time for family commitments."

Though she would never admit it to him, Jill saw herself taking that same route. Phillips' image flickered briefly, as if offering an alternative. She pushed the idea, as unexpectedly tempting as it was, away. Then again, what if she was infertile like her sister? She couldn't think about that either. She had to focus. Maybe she and the senator had more in common than she'd realized. At least he was cordial to her and seemed sincerely concerned.

"I should be on my way." He squared his shoulders and gave her a nod. "You let me know if I can help in any way. I don't mind being asked questions about anything that concerns you, Jill. Your father was my dearest friend and I won't have you worrying about a thing."

She thanked him and watched as he strode away. Maybe she and Paul should lay all their cards on the table for the senator, get his take. And his help. Maybe he wasn't even aware the chief was performing negligently where the murder investigation was concerned.

Claire eased the door open and stepped into the corridor. "She's sleeping, Jill. We might as well go on home." Her mother looked exhausted and more defeated than she'd ever seen her.

Jill looked longingly through the glass and said a quick silent prayer for Kate. The newest level of Kate's nightmare had just begun. As if she'd telegraphed those thoughts, Kate suddenly turned her head and stared at Jill.

Jill's heart all but stopped as she watched her sister's lips move. Whether it was Claire who reached for the door first or Jill, they both raced to Kate's bedside.

Kate turned to stare at them. "I took him some place safe."

Jill searched her sister's battered face. "What're you telling me, Kate? Did you take Cody some place safe?"

"Just stop, Jillian," Claire protested. "You have to stop this."

Kate's expression grew slack and the light in her eyes dimmed. She was gone again. Back to that place inside her that no one could touch.

Jill glared at her mother. "Are you satisfied?"

They didn't speak again as they exited the hospital. Jill was too furious. Claire was…God only knew what she was thinking or how she felt.

Outside the air was thick with humidity. The interior of the car was an oven. With the air conditioning set to max, Jill's thoughts turned to Paul as she pulled out onto the street. She couldn't wait to get to him and tell him what Kate had said. Surely this confirmed what she had thought all along. Kate would never hurt her son. There had to be a third party—the person or persons who had done these awful things. The question Phillips had asked her before the service nudged at her again. She'd never considered why she and her sister were both right-handed. It wasn't usually that way with identical twins. She'd read that somewhere. Maybe her parents had discouraged Kate's use of her left hand, Jill had always been a rightie.

She started to ask her mother, but her mother spoke first.

"You can't make anything of what she said, Jillian. Kate is very ill. She doesn't even know what she's saying." Claire fidgeted with her purse.

Fury lashed like a razor inside her and Jill bit her tongue to prevent saying too much. How could her mother be so blind? Not blind, no. She was hiding something.

It was all connected. Everything. MedTech. Benford Chemical. *Every-damned-thing*. And somehow Claire knew how or why it connected. But how did Jill make her open up? The sooner they were home, behind closed doors, the better. One way or another she was going to get her mother to talk.

"Don't go so fast, Jill," Claire pleaded. "You're frightening me."

"Don't be ridiculous, Mother. I'm driving the speed limit."

They were almost home. The Washington Street intersection was next. The light turned yellow then red. Jill braked. Nothing happened. Her heart stumbled.

She stomped hard on the pedal.

Like mush, it sank all the way to the floor, useless.

Fear constricted her throat.

Cars moved through the cross street and...she...could...not...stop.

"Hold on!" She crammed her foot down on the emergency brake and swerved away from the traffic.

Claire screamed.

The force and sound of impact obliterated all else.

Then the world went dark.

CHAPTER ELEVEN

Paul stood in the corridor outside the trauma room where the paramedics had taken Jill. Her mother was two doors down. Terror throbbed in his veins. A nurse or doctor or someone had tried to herd him back into the ER waiting area, but he'd refused to go.

The cop covering the so-called accident had taken one look at the rage in Paul's eyes and backed off. The paramedics had assured him that both Jill and her mother were okay, no serious injuries. But he wouldn't be satisfied until he saw her with his own eyes. Until he touched her…held her in his arms.

He closed his eyes and fought to keep it together.

He couldn't lose her.

That realization startled him.

A wayward neuron that misfired. A mental receptor that either absorbed too much or too little of a necessary chemical, triggering a primal response that he couldn't deny. Panic hit him in the gut like a sledgehammer.

He hadn't wanted to come here. To take this case. But he'd done it to get Lawton off his back.

What had he accomplished? Nothing. He was supposed to help but he hadn't made a difference fast enough. Hadn't kept Jill from harm. He didn't care what the police called it...Paul knew deep in his gut that foul play was somehow involved. The evil smoldering here had touched her...almost stealing her life. Just one more reminder of the balance of power. *They* were in control. Paul and Jill were fighting an uphill battle where the ultimate stakes and the rules of engagement were unclear. At this point they couldn't even name the bad guys.

But the evil was close...Jill was standing on the edge of a deep, dark abyss. One he knew well. Too well.

It wasn't until he'd gotten the call about the accident that he'd realized just how deeply she'd gotten to him. He wanted Jill on a level he'd denied himself for so long he'd forgotten it was even there. He thought of the feel of her skin beneath his lips when he'd kissed her earlier today. Why hadn't he driven them to the service? He swallowed hard, tasting the regret that served no purpose except to remind him that he was a fool too many times over.

"Dr. Phillips?"

His head came up at the sound of the nurse's voice.

"Yes."

She stood outside the door of Jill's room. "You can go in now. The doctor would like to speak with you."

Renewed fear collided with the knot of anxiety in his gut. "Thank you." He took a breath and opened the door. Jill was sitting on the exam table, smiling feebly, falsely. A fighter, he thought, she didn't give up so easily.

Uncertainty crushed in on his chest when he took in the whole picture. She had an angry red lump on her forehead above her left eye. Her neck and arms were covered in dried blood. Lots of it. His heart dropped to the floor.

"Her mother had a laceration on her forehead near the hairline. That's where the blood came from," the doctor explained quickly.

Paul nodded, relieved beyond words.

His gaze locked with Jill's watery blue eyes. "You okay?"

Jill laughed a dry, aching sound, blinked several times and demanded, "Are you nuts, Phillips? I totaled my car and almost killed us both. Of course, I'm not okay."

He managed a smile. "I saw the car. Hell of a job you did on it."

She released a shaky breath. "I guess we were pretty lucky." Her voice was a little thin, but steady.

Damn lucky. "So what's the prognosis, Doc?" He turned to the ER physician who'd waited quietly during their exchange. A spot or two of blood stained the right cuff of his lab coat. Mrs. Ellington's, Paul assumed. That image nudged him. The feeling was a familiar one that usually warned of things to come. *Bad* things. It soured in his gut.

"Shaken, but fine," the doctor said, drawing Paul from the trance he'd suddenly drifted into. "The head injury is only a contusion. She'll have a lot of bruising, especially where the seat belt held her in place. But, otherwise, she's in remarkably good shape."

"And Mrs. Ellington?" Paul knew head injuries bled more than most, but the amount still concerned him. Images of Jill holding her mother in her arms until help arrived flashed in his brain. Made his chest tighten.

"Shaken as well. Ten stitches near the hairline on the right side of her forehead. No broken bones, which was a concern since she's a bit older. As soon as I've written the discharge orders, they'll both be ready to go."

When the doctor left the room, Paul moved closer to the patient. "You scared the hell out of me."

She swiped at her tears and blew out a ragged breath. "Scared myself."

"What happened?" He wanted to touch her. No, he wanted to put his arms around her and hold her. But first, he had to know what took place in that car. If his instincts were on target, the enemy had just issued a major warning.

"I was in a hurry." She shrugged, then winced. "I wanted to get back to you and tell you what happened at the hospital. But I wasn't speeding. The light changed at the Washington Street intersection…I couldn't stop." Her shoulders sagged and she closed her eyes wearily.

He'd known it. Dammit! His tension shot to a higher station. "What do you mean, you couldn't stop?"

"The pedal went all the way to the floor. Nothing. No brakes."

"But you did brake, I saw the skid marks."

"The emergency brake." Fear glittered in her eyes as she obviously relived those terrifying moments. "It didn't slow us much, but it lessened the impact when we hit that brick wall."

The car had careened between two vehicles in the cross street, barely clipping one, and then slammed broadside into the brick retaining wall that bordered a residential lawn. The passenger side had been the one to hit the wall. Every time Paul pictured the scene he realized how much worse it could have been.

"Mother's head hit the passenger window," she said, her voice shaking. She pressed her lips together and tried to hold back a sob.

Paul put his arms around her and held her against his chest. "She's fine. You're both fine."

"But it was my fault," she murmured, her voice wobbling. "I should have reacted more quickly. I could have killed her. It's a miracle I didn't."

"You didn't do anything wrong. The brakes will have to be inspected but I'm betting they failed, not you. This isn't your fault."

"She asked me to slow down. I should have listened."

Her shoulders shook in his arms. He wanted to rip apart whoever was responsible for this. He'd known the moment the phone rang that it was something like this.

He held her. Held her and reassured her again and again that it wasn't her fault. Finally, when she'd calmed, they walked together to her mother's room. Jill and Claire hugged for a long time, shedding more tears, thanking God over and over that they were both safe.

But Paul had his own ideas about that.

He had a feeling that none of them were safe.

Not in Paradise.

* * *

Jill closed the door to her mother's room and moved quietly away. She was finally resting. Considering the head injury, which like Jill's was a contusion in addition to the laceration, Jill was to rouse her every two hours as a precautionary measure. She glanced at the clock hanging at the end of the hall. It was seven-thirty now, at nine-thirty she would check on her.

She'd had a shower and changed into lounge pants and a tee. Paul was waiting for her in the library to go over what they had so far. He looked up when she entered the room. Her heavy heart lifted at the sight of him. His smile nearly undid her. She saw it so rarely it took her breath every time he allowed it. The gesture softened the lean angles of his face and put a sparkle in those dark eyes. She could look at him like this forever and never grow tired of it. Her throat tightened whenever she thought of how close she'd come today to never seeing him again.

This bond they'd formed, both fighting it every step of the way, was damned strong. Pretending it didn't exist would be pointless. She needed him. No, it was more than that. She wanted him here… she wanted to be close to him.

"She's sleeping," Jill said in answer to the question that formed in his expression.

He nodded. "Good."

Jill collapsed in one of the leather wingbacks flanking her father's desk. "So what does all this add up to?" She had mentally grasped all the bits and pieces, but she'd been so distracted by other events she hadn't been able to put things together fully just yet. She was sure Paul had. When she'd told him what Kate said he'd only nodded but, like her, he recognized the revelation was significant. Her mother could pretend otherwise but Jill knew without a doubt that Cody was alive and out there somewhere—some place *safe*.

Phillips stared at her for so long she felt like squirming. "Is something wrong?" She'd had about all she could stomach this day.

He gave his head a shake, as if to clear it. "I was just thinking."

"Well, that certainly got me into trouble yesterday." She smiled, it felt good to do that when she had so little to smile about. He'd warned her not to look at him that way. Not happening.

When he continued to stare without saying more, she cleared her throat. "What are your thoughts so far?"

He blinked. "I think MedTech and LifeCycle are in bed together."

She shivered at the analogy "Go on."

"I believe there's some kind of cover-up going on here that goes back to Benford Chemical and the murder of its owner," he explained. "I also think there've been a number of human experiments."

"Like Cody and the boy in Lynchburg." She had been thinking along those lines as well. Maybe they'd both read too many novels or watched too many movies, but the incredible likeness between the children was impossible to ignore.

"Yes."

Fear crept along her spine. "They could be twins."

He nodded again. "They could be."

She refused to be put off by his obvious need to answer only her question. She wanted more—all of whatever was on his mind. "Do you believe my nephew is alive?" She held her breath. She needed him on her side about this. And if Cody were alive, whose body had the chief found? The possible answer to that question made her stomach churn with a new kind of fear. Could the chief be that kind of bad man?

Jesus, she'd known most of the people in this town her whole life.

"I believe the remains the chief would have us believe is your nephew are a decoy to throw us off the hunt. If your nephew is dead, there's no reason for you to hang around and look for him. Dotson wants you gone."

"What about my sister? The chief knows I won't leave with Kate's situation up in the air."

"I look for that to be resolved any day now. They—whoever they are—want rid of us. They're willing to take extreme measures to reach that goal."

"That's why the brakes failed." Her chest tightened with apprehension.

He tipped his head in silent acknowledgment, confirming but not elaborating. "They either know or don't care why Karl Manning was murdered. They simply want the case closed and the two of us out of their hair."

An icy cold swept through her as that reality sank in. On some level she'd known it was so…but she hadn't wanted to admit it. The whole idea was too scary, too unbelievable.

"Do you believe my sister is in danger?" Her lips trembled on the words. If her actions had put her sister in danger Jill would never forgive herself.

"If that was the case, she'd be dead already. They could've tied up the entire case with one big bow at the homicide scene staged in your sister's kitchen."

Made sense. "I want to hear all of it," she insisted. He was holding back, she sensed his reservations. "What're your instincts telling you?"

That dark gaze settled on her. "That MedTech and LifeCycle took advantage of the situation thirty-two years ago. Paradise was devastated and needed help. LifeCycle offered a deal no one outside the powers that be here in Paradise ever had to know about."

"A deal?" She mulled over the concept. "The kind of deal that gets you what you want and saves your pride. For a price?"

"A very high price."

"All everyone had to do was overlook whatever illegal and immoral experimentation was conducted," she suggested, her pulse pounding harder and harder at the scenario he painted.

"The residents might not *have* known the full ramifications of what they had agreed to."

"But what about Benford? Who murdered him?"

"Someone or several someones from right here in Paradise. A vigilante killing is my guess." He shrugged. "An eye for an eye."

"Dear God." It was too much. Jill shook her head in denial, then winced, groaning at the ache the move caused.

He was out of his chair and at her side in a heartbeat. "Do you need something else for that headache?"

She'd already taken a mild pain reliever. Anything else would put her in a fog and she needed her head clear for this. "I'm okay."

He sat down in the chair adjacent to hers. "You need to be prepared for where this is going. When we find the truth, you may be outing people you knew, respected as a child, maybe even your own father. He may have had a hand in Benford's murder."

"You didn't know my father," she countered. The suggestion was ludicrous. "He wasn't that kind of man."

"I'm sure he wasn't. But he knew about the chemicals. Knew about LifeCycle. He was too prominent a citizen at the time not to have been up to his eyeballs in the whole affair. And maybe he was desperate."

She wasn't sure she could accept that. The idea made her ache at the very core of her being. "As an attorney I understand that what you're saying is logical. But, as a daughter, I can't accept it." Not until she had evidence. She just couldn't.

"Do you think your mother will talk after what happened today? If I can produce evidence of tampering with the brakes?"

Jill sighed. "Maybe. She's coming around, opening up more. We could try talking to her in the morning."

"Keep in mind that we're still putting the pieces together. We may discover that we're off a little one way or the other. I could be wrong on some parts. I've been wrong before."

She searched his eyes. "Tell me how you know things. How it comes to you."

He didn't answer right away. She waited, understanding that sharing something so deeply personal wouldn't be easy.

"It's always been this way," he began quietly. He reached for his shirt pocket and the cigarettes there, but then apparently thought better of it. She hadn't seen him smoke since that first day. "I feel things...sensations. Vague images and sounds." He shrugged. "Nothing glamorous or dramatic. Not like in the movies. But those moments of perception eventually coalesce into conclusions and I'm usually right. When I want to be anyway."

Silence stretched between them. Jill allowed it to linger...remained patient, not wanting to push him. Watching him was enough. He was so complicated and strong in a way she was only now coming to realize. Something fluttered deep inside her. This strong, tortured man had touched her in a place no one else had ever reached. She respected him the way she had her father...respected the man beneath all else. Her trust and respect for others was typically limited to their professional façade because she never allowed the relationship to go beyond that level. With Paul Phillips it was different. Did he realize, she wondered, how deeply he affected her?

"I feel it first," he went on, "like a light in the back of my brain, a quickening in my gut. It slices through causing a kind of unbearable pressure. Then comes the darkness and the panic. The fear that it'll consume me this time. Drag me into the darkness so deep that I can't find my way back."

He released a heavy breath. "The deeper I get into the darkness the more I feel. And then I know the answer but it's in bits and pieces. Eventually it all falls into place...if I can deal with the cost of touching it long enough."

She ached for what he must suffer with each case he accepted...or turned away. She squeezed back the tears. It had to be a nightmare. "I'm sorry." And she was. "I appreciate your help more than you can possibly imagine. I couldn't do this alone."

Reaching out she took his hand in hers and studied the dark texture of his skin in contrast to hers. "It scares the hell out of me that you might be right about all this." If he was even half right, what they were about to uncover would hurt so many. "It'll be the fall of Camelot for a lot of people, including me. Nothing in Paradise will ever be the same."

"If I'm right," he said somberly, "change would be a good thing." He laced his fingers with hers. "I don't know yet how Karl's murder ties in, unless your sister discovered something he was up to. Even then there were other ways to handle it."

Jill stared at their joined hands. "She tried to get me to come home two months ago and I couldn't. I was too busy. I always had some sort of excuse. Maybe that's when she discovered the Lynchburg child." Another kind of regret settled heavily on her shoulders. "That could be when it all began to surface. The lies…the deception."

"I can't help wondering why she didn't just take her son and go to you."

"You had to know Karl." Jill had never liked that about her sister's husband. Too controlling. Too domineering. "He arranged every move she made. She was the perfect, obedient wife. She did exactly as he told her, just like she'd always done with our parents." Jill had spent a lifetime pretending that was just her sister's way. What if she'd been wrong? "Like a *Stepford Wife*." Another of those shivers danced up her spine. She kept coming back to that analogy.

"The two of you fought about that," Paul deduced.

Jill made a dry sound that hardly met the definition of a laugh. "Numerous times. I wanted her to be her own person, but she just wanted to be whatever the people she loved wanted her to be."

"You were the trouble maker...the rebel."

"You do read minds." She laughed again, the real thing this time.

"From time to time." He leaned closer to her, held her hand tightly in his. "Right now I'm glad you can't read mine." He kissed her lips, just a tender brushing of mouths.

Her heart leapt. Desire swirled deep in her belly. "Actually, I think I can."

He kissed her again. It was deeper, longer this time. The kind of kiss that promised so much more. And she wanted more.

The telephone rang. Jill jumped.

He drew back slowly. "You should get that."

She nodded, struggled to regain her composure. It could be the hospital calling. She stood and reached across her father's desk. "Hello." She squeezed her eyes shut, wished her voice didn't sound so husky. How had nothing more than a kiss turned her so inside out?

"Jill?"

"Richard!" Relief washed over her. She was glad to hear his voice and to have the intensity of the moment interrupted. Somehow she had to get her head screwed on straight. Nothing, not even her own needs, could get in the way of finding the truth.

"I'm glad I finally caught you."

"Have you been trying to call?" She didn't remember seeing any messages on the machine. She certainly hadn't gotten a call on her cell.

"A couple of times just to check on you. I didn't leave a message. How's your sister?"

"Not well I'm afraid."

Richard made a disappointed sound. "How are you?"

"I'm okay. Things are getting pretty complicated around here." She opted not to tell him about the car crash. She knew Richard too well. He would be suggesting she head back to Jackson pronto.

"Is Paul there with you? He's helping with the case?"

"Oh, yes, Dr. Phillips is here." Her gaze lit on the man in question and she was taken aback by the intensity in his eyes. Not the hot, sensual kind. Anger or something along those lines.

"Would you like to speak with him?" she asked, unsettled.

There was a moment of silence before Richard replied. "Just give him my best."

"I will." Jill felt really uneasy now. She'd thought he and Richard were friends but there was nothing friendly about the way Paul Phillips looked right now.

More of that silence strummed for a moment or two. "I'm worried about you, Jill. I wish you'd keep me posted as this situation moves forward. I feel completely out of the loop."

Richard's concern touched her. "I'm okay, really. We're being very careful." There was no point in making her old friend worry.

"You'll keep me up to speed then?"

"I will. I apologize for not having called already." She had called him for help, then dropped the ball when it came to keeping him apprised of the evolving events. But, giving herself grace, she'd been a little distracted. She stole a glance at Phillips but he looked away before she could read his face. What was she missing?

Paul struggled with keeping his resentment contained. Whatever had been or still was between Jill and Lawton was none of his business. He'd been a fool to kiss her the way he had just now. Just went to show that his control was slipping way too fast.

He pushed to his feet, fought the urge for a drink. He should focus on the investigation.

Jill ended the call and dropped the receiver back into its cradle. In spite of his best efforts, his mouth got the better of him. "How is our old friend?" Not such an unexpected question but his tone hit just a degree shy of sarcastic.

She frowned, clearly confused by his reaction to the call. "He's fine. He just wanted to check on me—us."

Me was the answer. Richard wanted to know if she was okay. Paul could be six feet under for all the bastard cared. There was a time when he and

Richard had been close…as close as father and son. But after the breakdown, Richard had pushed Paul to get back to his work at the Bureau…to carry on. *Be strong, not weak.* When Paul refused, the relationship ended. Or more accurately, he ended it.

"What's the story with you and Lawton?" The question startled him almost as much as it did her. But it was out now, he might as well have the answer.

"He was one of my law professors at Ole Miss," she said, avoiding his gaze.

Her statement was true, but at its heart it was a lie. He could feel the weight of omission. She didn't want to tell him and he had no right to question her about it.

"Were you lovers?" Dammit. Why couldn't he keep his mouth shut? He gritted his teeth. *Idiot.*

She looked him straight in the eye. "Yes. We were. Briefly." Her words were stiff, laced with a resentment of her own. "My father had just died and I needed someone. Is that what you wanted to hear?"

He'd gone too far. He'd been wrong. Normally he worked out his anger on a punching bag in his garage, but he wasn't in Memphis right now. He had no way to work off the layers of tension that had accumulated since meeting Jillian Ellington. Dredging up the past with Lawton only made bad matters worse for her and for hm.

He needed a walk to clear his head. Cool off. And then apologize. "I need some air."

She stopped him with a hand on his arm. "Don't go."

Her touch made him yearn for things he knew he could never hang onto. The need in her voice and the plea in her eyes gave her away as surely as if she'd said the words.

"Are you sure I'm what you want?" That's what she was asking. She didn't have to say the words. "I come with a lot of baggage, Jill. I go for days without sleeping. Sometimes I drink myself into oblivion. Maybe more than sometimes. Anything to avoid that mental darkness that stalks me. Even then, sometimes it catches up. No matter how you see me at this moment, I'm not a hero. I'm just a guy who's more screwed up than most."

Despite his warning she stared at him with a kind of awe and hunger that made him weak…made him wish he was more of the hero she thought he was and less of a coward.

"I want you." Her words were barely a whisper but the fire in her eyes was a roar.

"I won't hold it against you if you change your mind," he offered.

She leaned into him. Looked him straight in the eyes. "I'm not changing my mind so stop trying to change it for me."

"You seem pretty determined for a woman who still calls me Dr. Phillips." He had her there. At least he hoped. He was way too close to giving in to keep playing this game.

"Stop trying to distract me." She stared at his mouth a moment before lifting her gaze back to his. "I want you. Is that a problem?"

"No problem at all."

He whisked her into his arms. She gasped. He mounted the stairs, kissing her thoroughly as he climbed. Damn but he wanted this woman. By the time they reached her bedroom door, he was ready to rip her clothes off and toss her across the bed.

Instead, he settled her onto her feet and leaned in close, one arm braced against the doorjamb on either side of her. "You listen to me, pretty lady," he murmured, "you get back to me in a day or two if you still feel the same way. Then I'll be happy to give you all you want of me."

He backed off. Walked away.

Her door slammed hard enough to wake the dead.

Maybe he'd have that drink after all.

CHAPTER TWELVE

It was just past seven when Paul woke. With D.C. an hour ahead, he'd have time to shower and have a cup of coffee before Cuddahy got to his office. At one time he'd had the guy's personal cell phone number but he'd buried all that along with the man he used to be. Touching base with his old friend this morning might be a bit premature since until he knew more about MedTech and LifeCycle, where to go from here was unclear. One thing was certain, he had to protect Jill. If he'd had any doubts that she was in danger, yesterday had cleared those up.

MedTech and LifeCycle were the catalysts for the events that happened the past few days. Paul was sure of it. Benford Chemical had merely set the stage thirty odd years ago.

A setup to render the people of Paradise vulnerable and pliable enough to ensure they would welcome LifeCycle and MedTech and gladly agree to any and all promises.

It was a strategy as old as time. Make people desperate enough and they obeyed.

The scenarios he'd drawn were on the mark, or at least damned close. A familiar restlessness had started deep inside him. All he had to do was stay focused.

Just like in the Garden of Eden, something evil had permeated Paradise and he could feel it. That evil had presented itself as an entity both knowledgeable and helpful. It had offered hope. The ultimate temptation to a town suffering an unthinkable horror. And, like Eve, the good people of Paradise had grabbed on with both hands.

Little did they know the price they would pay in the end.

By eight, Paul was in the Judge's study, putting through a call to Cuddahy. "You have something for me?"

"Good morning to you, too."

Paul leaned back in the chair. "I won't know if it's a good morning until I hear what you've got." He swallowed the last of the coffee in his cup.

"I can't make any promises," Cuddahy tossed back, "but here goes. MedTech was the first in this country to be granted licensing for extended human cloning research. A thorough investigation revealed no reason not to grant licensing."

"In other words MedTech's squeaky clean." No surprise. Those bastards hadn't gotten to the top of the food chain without being damned smart. Brilliant maybe.

"On paper, yes," Cuddahy confirmed. "But to answer the question you asked of me, MedTech and LifeCycle have a long and solid relationship. LifeCycle is also, remarkably clean. They don't even cheat on their taxes."

Now Cuddahy was being cynical. "But you don't like what you see...on paper, as you say," Paul suggested.

Cuddahy hesitated before going on. "It's just a hunch. MedTech donates hundreds of thousands of dollars to all the right causes. Hell, LifeCycle even supports dozens of low-income women's clinics."

Paul's pulse rate picked up. "Like the Women's Clinic in Tullahoma, Tennessee?" Sarah Long had used that clinic.

"That's one of them."

He was holding back. "What is it you're not telling me?"

"Off the record?"

A new kind of tension rippled through Paul. "Definitely."

"Two months ago there was a call to the federal contractor whistleblower hotline. The unidentified caller threw out some accusations then hung up and never called back. An investigation I can't access was triggered based on that call. But I can tell you the call originated in Paradise."

The hum of awareness deep inside Paul grew to a roar. Two months. That was around the time when Kate tried to talk Jill into coming home. "Thanks, Cuddahy. I'll get back to you."

"What have you gotten yourself in to, Phillips?"

Paul hesitated. "Not that much. A murder. Missing kid…the standard stuff."

Cuddahy laughed."Yeah, right. The Bureau still needs you, you know."

Paul knew how the Bureau needed him. The Bureau had been using people like him since before the Nixon administration. Only then it had been a big secret. Now the stigma was softened with the right kind of education and job title. A psychologist was supposed to be able to read the human psyche, right? And, of course, a trained forensics man could read the clues left at a crime scene. Nothing else ever had to enter into the equation of what Paul Phillips did.

"Thanks for the help." Paul severed the connection, not wanting to discuss what the Bureau needed with his old friend or anyone else.

What *he* needed was to know what MedTech was up to. The solution to this mystery was there and with LifeCycle. Kate had known it. He'd bet his life she was the one who'd made the call. That knowledge would be another blow to Jill. No need to tell her just yet.

Kate had discovered what her husband was up to as CEO of MedTech and she'd tried to stop him. But first she'd taken her son to a safe place. The burned body the chief had shipped off to TBI wouldn't be Cody Manning's.

Other than her husband's blood, no foreign substances had been found on the clothing that Kate had been wearing when taken into custody.

If she'd burned her child's body, there would have been traces of soot and the accelerant she used. Human bodies didn't burn beyond recognition without a powerful accelerant. And no one burned a body that thoroughly without walking away with trace evidence in the fibers of their clothing, in their hair and on their skin.

Cody Manning was still alive.

"Good morning."

Jill stood in the open doorway. Dammit he'd forgotten about closing the doors. Before he could stop his traitorous gaze, he'd taken in every inch of her. She looked gorgeous, despite the bruise on her forehead. The good news was she didn't look mad at him.

He stood. Gathered his empty coffee cup. "Morning. How're you feeling this morning?"

"Thankful."

If he were lucky that was a good thing. "How so?"

"I'm thankful you prevented me from making a fool of myself last night."

Oh hell. He hadn't meant for her to feel that way. "Jill—"

She held up a hand. "I don't want to talk about it." Then she waved her cell phone. "Besides, I missed a call last night and I think it might have been important."

"From the hospital?" He hoped Kate hadn't taken a turn for the worse.

She shook her head. "It was Connie. My friend from high school. She said she needs to talk to

195

me. About Kate." Worry clouded her eyes. "She sounded…scared."

"Did you call her back?"

"Twice. No answer. I'll try again in a few minutes."

"How's your mother?"

Jill blinked, still distracted by thoughts of her friend. "She says she's fine but I know better. I threw together a fruit and cereal tray and took it to her room. She plans to stay in bed most of the day."

Paul nodded. "Good idea." He didn't want Claire out of the house on her own. Of course, with her agoraphobia, he mused, she shouldn't want to leave. Yet another of Paradise's mysteries.

"I'm going back to the library." Jill squared her shoulders and looked ready to argue. "I know I'm supposed to be taking it easy today but I want to follow up on something the senator said when he dropped by the hospital."

"You're not going anywhere without me." Paul grabbed his keys. "I'll take you."

"After yesterday, that's probably a good idea." She gave him a sad smile. "Considering my car is down for the count, I'm not going anywhere without you."

He could live with that.

* * *

Paradise Public Library

After just two hours Jill had to admit that the senator was right. There was the occasional year here and there during the past thirty where no births were announced in Paradise. But that concern had given way to a new and steadily increasing sense of horror more than twenty years back in her research.

There were numerous deaths of young children in Paradise and the surrounding smaller communities. At least four per year, sometimes five or six. Fear crept so deeply into her bones that Jill wasn't sure she could stand for a few moments. But she had to tell Paul. She hoped he might be able to give her some reasonable explanation as to how this could be normal. Why had she never noticed this growing up? Maybe because she hadn't personally known any of the children who'd died? No, that wasn't right... there was this one girl who'd died when Jill was six. They were in first grade together. The girl had always been sickly. Pale and thin.

Something cold and too terrible to examine critically knotted inside her. Why had no one questioned all the deaths?

She moved stiffly toward the computer station where Paul worked. The idea that she was suddenly referring to him as Paul lurked around the fringes of her thoughts. She dismissed it. He'd been calling her by her first name practically from day one. It wasn't because he'd mentioned any such thing.

Focus, Jill. What she needed were some comparisons. She pulled up a chair and sat. While she waited for him to notice she was there, she studied his profile. That intense yearning she'd felt last night started to build inside her, chasing away some of the chill. *Don't go there.*

He glanced at her. "You find something?"

She nodded. Dredged up the wherewithal to say the words out loud. "I think we need to look into another aspect of Paradise's history."

His gaze narrowed as she relayed the details of what she'd noted in the newspaper. Ironically, the obituaries had almost always been on the same page with the births.

"We'll need comparison data."

She held up her tablet listing the dates and deaths.

"You should call the house and check on your mom. We're going on a little road trip."

* * *

Jill sat in the passenger seat of the Land Rover too stunned to carry the thread of conversation Paul had tried at least twice to initiate. She couldn't talk right now.

They'd driven to two neighboring towns, both were about the same size as Paradise, and perused obituary records for the past thirty years or as close to that time frame as records were available. The task could have easily been done via the Internet but, after yesterday's incident, the goal was to prevent anyone from figuring out what they were up to. They couldn't take any more risks. Nausea roiled in her stomach even now at the thought of what she and Paul had found. Neither of those towns had the kind of child mortality rate that Paradise had.

Could the old Benford plant or even MedTech or LifeCycle be releasing something else harmful into the environment in Paradise? The EPA had seen to the cleanup of the old chemical plant. Or had they?

Were the deaths reported in the *Paradise Gazette* all of them? What if there were others? Paranoia soared and she suddenly felt as if she could trust nothing she saw, read or heard. Her whole perfect childhood was based on one lie after the other. No one or nothing was what it seemed. All this time she'd thought she and Kate had the idyllic storybook childhood. She just hadn't known there were so many skeletons in the closet—a whole other world of pure menace lying beneath that perfect facade.

"How do you feel about a little breaking and entering?"

The sound of his voice after the long minutes of silence startled her. "What do you have in mind?"

"I have grave reservations as to whether MedTech is going to allow us to take a look around or review their files." He flashed her one of those smiles that made her heart react. "Certainly the LifeCycle Center isn't going to."

"You want to break into one of those places?" Okay, reality check. "Paul, we can't do that. They have security guards with guns."

He laughed. It was the first real laugh she'd heard from him. The sound challenged her to take a blind leap of faith just because he asked. Twelve years ago he wouldn't have had to ask. But she had worked long and hard to transform herself from impulsive and emotional to level headed and reserved. Was she going to allow him to undo all that work in a matter of days?

She thought of her bold demand last night. Maybe he already had.

"No," he said patiently. "That would almost certainly ensure a trip to Chief Dotson's facilities. Knowing how the man feels about us, me specifically, I don't think that would be a wise move."

A frown tugged at her brow, reminding her that her head hurt. "Where do we need to do this breaking and entering?"

"Karl Manning probably kept a few working files at home. We need to check out your sister's house and see if we can find anything. Since, technically, it's still a crime scene, to enter, with or without the owner's permission, is illegal. You up to the challenge?"

This time she did the smiling. Why the hell hadn't she thought of that? "Oh, I'm more than up to it. I know where Kate keeps her spare key." She hoped the police hadn't added any additional locks.

There was only one way to find out.

* * *

Jill directed him to an upscale housing development high on a mountaintop overlooking Paradise. The view was nothing short of spectacular, the houses high end. Karl Manning had no doubt left a hefty estate. Paul wondered why the chief hadn't considered that as a motive.

Because they aren't really looking for one.

It wouldn't be dark for several more hours. There was no way to avoid the risk of being seen by the neighbors. Paul parked on the curb instead of in the drive. If the chief or one of his deputies showed up, he didn't want to be blocked in.

He surveyed the neighborhood as he emerged from the vehicle, then met Jill on the passenger side away from the street. "You get the key and go on inside just like you own the place. I'll be right behind you."

She nodded, then walked straight up to the front door without glancing about. By the time he stepped up behind her, she had the key in the lock and had turned the knob. She hesitated and he understood that it was about the crime scene notice right in front of her face. He reached past her and opened the door.

He followed her inside and checked the alarm system to ensure it wasn't armed. Probably hadn't been since the police arrived to find Karl Manning dead on the floor.

Jill closed and locked the door behind them. "Where would you like to start?"

"You take the upstairs. I'll look around down here." He didn't want her faced with the kitchen.

She headed for the stairs.

"Is there a basement?"

She paused, chewed her lower lip for a moment. He licked his lips, wishing it was him nibbling on that full bottom lip. He'd gotten way too much pleasure out of hearing her use his first name. Most likely didn't mean anything but it made him won-der...or hope.

"I think there's a storm shelter. I remember she said something about it when they built the house."

"I'll cover the storm shelter."

She nodded and hurried up the stairs. Didn't take a mind reader to see she'd rather be anywhere else and wanted this over as quickly as possible. But, like him, she recognized the need to examine this avenue.

They were just about out of directions to go. Without evidence calling in the state police or the Bureau was off the table. All they had right now was speculation and the Paul Phillips sixth sense, for what that was worth. Neither of which was admissible as evidence. If whoever was behind this nasty business was as thorough as they seemed so far, he doubted the follow up on that whistleblower call would garner any results either.

Finding the truth was up to the two of them.

Paul narrowed his attention to the task at hand. A formal living room and dining room flanked the entry hall at the front of the house. The furnishings were expensive and thoughtfully arranged. It smacked of professional decorating. Too many fine details woven too tightly together for a novice. A powder room and spacious family room. All large, elaborately appointed, and without the first hint of anything untoward. Karl Manning had chosen only the best for his family. A huge television, all the latest in electronic gadgets, expensive overstuffed sofas and elegant tables.

Mentally bracing himself he entered the final room on the first floor. The kitchen with its airy breakfast room and commercial grade everything. A chill settled deep in his bones. The kind he always experienced when he entered a crime scene where murder was involved. The blood had discolored the natural stone tile, seeped deep into each tiny crevice.

Whispers, shadows of sound, echoed all around him. His pulse reacted. He moved toward the island, stood at the very end of it and stared down at the place where Karl Manning had fallen…taken his last breath.

Blinding light shattered all thought, pain arced inside his skull. He leaned against the smooth granite counter, the feel of the powdery residue used for gathering prints gritty beneath his palms. He closed his eyes and looked inward, surrendering to the pull…to the voices and images.

Her hand shook, then closed around the handle of the knife. *Tell me. No!* Another hand, this one larger…male…withdrew a hypodermic needle from a jacket pocket. *Tell me or I'll use this.*

Pain sliced through his chest. The knife slid deep, clipping the atrium wall. He crumpled to the floor. Shock and disbelief rendered him speechless for those final moments as blood filled the thoracic cavity around his quivering heart. She peered down at him, then collapsed to her knees. Sobbing hysterically, she tried to pull the knife out, but her efforts only made matters worse. He could feel the life force draining away, bathing his heart and lungs, seeping around the sharp, stainless steel blade of the knife, soaking into his shirt.

Who would carry on with his work? No one else understood...his grandfather had warned him. Had told him that the world would never comprehend such beautiful, perfect work.

Paul jerked back from the darkness. He gulped in massive amounts of air, fighting the urge to vomit. He closed his eyes and shook his head. Calm the hell down. *Let it go.*

That was always the hardest part...turning loose. It grabbed him, sucked him into a vortex of sensory perceptions, lights, sounds, images. His mind and body absorbed the energy that hung in the air long after the event. Bits and pieces of positively charged ions floating about, waiting to be noticed. All one needed was the heightened senses to pick up on them. The constant hum of elevated perception was always there with Paul. Most of the time he refused to see or hear any of it. Pushed it away. But it was there just the same. Waiting.

He exhaled a heavy breath and mopped his brow with the back of his hand. He never got used to this. No matter how often it happened. It was like a waking nightmare. A blip in neuron transmission that went a-freaking-wry.

He dusted his powder-coated palms together and forced his attention back to the search. He avoided looking at the blood stained tile as he moved through the kitchen. Eventually he returned to the hall. If there was a basement, then where the hell was the door leading to it? He opened the one beneath the staircase and discovered a coat closet. He swore and started to close the door. Something in his peripheral vision snagged his attention. He opened the door wide and stepped inside, parting the mass of coats and jackets.

"Well, hello," he muttered. A pocket door, designed to slide into the wall, and painted to match, lay beyond the array of outerwear. Paul flipped the light switch next to the door and peered down the stairs. A perfect place for a storm shelter.

The narrow stairs descended for six steps, there was a landing and a left angle where six more steps led to the basement floor. Bright fluorescent lights shone from overhead. A large L-shaped metal desk occupied a corner. Along one wall was a long table with open files spread atop it. Metal filing cabinets lined the rest of the wall space. Karl Manning's private work files. The ones he dared not keep at the office.

"So this is where you kept your secrets." Maybe Manning had kept his secrets too well. Otherwise Paul felt confident the chief and his pals would have cleared out this place already. This could be what they needed.

Anticipation zinged through him, had his heart thundering. First, he surveyed the open files on the tabletop. Several times he noticed the word "Gemini Series." Each time, the chill already permeating his skin went a little deeper. One heading in particular captured his attention as he thumbed through a stack of manila folders. He flipped back to it. *Cannibalism in the Womb.* The file was filled with what appeared to be detailed studies but it was the page right up front that held his attention the longest.

> *One of the strangest instances of the vanishing twin within the womb is twin cannibalism, in which the surviving twin literally ingests, or absorbs the remains of a dead twin in the uterus...*

What had these bastards been up to?

Jill lingered at the door of her sister's home office. She wondered vaguely if Paul had found the basement or Karl's work files. She swiped her eyes and drew in a deep breath. Going through Kate's room, the one she'd shared with her husband, had been tough. But just looking through the doorway into Cody's room had torn her apart. His toys and stuffed animals were everywhere. Pictures chronicling his growth and accomplishments decorated the walls. She wept for long minutes. And then she prayed. Prayed with all her heart that somehow Cody was still alive as Paul suspected...that Kate really had taken him some place safe. And if he wasn't, she prayed that her sister had not done this unthinkable thing.

Okay, suck it up, she told herself. She had to look for clues, anything, that might give some reason for all that had happened. Or some hint as to where Kate would take Cody if she had hidden him away. The moment she entered the only room left on the second floor, she knew it was here, in Kate's office, hobby room, whatever, that Jill felt the closest to her sister. She looked at all the lovely pictures Kate had taken. As a young girl she'd dreamed of being a photojournalist for National Geographic or Discovery, but college, MedTech and Karl had changed all that. Still, Kate had documented their lives quite beautifully. Each photograph was carefully labeled in her neat handwriting.

Cody's first trip to the beach.

Karl at work.

Catching fireflies.

Each label was simple and self-explanatory with only one look at the photograph. Jill smiled, admiring the life that had so pleased her sister until just a few days ago. On one wall were photographs of places Kate had found interesting or pleasing to her critical eye. Jill's breath caught when she recognized several as having been taken at one of the villages nestled in the foothills of the Appalachian Mountains. As girls they'd heard the lore about the people who lived there and who refused to change their primitive ways of life and blend in with the rest of society. Kate had always sworn she would learn about them one day. It looked as if she had and that made Jill happy. The final photograph of the village caused her heart to stumble. The simple label at the bottom read: *A Safe Place.*

I took him to a safe place.

The doorbell chimed.

Jill jumped, her breath catching.

She snatched the matted photograph from the wall and hurried to a window on the front side of the house to see who had rung the bell. She fully expected to see the chief's cruiser. But the only car out front was Paul's SUV.

A neighbor, she decided. Someone who wanted to be sure that nothing was amiss. Jill took a deep breath and forced herself to walk, not run, down the stairs. She would be calm and cool. No one knew she wasn't supposed to be here, except the chief, of course.

Paul stood at the entrance to the formal living room, just clear of the front door looking into the entry hall. Though the glass in the door was textured for privacy, anyone outside would see movement beyond the glass.

"Female," he whispered.

He must have checked from a front window. Jill nodded and moved toward the door. Paul eased out of sight.

Still clutching the photograph, Jill swiped her sweating right palm on her slacks and reached for the door. She twisted the knob and pulled it open, plastering a smile into place. The nanny from the Radcliff home stared back at her.

The young woman's eyes widened. "Kate, is that you?"

Jill almost corrected her...but then nodded.

"I was afraid someone was snooping around over here." Suspicion slipped into her expression. "When did you get out of the hospital?"

"This morning," Jill lied. "I'm so glad to be home." The expression of grief at all her sister had lost didn't require any faking.

The other woman sighed. "I know you must be." She looked down for a moment. "It's just awful about Cody. Roman asks for him every day. He misses their playtime. Is there anything I can do to help?"

The woman looked sincere, but all Jill could think about was the fact that she had lied to her. She'd said the children never played together. And here she was acting like Kate's best friend. Checking up on who came and went into the Manning home.

"No," Jill said softly. Kate always spoke softly, never raised her voice for any reason, not even when she was angry like Jill was right now. "I'm managing. I appreciate your concern."

"Well." The nanny nodded. "Let me know if you need anything." She started to turn away but hesitated. "I met your sister the other day. She asked a lot of questions. Has something else happened?"

Jill shook her head. "She's just worried about me. That's all." She lowered her gaze meekly. "Thank you for stopping by. I really don't feel like talking right now."

"Sure, I understand," the other woman said, but her frown contradicted her words. "I have to go. The children are sleeping."

She didn't look back as she hurried across the adjoining yards. Jill glanced at the street then closed and locked the door.

"She lied to me." She met Paul's gaze as he stepped into the hall. "She told me she knew nothing about Kate and her son. That the children never played together. I don't understand why." She shook her head. "This makes no sense at all. And I think she figured out I wasn't Kate before she left."

The fire in his eyes had her pulse skipping before he even spoke. "You need to come with me. There's something you should see."

He'd found something. Jill's stomach executed an unsettling flip-flop.

Still clasping the photograph, she followed him into the coat closet and then down to what she presumed to be a basement.

"What is this place?" She'd had no idea her sister's storm shelter was…like this.

Paul glanced around the room, then up at the ceiling. "I think it's a large vault. Looks fireproof. Concrete and really thick. The house plans likely listed it as a safe room." He motioned for her to join him at a table. "Pull up a chair and take a look at this stuff. I'm going through the file cabinets."

Disbelief and horror clawed its way into her throat as Jill scanned folder after folder. No one would really perform these kinds of experiments on humans? Would they?

But they had. The reports...detailed descriptions. Dear God. Jill shook her head. No. God didn't have anything to do with this.

She wasn't sure how much time had passed when she finally looked up, stretched her neck. Paul was still poring through drawers of files. None of the subjects were named. All were designated by a number. Somewhere there had to be a database that linked these numbers with names.

"This is...unbelievable." Her throat had gone dry, her heart felt strangely distressed. "I'm not sure I can quite grasp that it's real." Genetic tampering, strange experiments that she didn't know how to begin to describe. Transplanting embryos, cloning. It was too incomprehensible.

Paul paused long enough to look at her. "It's real all right. The really scary part is that it's probably just the tip of the iceberg. I'm—"

A muffled sound echoed overhead.

"Stay put," he ordered.

If someone was in the house they would notice the closet door standing open and then...

Fear tightened around her throat. Paul took the stairs two at a time. What if it was the chief? Or...? She couldn't label the other threat. It was too enormous to encompass with a single individual or entity. Too awful to name.

She reached for the photograph she'd taken from Kate's hobby room and clutched it to her chest. Was there any place safe from what lay outside these walls? Jill was certain that for her and the people she loved, there wasn't.

"Jill!"

She moved to the bottom of the stairs. "Who's up there?" Fear pounded through her veins.

Paul was halfway down the stairs now, reaching for her. "We have to get out of here."

Her nose wrinkled at the acrid smell of smoke following him. Fire?

"Hurry! The house is on fire!"

CHAPTER THIRTEEN

"You've destroyed evidence. I could get you disbarred for this!" The chief glowered at Jill.

"We didn't start the fire, chief." It took every ounce of resolve Paul possessed not to lose it right now. But he couldn't do that...not and protect Jill. Not and find the truth.

"And you!" The chief stabbed a finger in Paul's face. "I should haul your ass—pardon my French, Miss Jill—to jail. You crossed the line, mister!"

"We have nothing to hide, chief." Paul held his hands up surrender style. "Do what you think you have to do."

They were alive. That in itself was a small miracle. The front door and rear entries of the Manning home had been fully engulfed. He'd thrown a chair through one of the large front windows, creating an escape route.

Too close for comfort. That's what it was.

Kate Manning's home was completely destroyed. The fire department had gotten the flames put out, but other than the still standing brick, the house was gutted. The second floor had collapsed into the first.

"Well, that fire didn't start itself," the chief accused. "If I find one shred of proof that you're involved in this clear cut case of arson, you'll wish you'd never set foot in this town, Dr. Phillips."

His control slipped. Paul leaned in close to the shorter man who just wouldn't let it go. "Bring it on, Chief. I've already told you we have nothing to hide, can you say the same?"

Difficult as it proved, Paul walked away, ushering Jill down the drive and to the Land Rover. They'd both been through enough today. He didn't want her exposed to anymore of the chief's groundless accusations or the suspicious looks of all the rescue personnel who'd showed up to save the day.

He and Jill were walking away.

That wasn't supposed to have happened. Paul couldn't shake the feeling. They were supposed to have died in that fire. The fire marshal would find evidence of arson all right. A high-powered accelerant had been used. Probably the same one used to burn that small body the chief wanted them to believe was Cody. An accelerant of that caliber was the only way the house would have become so widely engulfed before the smoke even reached the basement. Particular attention had been paid to the front and rear entrances. A trail of fire had run from the front door to the staircase. The arsonist hadn't wanted the smoke or flames to warn them until it was too late to escape.

His plan might very well have worked had the textured privacy glass in the front door not shattered.

The sound had echoed down those basement steps like a rifle blast.

They were safe. That was all that mattered. The chief and his arson investigation could go straight to hell.

"Jillian!"

Standing in the vee of the Land Rover's open passenger door, Jill turned to see who had called her name. Paul went on instant alert. Whoever it was, he wasn't happy. Her name had been uttered sharply, vehemently. A politician, Paul determined when the man got a little closer. Five hundred-dollar suit and enough arrogance to provide hot air driven energy for a small country. Recognition flared. *The mayor.*

Paul had to physically restrain the urge to punch the older man when he marched right up to Jill, his face red with rage, and started ranting.

"You've gone too far!"

"Mayor Hammersly," she said, acknowledging his presence and ignoring his accusation.

"We were just leaving," Paul cut in. "As you can see, we've had a bad day."

Hammersly glowered at Paul, then pointed that cutting gaze at Jill. "This is enough, young lady," he warned. "How dare you come back to this town and try and tear down all we've built. Your daddy would be ashamed of you." He harrumphed. "What am I saying?" He glared at Jill even harder. "He *was* ashamed of you and those ridiculous antics of yours. Always getting into trouble...running off to Ole Miss and thinking only of yourself. You're a disgrace to your family…to this town."

Fury whipped through Paul. He moved in, forced Hammersly back a step, as he got between the man and Jill. "I don't think you want to say anything else."

"Just ask her, if you don't believe me," he hurled the words at Paul, too blind or too stupid to be afraid. "Ask her how she hurt her daddy all those years ago."

"I said, shut up." Paul reached for him, his fingers itching to wrap around that scrawny neck, to squeeze until the bastard shut the hell up.

"No." Jill tugged at his arm. "Please, Paul, let's just go."

Obviously having come to his senses, the mayor stumbled back a couple of steps. "Tell him, Jillian. Tell him how you drove your daddy into an early grave. Maybe you want to do the same thing to your mother."

"Get in the car and wait for me," Paul said, his throat so taut he could scarcely speak. At the moment he didn't care if he spent the rest of his life in prison, this guy was about to eat his words.

"Please, Paul," she pleaded. "Take me home."

Unwilling to cause her more pain, he turned his back on the bastard and rounded the hood. He settled behind the steering wheel and slammed the door. Forcing his complete attention on getting the hell out of here, he pulled away from the curb and eased through the emergency vehicles parked this way and that on the cul-de-sac.

They didn't talk as the dying embers of the Manning house faded into the night behind them. There was nothing to say. They were alone in this... had no proof of their beliefs and no one on their side.

"Paul."

He glanced at her, an ache starting deep in his chest. Her cheeks were smeared with soot, tears clearing a path through the dark smudges.

"Yeah."

"These conclusions you reach, are you always right? I mean, if you really try." The little hitch in her breathing tugged at his heart. "I need to know... if you're right this time."

For the first time in his entire life he was genuinely afraid for someone to know the whole truth about him and it had nothing to do with avoiding the media or exposure to some scam. He didn't want her to look at him any differently. To see the freak he had been accused of being by his peers and the media.

"I...I need you to be right," she murmured, the misery in her voice tearing him apart one tiny piece at a time.

"I have a heightened sense of recent memories made by others, especially the deceased. I refuse to call it anything else." He hadn't meant the words to sound so harsh, but his chest felt ready to implode. "I pick up on some things from the living, but I'm better with the dead." He exhaled slowly, deeply. "I'm right most of the time. When I really try."

She appeared to consider his answer for a time. "Then, when you said my sister murdered her husband, you were fairly certain? You…saw it?"

Another not so easy to answer question. "I didn't see her do it. I *felt* her do it."

Her sharply indrawn breath made him flinch. He didn't have to look to know she'd just recoiled physically.

"How do you cope with those feelings?"

To his surprise there was no accusation in the question. No pity…no horror. Just concern. He looked at her this time. A long, lingering look that forced him to come to a near stop in the street. *I don't*, he didn't say, which was the truth. He hid from it, locked it out. Sometimes he tried his level best to drown it.

"I…" He forced his gaze back to the road and his right foot on the accelerator. "I keep it turned off as much as possible. But to answer your question, yes, I believe Kate killed her husband."

Silence stretched between them. It wasn't a bad kind of silence…not wrought with building tension or unspoken censure…just a quiet time to slowly assimilate those things which were simply too big or too overwhelming to accept all at once.

"So," she began again as they rolled into Paradise proper, "when you said my nephew was alive…somewhere, you feel that with the same certainty?"

He braked for a red light and rested his gaze on hers. "Yes. I believe he's alive."

Slowly, as if fearing the wrong move might trigger some terrible chain of events, she showed him the photograph she'd been clutching since escaping the burning house. The streetlights and dash lights provided enough illumination for him to make out most of the detail.

"This is where he is," she said with complete certainty.

He studied the small village in the photograph, then the label that dubbed it *A Safe Place*. His gaze settled on hers and that same certainty moved through him. "You know where this place is?"

"Sort of. See that bald spot in the forest on the mountainside?" She pointed to the photograph. "I know where that is. From there I should be able to find this village."

A safe place.

"She told us," Jill said, hardly believing it could have been so simple. "Kate told us she took him to a safe place."

Paul leaned across the seat and kissed her cheek. "We'll find him."

He would not let this woman down. Whatever it took. Whatever it cost.

* * *

Showered and changed, Jill had calmed down considerably since the confrontation with the mayor. She'd even managed to go over everything that had occurred with her mother while Paul delved into a search on the Internet. He'd said he had more research to do. She'd also tried to call Cullen Marks again to give him an update, but, just like last time, he was unavailable. Jill was more than a little perturbed at his evasiveness. Another attempt to reach Connie had failed as well. She couldn't sit around waiting for either of them to call her back, she had to do something. If she closed her eyes or stopped long enough to think those hateful words taunted her.

You drove your daddy into an early grave.

Some small part of her had believed that all along, the accusation had hovered over her like a dark cloud all these years. But hearing it out loud from someone else was so much more painful. As raw as the memory was, it was done...she couldn't change the decisions she'd made any more than she could change the ones her father had made. She had loved him, still did. But he was gone. Her mother, on the other hand, was still here. Maybe if she could make her see...but even after her detailed explanation, Claire Ellington remained skeptical.

"Mother, don't you understand what this means?"

Claire sat on the sofa in the family room, purple bruises across her forehead. She looked distraught rather than relieved by Jill's revelations.

"But the body. I identified the..." Her voice quivered. "We have to come to terms with Cody's death, Jillian. Denial won't do either of us any good."

Jill took her mother's hand in hers. "I'm trying to make you see this whole thing is wrong. We can't trust anything we've been told. We don't know what set off this chain of events but the chief is covering up something. We can't be sure that's Cody's body. We only have the chief's word."

Her mother looked away. "That's just too unbelievable. I refuse to listen to such nonsense. You're grasping at straws."

Calm, Jill told herself. *Stay calm.* "Mother, this is what Paul does. He knows the truth. I know the truth. My God, what about Benford Chemical and all those dead children?"

Claire shook her head. "Benford Chemical was a long time ago. People try to put nasty business like that out of their minds. I don't know what you mean about the dead children. I'm sure we don't have a higher child mortality rate than any other town."

"But we do," Jill said gravely. "I checked."

Her mother's gaze snapped to hers. "You must be mistaken."

Jill shook her head. "I'm not mistaken. Whether you choose to believe it or not, it's true."

Claire paled, looked away once more.

The idea that her mother was hiding something niggled at Jill. "What is it you're not telling me? You begged me to forget this investigation. What is it you know that scares you so badly?"

Claire shook her head. "I can't talk about it. Please don't ask me to."

Tension stiffened Jill's spine. "At least tell me this much, are you keeping quiet because you're afraid?"

Claire's gaze collided with hers. "I'm terrified."

* * *

The search box appeared on the screen and Paul typed in: Josef Mengele.

A few seconds later dozens of subject lines filled the screen. He selected the first: Josef Mengele, The Angel of Death. Words jumped out at him...Hitler's henchmen...hideous crimes against humanity... willfully and with bloodlust. Twins were the focus of his madness. They were rescued from the NAZI gas chambers only to fall victim to a decidedly crueler fate.

Twins were selected and placed in special barracks. Auschwitz offered Mengele unlimited specimens where twins could be studied at random. One could serve as a control while the other endured the experiments. Experiments included injecting blood samples from one twin into another twin of a different blood type and then recording the reaction. The injection of dye into the eyes of several twins to see if eye color could be altered. If the twins died, Mengele would harvest their eyes and pin them to the wall of his office.

Isolation cages housed twins who were subjected to a variety of stimuli to see how they would react. Castration, sterility. The removal of limbs and organs without the use of anesthetic were performed routinely. Injections of infectious diseases to see who would succumb and who would not and how long it would take. Why did this one live and that one perish? Ultimately the corpses were dissected.

Paul stared at the screen, no longer seeing. A cold hard fist of fear had taken hold of his gut. Though cruder and much less humane, these experiments bore a striking likeness to those he'd read about in Manning's files.

But Manning was in to far more than Mengele had been able to do in his time under the Hitler regime and with the knowledge and equipment available. Genetic alterations, cloning. One of Manning's favored experiments zoomed into vivid focus in Paul's mind. Cannibalism in the womb. He quickly typed those words into the search box.

When identical twins were conceived, one fetus was destroyed invivo. After absorption occurred, the surviving twin was then studied to see if a higher cognitive ability resulted. Stronger physical attributes. A heightened sense of survival…heightened senses period.

Paul closed his eyes and banished the words from his mind. Manning was all that Josef Mengele had hoped to be. He'd secretly carried out hideous experiments for years right here in Paradise. The whole town had been bought and paid for with the promise of offspring. In exchange for the promise of heirs the citizens who had made the original deal would take the secret to their graves. No one would ever know. Manning had the perfect setup. An entire town as his lab. Only something went wrong. Kate found out. Or somehow her son was threatened and she fought back.

The certainty that Cody Manning was being sought behind the scenes for a particular reason wouldn't let go. Kate and her son were at the center of this, as was Jill...somehow. Simply being a twin wouldn't be enough for the boy to be so important. It had to be cloning. Manning had likely been conducting those experiments well before being granted license to do so. Paul's thoughts went back to the child in Lynchburg and he wondered...could Cody and the other child be MedTech's first successful venture into cloning?

Paul rubbed at his eyes. Damn he was tired.

He had to rest...just for a few seconds. Jill needed him. He couldn't function without a little shuteye. He leaned back in the chair and surrendered.

Help me. Please help me. The small, frightened voice sobbed.

He was there. In that dark, dank cave. With the girl he'd failed...the first of several.

Help me, please.

Paul tried to pull back from the darkness but he couldn't. That black abyss sucked at him, drawing him deeper...deeper.

You have to help me.

The voice was different now. No longer a frightened little girl's.

I told you what they'd done.

The voice sounded like his...was his.

They sacrificed me for you.

Now do you see?

I'm dead...because of you.

In the dream he stared at the reflection in the mirror...his reflection only not him.

Paul jerked awake. He sat up straight, blinked at the lights. Focused on the ticking wall clock. Five minutes. He'd only been asleep five minutes.

He wasn't in the cave anymore. He was here... with Jill.

He forced his heart rate to slow...took long, slow, deep breaths. Just a dream. The same one he'd had a thousand times.

I'm dead...because of you.

Sweat slicked his skin. The voice was his. The face was his...but it was someone else.

Paul scrubbed a hand over his face then slammed the laptop closed. He didn't want to look anymore. He didn't want to think about the evil...the sick madness of men like Manning.

What about all the dead children? a voice demanded from one dark corner of his mind.

What about all those who don't know?

He forced the voices away. He couldn't save the world. He couldn't save those children. It was too late.

Paul pushed back from the desk and stormed out of the Judge's study and through the front door. He had to have air. Had to clear his head.

On the wide verandah, he shook a cigarette from his half empty pack and lit it. He couldn't even remember when he'd smoked last, but he damn sure needed it now. Hell, maybe he needed a drink too.

Then he thought about the fire and the failed brakes and he rejected the idea of a drink. He had to keep his head on straight. Someone was out to shut them up.

He drew deeply on the cigarette and exhaled the smoke after his lungs had grabbed up enough nicotine to send a little buzz through his system. He should never have allowed Jill in the Manning house and he should have beaten the hell out of that mayor. Maybe he still would. But then he wouldn't be here to protect her.

Another long drag. Maybe it was time to call Cuddahy and spill the beans. Solid evidence or no, things were getting a little too hot around here, no pun intended. Most of Manning's basement files probably survived the fire. The place was like a vault. The Bureau could bring in a recovery team. He flicked the fire from the tip of his spent cigarette butt, pinched the end to make sure it was out and stuffed the butt into his pocket. He didn't know why he even bothered to smoke. It was more trouble than it was worth.

The front door slowly opened behind him. Jill came outside, looking tired, but like heaven on earth to a man accustomed to nothing but hell.

"There you are," she said, a weary smile on her lips.

"Here I am."

"Mother won't talk about what she knows." She massaged her temples. "I don't know what else to do."

He ached to make her forget for just a little while but that was far too risky to his ability to maintain control. "We've done all we can today."

The door jerked open behind them. "Jillian!"

Claire stood in the doorway, the entry hall light silhouetting her trembling frame.

Jill went to her mother. "What's happened?"

Paul steeled himself for bad news.

"Ruth Neil just called."

"Mrs. Neil? Is everything all right?"

Paul remembered the name. The girl who had been Jill's best friend back in high school was a Neil. She'd behaved strangely since Jill came back to Paradise. Friendly one minute, avoiding her the next. She'd left a voicemail but Jill hadn't been able to connect with her since.

Tears streaked down Claire's cheeks as she shook her head adamantly. "They've just found Connie." She pressed her fist to her mouth for one fleeting second. "She's dead, Jill. *Connie's dead.*"

CHAPTER FOURTEEN

Sunday, July 17

Jill and her mother sat on the parlor sofa, holding hands, faces weary, eyes red rimmed and underscored with dark hollows, painful testimony to a sleepless night and far too much grief suffered in too short a time.

Paul had taken a position next to an overstuffed side chair, his hip resting on its sturdy arm, choosing to simply observe for the moment. Separating himself from the women was a strategic maneuver designed to enhance sympathy for the grieving and allow scorn a different place to fall. He didn't want the chief's dislike for him projected elsewhere.

Chief Dotson stood at the opposite end of the sofa, his back to the wall rather than the door, like any good cop, and facing the room at large so that his attention could shift easily to anyone gathered. His uniform was freshly starched, his leather dress shoes buffed to a high sheen. Here was a man come to deliver news. The kind that forever changed lives and the course of what was to come.

"Ms. Claire, Miss Jill," he said somberly, slowly rotating his hat in his hands. "There's been a major break in Ms. Kate's case."

Jill's face reflected the surprise she felt. "She's all right, isn't she? We called the hospital at eight this morning and she was fine."

The renewed sense of panic in her voice scraped over Paul's already raw emotions. This intense aspect of the bond between them was new territory and he was having a hell of a time maintaining objectivity.

"Yes, ma'am," the chief assured her. "Ms. Kate is just fine. Just fine." He nodded once and drew in a deep, bolstering breath as if bracing for what he was about to convey. "What we have this morning is new evidence that completely clears her of all wrong doing." His gaze moved from Jill to her mother and back, avoiding Paul altogether.

Claire eased forward a bit, drawing her daughter's hands tighter to her chest. "I don't understand."

The chief stared at the floor for a time. "Well, ladies, I'm sure you've heard that we discovered Connie Neil's body late last night."

Both women nodded. "What does that have to do with Kate?" Jill wanted to know.

"She was young, you know," the chief went on. "Like you and your sister. I believe you girls attended school together."

Jill nodded jerkily. Connie's death had troubled her deeply. Last night she kept replaying the last time they spoke and the fact that, like her sister's call, Jill hadn't been there for Connie when she called. Paul couldn't completely console her though he'd held her in his arms until, exhausted, she'd fallen asleep. There weren't any words to make this kind of cumulative hurt go away.

"Anyway," the chief continued, "she took an overdose of her own sleeping medication." He shook his head as if he couldn't comprehend such a thing. "It's just so hard to believe that a pretty young woman with a good job and her whole life ahead of her would do something so foolish."

Paul tensed when a flash of light seared through his brain. Edith Scott's image followed close on its heels. Her husband forcing her to take pill after pill as she begged him to think of their children. Memphis PD had been prepared to close the case, certain the poor woman had ended her life. Multiple Sclerosis patients did that sometimes. But her grown children hadn't been convinced. They had come to Paul. Once he'd opened her case file, Edith had haunted him until he'd gotten Memphis PD to take a closer look at the husband.

With effort, he pushed the mental pictures away, dragged his attention back to the chief. "You're sure it was suicide?"

"Positive." The chief looked at him for the first time, his disdain evident. "She left a note." His attention shifted back to the women. "A long, startling one." Dotson shook his head. "It's still hard for me to believe, but it was her handwriting. Her mother and sister verified it."

"What does this have to do with Kate," Jill pressed. She was growing impatient.

Paul had already gone way beyond that. He wanted the chief to get on with this. He had other questions for him. Questions the man wasn't going to like.

"It appears that Miss Neil had an obsession with Karl Manning."

Claire gasped, the sound echoing in the quiet room. Jill looked stunned.

"As you probably know she'd worked at MedTech as one of Karl's personal assistants for several years." The chief shrugged. "We're not accusing Karl of anything, mind you, but Connie's letter indicates that an affair had been ongoing for most of that time. She related she'd finally gotten tired of his promises that he would leave Kate. Unfortunately, she decided to take matters into her own hands. She kidnapped Kate and Cody, with the intention of murdering them both so Karl would be free. The details are somewhat vague. She rambled a bit there. We know, of course, that somehow Ms. Kate managed to get away."

No one said a word while the chief took a moment to catch his breath. What was there to say? The man was lying through his teeth.

"When Connie confronted Karl in his home with what she'd done," the chief cleared his throat as if emotion had lodged there, "he was devastated and outraged. He was going to call the police. In a fit of rage, Connie killed him. She even said she'd tried to cover up what she'd done by wiping away her fingerprints."

The chief shifted from foot to foot before he continued. "Since Ms. Kate got away before Connie could finish her off, we're assuming she made her way home just before the police arrived on the scene. We figure Ms. Kate tried to save her husband. Got her prints all over the knife and blood all over herself. It's possible she may have been forced to watch what this crazy woman had done to her son. I can see how that would push the poor thing over the edge. With her unresponsive and suspected of the crimes, Connie figured she was off the hook."

Silence thickened in the room.

Paul restrained the urge to stand up and applaud. He'd never heard such well-rehearsed bullshit in his life.

"When you came back to town, Miss Jill, Connie was afraid you'd discover what she'd done, but she couldn't bear the thought of killing anyone else. So she killed herself instead."

How convenient. "And she left all this in a note?" Hell, why didn't she just write a book. Sounded like a bestseller to him. It was assuredly all fiction.

"It was all there," Dotson assured them. "Just the way I told it." He cleared his throat again and turned his attention back to the ladies. "We also discovered Prozac in her medicine cabinet. This morning her personal physician confirmed she'd been coming to him for some time citing sleep and depression problems."

Paul supposed her physician was a friend of Dotson's and a lifelong resident of Paradise. But what he wanted was to see the body. No, he *needed* to see the body. "When can I see her?" he asked, standing now, anticipation surging through him, overriding any sense of decorum he'd pretended to possess. This had gone far enough. The chief and his cronies were getting away with murder *again*.

The chief looked confused. "See who?"

"Connie Neil."

Astonishment claimed the older man's features. "I'm afraid that's impossible, Dr. Phillips."

"And why is that, Chief Dotson?" One way or another he was going to stop this guy and whoever the hell else was in this with him.

Jill was standing now, evidently picking up on Paul's agitation.

"Mrs. Neil asked that her daughter's body be cremated. The crematorium from up near Nashville picked her up first thing this morning. There'll be a service tomorrow afternoon. Under the circumstances, Mrs. Neil wants this nightmare behind her as soon as possible. Surely you can understand that."

"The coroner didn't request an autopsy?" How the hell had they gotten around that one? It was an unaccompanied death. An autopsy was standard operating procedure. Then again the coroner was probably in on this whole damned thing. Where did it end?

The chief adopted a look of incredulity and shook his head as if Paul had lost his mind. "There was no need. She left a suicide note. Swallowed her own pills. A blood test at the hospital verified what was in her system. There was no indication of a struggle or any other signs of foul play. There was absolutely no evidence to support recommending an autopsy. Why put the family through that nightmare? I don't know how you big city fellas do business, but in Paradise we try to consider the feelings of the family as long as it doesn't conflict with the law."

"Chief," Jill said quietly, a soul-deep pain in her voice.

He turned to her, his expression immediately turning compassionate. The chief was in the wrong business. He should be out in Hollywood. A muscle flexed annoyingly next to Paul's right eye. It was all he could do to keep quiet…to restrain the urge to jerk the weapon from the chief's utility belt and force him at gun point to tell the truth for once in his life.

"Since my sister is no longer under suspicion, is there any reason why we can't have her moved to a private facility?"

The chief shook his head. "None at all. I've got my men working overtime to finish up all the final reports so we can close the books on this one for good."

And therein lay the motive for Connie Neil's murder. They needed a scapegoat. A way to tie up all of the loose ends into a neat little package and close the case. She may have done something at MedTech that put her in the cross hairs or she might simply have been handy and unlucky. The bottom line was: it was finished in the eyes of the law.

Then Jill would stop her investigation and go home. That was the goal.

The chief tucked his hat under his arm, moved to Jill's side and took her hand in his. His expression of humility and compassion was so over done that Paul had to look away or laugh out loud.

"Miss Jill, Ms. Claire," the chief shifted his attention down to the mother for a moment before continuing, "I can't tell you how sorry I am that any bad light was shed on Ms. Kate for even a single moment. I promise you we were only doing our job and would never have suspected her in any capacity otherwise."

Claire stood, swayed slightly until Jill steadied her. "I appreciate you coming in person to give us the news, Arvel. Thank you."

"You are most welcome, Ms. Claire." He took her hand in his and patted it kindly. "Miss Jill sure showed her mettle, didn't she? She knew Ms. Kate was innocent all the time." He beamed at Jill, then at Claire. "You should be very proud of her."

Paul shook his head. Another perfect knot in the bow atop the flawless pre-packaged ending to the story. The chief had taken yet another step toward undoing the hurt Jill had suffered, with only one goal in mind—getting rid of her quickly and on an upbeat note.

"I appreciate your saying so, chief," Jill said, a tremor in her voice.

God, don't let her be fooled too. She was too smart to fall for this act.

"I wonder though," Jill began suddenly, "why Connie didn't simply leave town...cut her losses and disappear?" She said the words quietly, without accusation, like a thought voiced for her own ears to analyze. She frowned, evaluating the theory. "It seems odd that she didn't consider the possibility that Kate might recover. So many days went by without reaction." Jill looked at the chief. "Doesn't that strike you as strange, chief? Maybe you should have ordered an autopsy."

Good girl. Paul kept the smile that wanted to emerge carefully tucked away.

"Well, Miss Jill," the chief scrubbed a hand over his chin "I see what you mean, but we have to remember that we aren't dealing with someone like you or me. Connie Neil was clearly unstable, mentally speaking."

"You think she set the fire at Kate's house too?" Paul suggested. "I mean, why not just be rid of the problem altogether. Maybe she tampered with the brakes of the car Jill was driving just the other day. With Jill out of the way and her sister mentally incapacitated, Connie would be home free? You think she killed herself because she failed in all those murder attempts? I mean, a person can only take so much failure."

The color drained from the chief's face. "Who said the brakes on Miss Ellington's car had been tampered with?" he demanded. "I haven't been informed of any such thing! Why would Connie have suspected Jill was on to anything? There was nothing at the house that incriminated her."

Why, indeed.

"The fact is we think the fire at the Manning's house is related to a couple of other incidents that were reported during the wee hours of this very morning."

"What incidents?" Paul's instincts sent up a warning.

"Well, I don't have all the details, but I can tell you that MedTech's security was breached early this morning, there were some retired research files stolen. If that wasn't bad enough, a clinic over in Tullahoma was burned to the ground." He heaved a big breath. "The chief over there thinks it might all be related to pro-life. Apparently a rumor went around that abortions were being performed at the clinic and we all know that MedTech was licensed for cloning research."

Tension nested like a rock in Paul's gut. They were in housekeeping mode already. He wasn't going to be fast enough. Defeat dragged at his confidence. Still, there were the files in the Manning home. Or were those taken care of already too?

"The forensics techs might find something the others missed at the crime scene when they go through the Manning house," Paul suggested, blatantly alluding to the files in the self-contained, no doubt fireproof basement.

Something sinister glittered in the chief's eyes. "Oh, didn't you hear, Dr. Phillips? They aren't going to find a thing in the Manning house. That whole end of the block blew up last night. I told you there were some strange things going on last night. I guess it was the full moon."

Paul couldn't keep the surprise from his face or the ice from sliding through his veins. "There was an explosion?"

The image of all those files, of all that research—research eerily similar to that done by another monster during the days of Hitler's regime—being obliterated bloomed then expanded to fill his mind's eye. *All those damaged and dead children from Auschwitz.* Like the damaged and dead in Paradise. Fury melted away the ice chilling Paul's blood. It would not end here. He would find a way to prove what Karl Manning had done. But he had to act before any more evidence was destroyed. He might have to drag Cuddahy and the Bureau into this sooner than he'd anticipated.

"That's right, you two had already gone by then," the chief said innocently. "There was a natural gas leak. We had to evacuate all of High Point. The explosion shook the whole mountain."

"Was anyone hurt?" Jill wanted to know.

"Fortunately, no," the chief assured her. "Everyone was clear when the blast occurred. My men did a hell of a job keeping folks safe." He puffed out his chest. "Well, I'll be on my way, ladies. As sorry as I am for the Neil family, I'm sure glad I could deliver the news about Ms. Kate. I know you're relieved that's behind you." His gaze lingered on Jill for a moment. "I'm certain you're anxious to get back to Jackson."

She only smiled, but it wasn't her usual pleasant one. It was brittle...forced. "I do have a job to get back to."

Paul wasn't through with the chief just yet. "One final question," he said, drawing the chief's attention back to him before he could escape.

"If I can answer it, I surely will," Dotson said congenially. He was certain he owned this round.

"Why didn't the smoke detectors work in the Manning home? We had no warning at all that a fire had started and I know detectors were in place. I saw them."

A broad, knowing smile split the chief's face. "Why that's elementary, son," he said, visibly struggling to hold back a grin. "The smoke detectors in the Manning home were tied in with the alarm system. That's how the police were summoned to the house the day they found the body. The alarm had tripped and the first officer on the scene couldn't shut it off. The alarm company shut down the whole system to facilitate our investigation over the next few days."

"Even the smoke detectors?" Paul wasn't convinced.

"Even the smoke detectors. Now, if you have any other questions just let me know." The chief tipped his head to the ladies and left without another glance in Paul's direction.

Paul had only one more question that pertained to the Manning house but he had no intention of asking the chief. Who set the alarm so that it would go off when Kate arrived home to find her husband's body? Karl Manning was dead when his killer left him, if one went with the chief's theory. Assuming that to be the case, who rearmed the alarm so that Kate's arrival triggered it? Thus summoning the police. Maybe the killer got in and out so fast the triggered alarm was of no consequence. Didn't speak well for the local cops. And there was still the question as to why the chief hadn't issued an Amber Alert on Cody as he claimed.

The chief may have won this round, but the game was far from over.

"I'm calling the doctor to see what kind of arrangements he would suggest for Kate," Claire Ellington announced, relief wreathing her face.

Jill watched her mother leave the room and had to remind herself that the woman who'd just taken the lead on a matter, any matter, was her mother. Maybe leaving the house for the service had finally broken down the barrier of self-imposed exile. All that time her mother had claimed to be agoraphobic was obviously just her way of hiding from reality. With all that she now knew and suspected, Jill could scarcely blame her. She closed her eyes and forced the chief's words from her mind. She would not believe the things he'd said about Connie. No matter how odd Connie had behaved after Jill mentioned the investigation she knew her friend couldn't have done all those things any more than Kate could have. It was insane. And Cody was alive, dammit. She refused to believe anything else.

"You understand what they've done, don't you?"

Paul's deep voice brushed over her nerve endings. Reminded her she wasn't alone in this. "I'm not sure I want to think at all right now."

"That's the goal, Jill. Make it all so complicated and painful that it's easier to look away."

He was tense, his voice clipped. She searched his face, attempted unsuccessfully to read him. "Can't I have just one moment of peace before I face reality?" She was so tired. If only she hadn't missed that call maybe Connie would still be alive.

"Your friend is dead because they needed a patsy. They've sewn everything up nice and tight in hopes you'll walk away. Is that what you plan to do?"

She closed her eyes and thought of her friend. Of the vibrant young woman Connie had been. She thought of her nephew and all the other children caught up in this nightmare. Then she thought of her father. He would never have walked away from something he believed in. That was the one thing that gave her comfort in all this—her father could not possibly have been involved. Maybe her mother knew certain things—God knew she'd been behaving strangely. But there was no way the Judge had any hand in this.

"No," she said in answer to Paul's question. "I want to know how all this happened and I want to stop it from happening to anyone else. And I want to find my nephew and bring him home. I can't do that unless we stop these monsters." She looked up at Paul again, into that face that was so familiar and dear to her now. "You think the clinic in Tullahoma had anything to do with MedTech or Karl Manning?"

"I know it did."

"How do you know?"

"That's the clinic Sarah Long used. I asked her."

No further explanation was needed. Sarah's son had to be Cody's twin. It was the only possible explanation.

Well...except for cloning and Jill just wasn't ready to go there yet. Animals were one thing. But humans...she refused to consider the possibility. Somewhere in the recesses of her brain, a part of her knew it was more than simply possible.

"Jill," her mother called from the entry hall. "There's a call for you."

"Coming." She glanced at Paul, wondered how he planned to proceed. "Don't go anywhere without me."

"Wouldn't think of it."

The ghost of a smile that lingered around his mouth made her want to throw herself into his arms and just close out the world for a little while. Soon, she hoped.

In the front hall, Claire passed her the phone. "Thank you." Jill didn't recognize the number on the caller ID. "Hello."

"Jill?"

"This is Jill. Who's this?"

"Kelly Neil."

Jill's heart fluttered painfully. Connie's younger sister. "Kelly, I'm so sorry about Connie."

"I don't...." Pain echoed in her voice. "I don't have much time. I need to meet with you some place away from here. It's important I talk to you but it can't be here. It's about my sister and her memorial service."

A surge of adrenaline burned through Jill. "Just tell me where and when, I'll be there."

A shaky exhale. "Go to Winchester. There's a restaurant, Rafael's, next to Walmart. One hour."

The call ended.

Jill hit the off button and placed the phone on the hall table. She wasn't sure she believed that Kelly wanted to talk about the service. But whatever it was, it was urgent. The possibility that Kelly knew something that pertained to the investigation set Jill's nerves on edge. Then again, maybe she blamed Jill for Connie's death. Jill's heart ached. When would this end?

"Anything important?"

Jill jumped, startled. Her hand flew to her chest. "You scared me half to death."

Paul lifted a skeptical eyebrow. "I scared you or the call scared you?"

He was a mind reader, whether he admitted it or not. "The call was unsettling, yes."

He reached out traced the line of her cheek with one finger, sending warmth flooding through her. But it was those dark, dark eyes that lit a fire in her belly. God, how could he have that much power over her? That he could heat her skin with just a look... just a touch...despite all that had happened.

"Are you going to tell me who it was?"

"Kelly Neil, Connie's younger sister. She wants to meet."

Paul's posture changed. His gaze grew guarded. "Did she say what this was about?"

"Connie's service but I don't believe that's what it's about." Jill swallowed the lump of emotion welling in the back of her throat. "She said it was important. She sounded nervous."

Paul scrubbed a hand over his jaw. "She could know something that would help us." His gaze leveled on Jill's. "Then again, she could have more personal reasons."

Jill nodded. "I considered that but I don't think I can ignore the call. If she knows something, we need to hear her out." She set her hands on her hips, felt torn. "I'd planned to suggest we start looking for the place in the photograph in hopes of finding Cody." *The safe place.* "But she wants to meet with me in an hour. It'll take every bit of that to get to Winchester."

"You mean she wants to meet with us."

"If she gets me, she gets you," Jill agreed, her lips drawing down into a frown as she recalled something Paul had said to the chief. "I thought the mechanic said there was no conclusive evidence of foul play with the car."

Paul shrugged. "He did. I just wanted the chief's reaction. Besides, no conclusive evidence means no evidence either way, counselor."

Jill felt some of the tension lighten. Somehow he always managed to make her feel a little better about things.

"How old is the sister?"

"Twenty-four maybe. Kelly was in middle school when Connie and I were in high school." She realized where he was going with the question then. "She's old enough to be a reliable source, if that's what you're asking."

"I say we meet with her and see how it plays out."

"I'll check on Mother and then we can go."

Jill was anxious to hear what Kelly had to say... at least, she thought she was. Paul was right about Connie too. It was all too open and shut. Too perfect. Like everything else in this damned town. A polished veneer of perfection had been hiding a world of evil for more than three decades.

* * *

Winchester, Tennessee, was about the size of Paradise, and though lovely in its own right, it lacked Paradise's picture perfect setting. The focal point of the town square was a well-restored late nineteenth century courthouse. The Oldham movie theater that graced the end of one block was the old fashioned kind rarely seen anymore, even in small southern towns. The streets were fairly busy, the lunch crowd, Paul surmised. He'd made a stop on Decherd Boulevard to get directions. Jill hadn't been here since the new Walmart was built so she was as lost as he was.

That was one thing you could count on in small southern towns: everyone knew where the Walmart was located.

He parked the Land Rover near Rafael's, a small Italian restaurant shoehorned between a jewelry store and a clothing boutique.

"Let me go in first," he said. "I'll get the lay of the land and then come back for you."

"Let's just go in. If she wanted revenge she could have gotten that in Paradise."

Revenge or not, Kelly had an agenda and that worried him. Whoever was behind this puzzle was getting nervous…panicking. Anything could happen if Jill pursued the investigation from this point. The chief and his cohorts had given her an out, if she didn't take it, they might just turn desperate enough to finish what they'd hoped to accomplish with those faulty brakes. Paul was certain it hadn't been an accident.

"Point taken," he relented. "But you stay behind me until I've assessed the situation."

Jill gave him a two-fingered salute. "Yes, sir."

At least she still had a sense of humor. And that was saying something under present circumstances.

The midday sun bore down relentlessly. It was impossible to cross the hot pavement without breaking a sweat. Inside, the cool air instantly chilled his skin. A small waiting area designated for arriving customers provided the opportunity for Paul to scan the crowded booths of the dining room. He spotted the brunette sitting alone.

"Is that her?" Paul jerked his head toward the brunette.

"That's her."

As they neared Kelly Neil's head came up. She put on a smile, but it was strained. Her face was ravaged from crying and she looked ready to start all over again.

"Hey, Kelly." Jill slid into the booth opposite her and reached across the table to cover her hand with her own.

Kelly glanced at Paul. "Who's he?"

Jill gave her hand an encouraging squeeze. "This is Paul Phillips. He's a friend. You can trust him."

Kelly looked ready to bolt. "I'm not sure about this."

"I used to be with the FBI," he explained, hoping to reassure her. "I know you didn't ask Jill to meet you here to talk about the service for your sister. We want to help."

"They killed her," Kelly said quietly, agony shadowing her face.

"Can you tell us who *they* are?" Jill held her breath. They needed a name. A starting place.

She shook her head. "I just know that all that stuff they said about Karl Manning was nothing but lies." She blinked back a new onslaught of tears and glanced around. "My sister hated the guy. She wouldn't have had an affair with him if he'd been the last man on earth. Someone made her write that letter."

Jill nodded. "I believe you. I remember Connie's type back in high school, Karl Manning would never have survived the first cut."

Kelly managed a wobbly smile. "She was scared, Jill. Like really, really scared."

"Did she ever say what had her so scared?" Paul prodded gently.

How could a man who wanted to feel nothing, who'd shut the world out, sound so kind and caring? Because he was, Jill decided. The don't-give-a-damn image was just to keep people at arm's length.

Kelly swiped her eyes and leaned forward, speaking for their ears only. "About six months ago Connie was pulling some old reports for Mr. Manning. One caught her eye. It mentioned several test subjects by name, one was our mom. So Connie read through it. She wouldn't tell me what all it said. She just kept saying it was bad. Real bad. Anyway, that got her to worrying about what else was going on at MedTech. So she started digging in places where she wasn't supposed to, I guess."

She sucked in a deep, emotion-filled breath and rushed on. "She said they were doing some really weird stuff. Experiments on" she glanced around "fetuses and, you know, actual humans."

Jill knew exactly what she meant. "And they killed Connie to keep her quiet."

Kelly nodded. "She got away with it for a long time, but a few days ago a couple of guys started following her."

Paul's tension moved to a new level. She'd glossed over something significant. He needed to know what that was. "She got away with what?"

Kelly looked at him, clamped down on her bottom lip for a second, then said, "On copying some of the files. She had to do it a little at a time on one of those flash drives."

Paul and Jill exchanged a look, one fraught with hope and an underlying fear that both were too smart not to acknowledge. Damn, but they needed those files.

"Kelly," Jill turned back to her "do you know where Connie kept the flash drive?"

"Yes," she whispered. "She told me the day she died if anything happened to her I had to tell you where to find it...that you would know what to do. She kept it in a place no one would ever think to look—in a loaf of bread right there on her kitchen counter." Kelly smiled faintly. "Who would ever look there?"

Pain nagged deep in Paul's skull. The nudge familiar, determined. He had to know. Without warning, he reached across the table and took Kelly's hand. Startled, her gaze bumped into his. *Tell Jill where to look. No one else. Do you hear me, Kelly? No one else can know...not even Mom.*

He held onto her hand when she would have pulled away and soaked up the sensations. "I know this is difficult, Kelly," he said quietly, struggling to keep his voice even, "but I need to know the answer to one more question."

She nodded, more tears seeping past her lashes.

"Who found her?"

She squeezed her eyes shut briefly as if to block the images. "I did," she murmured, sobbing. "I found her last night after the movie. I went by to tell her that it sucked and not to bother going."

That explained the sensations he experienced in her presence. She'd touched her sister.

"It was too late. She was already gone. I shook her, listened for breathing." Kelly wagged her head in denial. "She wasn't breathing. I started to do CPR...but she was so cold." Her gaze turned distant as she relived the horror in her mind. "So cold. Her lips were already blue. I was too late."

"It wasn't your fault." Paul squeezed her hand. "You didn't do this."

She looked straight at him and answered the next question before he even asked. "The worst was her eyes. They were wide open..." Another sob tore through her. "She was dead, but I could still see it..."

"What did you see, Kelly?" The connection between them was humming...he could almost see through her eyes...could almost envision the devastating memories.

And then he saw it.

"Fear," she said. "I saw fear."

* * *

Jill felt cold as they drove away from the meeting with Kelly. No matter that it was ninety-five outside. She was freezing.

They—whoever the hell they were, thugs from MedTech—had killed Connie. It was no surprise, not really. On some level she had known even as the chief related the news. Jill closed her eyes and fought the flood of tears rising. How could she and Paul hope to fight this? Somehow it was all tangled up together. All of it. The deeper they dug...the more lies they discovered but no evidence. And the players and the game kept changing with another murder or another element that didn't quite fit. Two plus two turned out to be five every time. And she was so damned tired of it. Where was her nephew? Was he really some place safe? The picture...*A Safe Place*...bobbed to the surface in the river of worries swirling in her brain.

Please let him be there. Just let there be one good thing in all this.

If those were his remains at the TBI lab in Nashville—she couldn't even finish the thought. It hurt too much. She'd suffered all the hurt she could for one day. She almost laughed. For a lifetime, she amended.

Nausea roiled in her empty stomach.

Panic hit her head on.

"Stop at that gas station," she blurted, uncertain if she could make it that far. She had to get out of this car...had to do something besides replay all those awful thoughts.

Paul cut sharply and bounced into the parking lot. He screeched to a halt in a slot at the side of the building.

"Ladies room," she mumbled as she scrambled out.

Halfway to the entrance she heard his door slam. He would follow her. She didn't care. She just had to splash some cold water on her face…move around a bit…something…anything.

She grabbed the key at the counter and rushed to the back of the store. She locked herself inside and sagged against the door.

The tears gushed, unstoppable. She cried hard for several long minutes uncertain if she would ever stop. Finally, when the last tear had trekked down her cheek she washed her face with cold water and stared at her reflection in the mirror.

What had happened to her life?

Everything she'd thought was good was a nightmare…something from a Dean Koontz novel. With all that she'd discovered in the past few days, there was nothing left of her past to consider a truly good memory. It would all be permanently underscored by evil.

A soft knock sounded at the door. "You okay?"

She moved to the door. Told herself to open it but she pressed her forehead against its cool surface instead. "No…but I guess I'll live."

"Let me in."

The sound of his voice…the words…her heart burst with need. She flicked the lock and stood back for him to come inside.

He squeezed in, made the room feel impossibly small as he locked the door behind him.

She stared up into his dark eyes, wondered how in the world she would ever go on with her life without this man in it. She was falling apart and he was all that was holding her together.

"Believe it or not, it may get worse before it gets better."

She gave her head a little shake. "I don't see how outside finding out my nephew really is dead. I'm numb, Paul. Completely numb. I don't know what to believe in anymore." She trembled with the weight of that admission. "Don't know who to trust or what to feel."

He pulled her close. Pressed his lips to hers for an urgent kiss that was over far too soon. "You can trust me," he murmured against her mouth.

"Make me forget the rest, Paul." She curled her fingers in his shirt, wished she could touch his skin. That was what she wanted. More than anything. Right now. Right here. She wasn't waiting another moment. "Please."

He kissed her, so slowly at first that she thought she might cry and, still, she couldn't resist. His hands moved down the length of her dress, hiked it to the tops of her thighs and lifted her so that she could wrap her bare legs around his waist.

She moaned as he slowly turned until he pressed her back against the door. His fingers slid along her panties. Teased her. Stole her breath. She arched into his touch. He fumbled with the fly of his jeans. She wanted to help but she couldn't stop touching him, tracing each line and angle she already knew by heart. His chiseled face. The length of his neck and those broad shoulders that helped her carry the weight of so many horrible secrets.

He pushed into her. She gasped and pressed down to meet him, her body shuddering. He groaned, kissed her harder. She couldn't remember the last time she'd been with a man but she had never been with a man like him. He made her want things she had never wanted before…made her feel *whole*.

They came hard and fast, both panting for air.

She closed her eyes against the tears. Didn't want to cry. Not now. But her world was crumbling, falling apart piece by piece.

He kissed her tears. "I won't let them win," he murmured.

No matter how foolish it seemed, she believed him.

CHAPTER FIFTEEN

"End of discussion," Paul snapped. He immediately regretted his words. She'd been through enough without him biting her head off. But she just wouldn't listen to reason. They'd argued the better part of the trip back to Paradise.

He wasn't going to argue with her any more on this point. He was taking her back to Ellington house and he was going to Connie Neil's place to retrieve the hidden flash drive *alone.*

End of story.

His hands still shook with each time he thought of those too-short minutes of getting lost in each other. He shouldn't have allowed that to happen. She deserved better than he'd given. She deserved better than him. But he'd been weak and needy.

"No," she repeated, her arms crossed over her chest. "I won't let you go without me."

"Dammit, Jill," he growled, "listen to reason."

She was one damned stubborn lady. As much as he liked that about her, that stubborn streak was going to get her killed. Still, he had to respect it.

"What's that?" She leaned forward and peered through the windshield.

Up ahead blue lights flashed. A tow truck was backed up to the edge of the highway's shoulder. Several cars were stopped awaiting instructions from the officer flagging traffic. An ambulance, sirens silent, pulled away from the scene, headed into Paradise. It wasn't more than another couple of miles.

"An accident," she murmured, then looked away. She sat in the passenger seat, her arms still hugged protectively over her chest. Those long, toned legs crossed making him think of how they'd felt squeezed around his waist.

Bad timing, pal. Bad idea. Only a selfish prick would take a woman on the edge of breaking in a damned bathroom. *You're an asshole, Phillips.*

"You're not going with me," he reminded her. "It's too risky."

"You can't stop me."

Their disagreement died a natural death in light of the somber business taking place in the road ahead. Trapped in traffic several vehicles back from the accident, Paul could just make out a small blue sports car. Looked as if it had left the asphalt and hit a power pole.

The tow truck's wench whined. Slowly, but surely the small blue sports car was dragged from the deep ditch by its rear end. The truck pulled forward, hauling the damaged vehicle behind it. Paul surveyed the crippled car. The hair on the back of his neck stood on end. The damage to the front end of the vehicle was extensive. Not a full frontal collision, but one of the offset kind that killed more often than not. The condition of the vehicle combined with the silent ambulance spelled DOA.

Jill made a frantic sound in her throat…a painful mewling. He followed her gaze back to the car and then he saw it too. The vanity plate, remarkably still intact.

K-E-L-L-Y was scrawled in bold pink letters on a pale blue background.

Kelly Neil.

He didn't have to ask one of the officers what happened as they were allowed to roll slowly by. Paul sensed the answer deep in his gut. He also understood there was just one outcome.

Kelly Neil was dead.

Just like Jill would be if she pursued this—whatever the hell it was—any further.

"That's it," he said, his tone hard, every muscle in his body rigid with fury. "I'm taking you, your mother, and your sister to safety."

To his surprise, Jill turned to him and said, "I know just the place."

* * *

It took less than half an hour to check her sister out of the psychiatric ward of Paradise General. One brief telephone call to the doctor on record and Kate was free to go with any member of the immediate family willing to sign for responsibility. The chief had no doubt paved the way already, hoping to facilitate Jill's departure from his jurisdiction.

Too upset by the useless and tragic deaths of the Neil sisters, Jill hadn't even thought of bringing clothes. The ones Kate had arrived in at the hospital had been seized as evidence. Paul picked up a Paradise tee and lounge pants at the hospital gift store for the trip home.

Jill intended to see that her mother and sister were safely tucked away before she and Paul did what had to be done. Whether he liked it or not, she was going with him to Connie's townhouse. She would help end this and bring these bastards down or die trying.

Her throat parched at the idea. She hoped no one else had to die. She stole a glance at the driver. Especially not him. Paul Phillips had suffered enough already. She now saw the other side of all those ugly headlines she'd read about him. Understood the pain he'd endured. He deserved a better life. Jill had brought him here, dragged him into the middle of that same kind of agony. She didn't want this to cost him anymore than it already had.

Kate sat quietly in the back seat as they drove through town, eventually turning onto Washington Street. If any part of the passing landscape struck a chord with her, she didn't make a sound.

When they arrived at the house, Claire met them at the door. "What's going on?" Her attention settled on Kate. "Katie, honey, it's good to have you home."

Kate merely looked at her mother as if aware she was being spoken to but incapable of understanding why or forming a response.

Claire took charge of Kate immediately, settling her on the sofa in the family room where she could watch television. The nurses had said that Kate preferred the television on, but the sound muted. Claire quickly attended to that detail. Then she moved back into the entry hall where Jill and Paul still argued about who was doing what.

"Why wasn't I consulted before you signed your sister out of the hospital? I wanted to speak with the doctor before making a final—"

"There's no time," Jill cut her off. She wasn't having this discussion with her mother. "Kelly Neil is dead."

Claire frowned, clearly confused. "What are you talking about? Her sister is—"

"She called me this morning." A dull ache pierced deeper into Jill's heart. "Right after the chief left this morning, remember?"

Claire's confusion visibly deepened. "I remember a call."

Jill's patience snapped. "It was her. She told us about the evidence against MedTech that Connie was hiding. The evidence that got her killed."

There was no missing the subtle shift in Claire's posture, the way she averted her gaze. She was hiding something. And she was on the edge...on the verge of telling all. Jill's pulse reacted to the bloom of hope in her chest.

"But Arvel said—"

"The chief lied." If the local police could be trusted they wouldn't be having this conversation. But no one could be trusted...no one but Paul. "Chief Dotson lied about everything, Mother. *Everything.*"

Paul opted to keep his mouth shut. Worked for Jill. She had this.

Claire shook her head. "That's ridiculous. Why don't you let this madness go? Let them close the case so we can get on with our lives!"

Wasn't she listening? "Your grandson is alive. He's out there somewhere and I intend to find him. I also intend to know what MedTech and LifeCycle have been doing to the people in this town and in the surrounding communities." Walking away was out of the question. "I won't let them get away with this. I will find the evidence I need and then I'll take it to the proper authorities."

"Jill, you must know how foolish this all sounds." Her mother laughed nervously. "We've known Arvel Dotson our whole lives. He's not a bad person."

"Isn't he?" Jill countered, livid now. "Tell me the truth, Mother. You know at least some of what's going on here. Why are you hiding it from me? It almost cost us our lives once. Connie and Kelly are dead because of it. How many more have to die before you tell the truth?"

A deafening silence echoed for what felt like an eternity.

Claire conceded first. "I…I'm sure I don't know what you mean."

Enough! Jill took her mother by the shoulders and forced her to meet her gaze. "I know about Benford Chemical. The births and deaths…the experiments and tampering with genetics. What I need to know now is who and why."

Claire moved her head side to side. "I have no idea what you're talking about," she insisted but all conviction had deserted her tone as well as her expression.

"What's it going to take?" Jill pushed harder, fury overriding any softer emotions that tried to intrude. "They'll kill me if I don't stop digging and I won't stop until I have the answers. Are you willing to stand back and let that happen?" Jill threw her arms up in exasperation. "Why not just do it yourself?"

She saw the change in her mother's eyes. Watched the scale tip to in their favor. A helpless sound issued from Claire's throat, then she broke. She sobbed hysterically. Jill hugged her mother close and cried with her.

When Claire had collected the scattered pieces of her composure, she seemed to stiffen her spine. "We should sit down. This is going to take a while."

Gathered around the family room, Kate's attention still glued to the television screen, Claire Ellington began her story. "When we discovered what Charles Benford had done and that nearly everyone had been affected, rendered sterile…" She shook her head, dabbed at her eyes with a tissue. "We were devastated."

After a moment, she continued, "Your father was the DA back then. He was the first to find out and he wanted to pursue criminal charges against Benford. Austin Hammersly was the chief of police and he agreed. Arvel was the ranking deputy. He was ready to do whatever everyone else wanted. Ken Wade was in the middle of a senatorial race. He couldn't be of much help, but offered to do what he could monetarily. The next thing I knew Benford was dead. Murdered."

"Do you know who murdered him?" Paul asked the first hard question. The answer to which could carry criminal charges.

Jill sat on the edge of her seat, scarcely able to breathe.

Claire nodded, her hands twisted together. "You have to understand, the federal authorities had decided to cut Benford a deal if he spilled the beans on some of his more high powered associates who were doing even dirtier business."

"That's the feds," Paul noted, "always looking for the angle that makes their job easier."

"Your father and the others were justifiably upset. We all were." She dabbed at the tears in her eyes again, then took a big breath. "So, before the federal authorities could whisk Benford away, Austin Hammersly, Arvel Dotson and some of your father's other friends tried him in a mock trial. Your father attempted to stop them but they wouldn't listen.

They found Benford guilty and after getting drunk enough they executed him. Your father wasn't involved but he kept their secret by looking the other way. He and the others insisted the old chemical plant was to remain standing as a reminder of how much carelessness and indifference could cost."

Too stunned to speak, Jill kept quiet.

Claire searched her eyes, a plea in her own. "Your father was a good man, Jillian, this was his one and only transgression in a lifetime of goodness."

Jill moistened her lips and blinked back tears. "Please," she said softly, "go on. I need to hear it all."

Claire cleared her throat. "About two months later, your father and Hammersly were approached by executives from MedTech and LifeCycle. I'll never forget that night. They were all here." She frowned, looked around the room as if remembering. "Except for Ken. He'd been traveling about in his pursuit for the senate. He was the only one who wasn't in on the final deal."

She folded her hands in her lap, visibly struggled to keep them still. "Anyway, the three men, uppity-ups from MedTech and LifeCycle, came to dinner. They outlined a beautiful plan for restoring everyone's ability to produce offspring. They wanted to build their first major facilities here and their primary goal during the first ten years would be to ensure the fertility of those affected." She fell silent for a moment. "It sounded so good at the time. Like a second chance—a gift—straight from God. They would offer twice as many jobs as Benford Chemical.

The town would prosper in more ways than one. We didn't know it was all about money...all about a ruthless science and technology race."

"But we look so much alike." Jill shook her head. This made no sense. "How can you have been sterile?"

"Your father was sterile. I simply stopped ovulating," Claire explained. "But I had still had viable eggs."

Jill fought another onslaught of emotions at hearing that news. Thank God.

"It was all just perfect for more than twenty years." Claire shook her head in long overdue defeat. "Paradise thrived, becoming a landmark of both beauty and tranquility." Her gaze settled back on Jill. "Seven years ago your father found out about those awful experiments they'd been doing. He also found a link between our new saviors and old Charles Benford. A link that led him to believe we'd been setup to be more receptive to MedTech and LifeCycle. That none of what transpired was by chance."

Jill's heart sank. Dear God. It was true. She and Paul had discussed this very scenario. At the time it felt too surreal...something out of a bad science fiction movie.

Claire shrugged, a weary gesture. "Your father didn't say how he discovered the information, but it was just awful." She shuddered. "He couldn't believe we'd been fooled so badly by those awful people. Hammersly and Dotson didn't want to rock the boat.

Life had been too good. But your father was having none of it. He was the judge by then and could make big trouble." She frowned. "The senator wasn't in on that part either, I don't think." She dismissed him with the wave of a hand. "He was gone so much with his political career I doubt he's aware even now just how bad things got."

"What did Father do?" Jill asked, her voice small and fragile. She could hardly bear the idea of what she knew in the deepest recesses of her soul was coming next.

"Why the same thing you've been doing, he butted heads with them. Tried to make them see that he wouldn't stand for what they were doing to his town. The Judge, as you know, thought of Paradise as his town."

"What happened?" Jill demanded. She had to hear it all.

Claire's shoulders sagged and she closed her eyes to the painful memories. "He didn't get to do anything. They killed him."

Jill grabbed the arm of the sofa and steadied herself. Before she could gather her wits, Paul was at her side, sliding in close, draping a strong arm around her shoulders, giving her the strength to continue listening to the unthinkable. No matter that she had suspected that was the case, she hadn't been adequately prepared.

"They claimed it was a heart attack," Claire said bitterly, "but I knew better. They killed him, just like they killed anyone else who ever got in their way. I don't know exactly how because I didn't dare order an autopsy. But I know they did it."

"You're sure about all this?" Jill needed to know everything. To discover her father had known and was possibly murdered had fury and outrage lashing through her.

"Why do you think I've spent the last seven years locked up in this house?" She pressed her fingers over her mouth for a long moment before going on. "I was scared to death I would say or do something wrong and then I'd be killed too. I hoped if I stayed in the house, didn't go anywhere and didn't talk to anyone, I'd be safe. That way I'd be here to make sure you and your sister were safe from what we'd done." She looked longingly at Jill now. "That's why I did all within my power to discourage your visits. I was afraid for you. Afraid you'd figure out something was wrong. I didn't even want to call you back here for this, but I knew you'd come anyway as soon as you heard."

Jill felt numb. "All this time you've feared them?"

Claire nodded. "For you and Kate." She gestured to poor Kate. "She was married to one of them. He could easily have killed her just to get back at me." She turned back to Jill. "Or you. I couldn't risk invoking their fury or their suspicions. I learned to keep it all inside and never to make waves."

It was all just too incredible.

"Mrs. Ellington," Paul said, "can you tell us who *they* are?"

That was the question no one seemed able to answer. The guardians of the secrets were obvious.

The mayor, the chief…Jill's own father and mother. But who were these monsters?

"I can't tell you their names because I never knew them. The visitors we had that night were introduced by first name only. But thirty-two years ago three men approached us. I think one of them was a relative of Karl's. A grandfather or uncle. He had an accent, German or Austrian, and looked very much like Karl. You know, handsome, distinguished. Nordic." She wrung her hands. "With Karl gone, I have no idea who's running things now."

"And Cody?" Jill urged. "Do you know where he is?"

Claire's gaze rested on Kate. "Two months ago she was in Lynchburg and she saw a boy who looks exactly like Cody."

Jill bit her lips together to hold back the questions. She had to let her mother talk.

"She confronted Karl. They had a terrible argument. She tried to call you." Claire made a sound, almost a moan of agony. "I begged her not to drag you into this. Pleaded with her to just be calm and not to make a fuss." Her lips trembled. "But she was a lot more like you than you realize, Jill. She made a plan. Told me that someone at work was going to help her stop them. It must have been Connie. Kate was going to hide Cody and then she was calling in the FBI." Claire drew in a big breath. "That's all I know. The hope that Cody is safe is all that kept me sane through this." Her eyes begged Jill to understand. "But I had to protect you. So I played the part.

I couldn't let them suspect what I knew. My single goal since the day you arrived was to get you out of here alive."

Jill blinked back the tears standing in her eyes, steely determination rising to replace all other emotions. "Some place safe," she said knowingly. "He's been there all along." She closed her eyes. "Thank God."

"If we can get those files," Paul said in the silence that followed, "with what your mother has told us, we might have enough evidence to ignite a full-fledged federal investigation."

"They'll kill us," Claire said resignedly. "They'll figure out what you're doing. There are no secrets in this town." She looked away a moment, then confessed yet another sin. "They made me drug you the other night."

Jill stiffened. "What?" The memory of the nearly forgotten spider bite zoomed to the forefront of her thoughts. She couldn't say why it came to mind, but she'd found it the morning she'd awakened so groggy. After...the warm milk. She turned to Paul. "I thought I'd been bitten by a spider." She reached around, tried to touch the spot. "It's right there between my shoulder blades."

The lethal look in Paul's eyes stole her breath. "How the hell did they come into your room with me right down the hall?"

"They said they needed a control specimen from you or Kate would die. That's what Arvel told me." Claire started to weep once more. "I didn't want to do it, but they said she'd die and that they'd kill you if that happened."

Jill moved to her mother's side and tried to comfort her. "It's okay. They didn't hurt me." She glanced at Paul. "Why would they need a spinal fluid specimen?"

Paul shook his head. "I should've stayed with you that night."

Jill had wanted him to but he'd resisted. "You couldn't have known."

"You don't understand how ruthless these people are." Claire looked from Jill to Paul and back. "They won't stop...not for anything. Coming into this house undetected is nothing." She turned to Jill then. "You don't know how your father and I longed for children. How badly we wanted you. We knew when you came that you and your sister were very special gifts. It didn't matter how we'd come to have you. We loved you more than life. That's why I've protected them all this time...to protect you. It was the only way."

"All right." Paul stood, agitation showing in his posture. "We've wasted enough time. I'm taking the three of you to safety."

Jill got up, sent a warning look in Paul's direction. She would not argue with him further. "Mother, throw a few things for you and Kate into a suitcase."

Claire pushed to her feet, looking weary and confused. "Where are we going?"

Jill moved to the other side of the room. She retrieved the photograph she'd brought from Kate's house and showed it to her mother. "This is where Cody is, I think. We're going there."

"A safe place?" Claire read, realization dawning. "That's what she said…"

Jill nodded.

"We'll be safe there," another feminine voice said.

Jill and her mother spun toward the sound of Kate's voice. She was standing up now. Hope sang through Jill's veins.

"Cody's there," Kate said, pointing to the photograph. "Safe."

* * *

The sun was melting into the western horizon at their backs by the time they reached their destination.

"We used to come to the mountains when we were kids," Jill said, wonder in her voice. "Mother would bring us. We'd go exploring. Kate would photograph everything from bugs to the sky. I spent all my time daydreaming."

He smiled. "I won't ask about what."

"It's best you don't." She surveyed the beautiful mountains. "No wonder Kate brought Cody here. I'd forgotten how beautiful it is here."

"And remote." Paul suspected that was Kate's intent. To get her son to a place where no one would look.

"You see there?" Jill pointed to a distant ridge where the bald spot in the forest stood out like a scab on the mountainside.

"I see it."

"It's the one in the photograph. We need to start moving northward, toward it. There should be a left turn coming up soon."

Kate hadn't spoken another word since announcing that her son was there…*safe*. Paul still wrestled with the idea that they had gotten to Jill right under his nose. It wouldn't happen again. He had taken great pains to ensure they weren't followed out of Paradise. He'd been watching his mirrors the entire two-hour trip. So far they were in the clear.

He saw the turn off and took it. The road was narrow, overgrown, just what they needed for getting completely lost.

"What caused the bald spot?" It didn't look quite like an area that had been strip-mined. Not that he really cared, but it was a distraction and they all badly needed one right now.

Jill rubbed at the bruise on her forehead. Both she and her mother were likely still sore from the accident.

"If I remember correctly, Daddy used to tell me—"

"A highland flood," Claire cut in. "A storm passed over and dumped massive amounts of water in a concentrated area in a very short time. It acted like a highland flood, washing away all that was in its path, down to the bedrock."

Jill looked back at her mother and smiled. "He said nothing would ever grow back there. It was a sign…"

Her words trailed off and this time her mother didn't finish the story for her.

"What kind of sign?" Paul asked.

"A sign of displeasure from God," she said softly. "Well, at least we know now what He was unhappy about."

The rest of the trip was made in silence.

Paul recognized the village instantly. It looked just like the photograph Kate had taken.

Uncertain as to how the villagers would feel about the automobile, he parked the Land Rover well outside the populated boundaries. Jill walked beside him, her mother and Kate bringing up the rear as they approached the small settlement.

The dwellings were rustic, mostly made of hand-hewn logs and mud chinking. Children scurried for home as the strangers approached. They were barefoot and healthy looking. A welcoming committee waited in the center of what they likely considered town. One dwelling looked like an old fashioned general store. Another served as the meat market, with hunks of fresh kills drying in the balmy air. Paul was vaguely familiar with the process. Those who chose not to refrigerate or freeze their meat cured it. He was also familiar with this type of primitive community. There were lots of small settlements in Appalachia. Dirt poor and seriously superstitious groups who lived their own way of life and avoided civilization.

An elderly woman stepped forward, leaving the younger woman and the man waiting two steps behind.

"Kate Manning has returned," the woman said, looking beyond Jill and Paul.

Paul was surprised that she so easily distinguished one twin from the other. He knew Jill by her eyes and her scent. But this woman was not yet close enough to see their eyes or pick up their scents.

"I'm Jill, her sister." Jill offered her hand as they moved closer.

The woman gave it a shake. "Have you come for the boy?"

A sob broke loose from Claire Ellington. Jill blinked back her own tears. Paul could see her struggle to keep her composure.

"Yes," she whispered. "We're here to see the boy."

The woman gestured to them. "Follow me."

As they moved deeper into the village, she said, "My name is Willa Dean. I became acquainted with your sister four years ago."

Paul sensed that she recognized something was wrong with Kate and spoke about her instead of to her.

"She came here to do a study on how health related to environment. I persuaded the people here to trust her."

Jill, ever the attorney, asked, "What made you trust her?"

The woman paused and smiled. "She has a good heart." She looked back at Kate. "She has troubles now."

Jill nodded. "Yes."

Willa Dean sighed. "Come, the boy will be happy to see his family." She glanced at Paul. "This is your man?"

Without hesitation, Jill answered, "Yes." Her gaze moved to his and something passed between them, a feeling that was too precious to name. He was hers… for as long as she wanted it that way.

He would not allow anyone or anything to hurt this woman.

Paul didn't analyze the epiphany instead he followed Jill and Willa Dean to a large dwelling on the far side of the settlement. The log house sat nestled against the base of the mountainside. He glanced around and couldn't help getting caught up in the beauty of it. A spicy evergreen scent tinged the fresh air. His gaze drifted back to Jill. She would be safe here.

If he could only convince her to stay.

Willa Dean called out to someone named Dottie. The door to the dwelling opened and a young girl leading Cody Manning by the hand emerged. His blue eyes lit up and he flew toward his mother.

Like Willa Dean, he moved right past Jill and hugged Kate's legs.

"Mommy, mommy!" he cried.

Claire and Jill sank to their knees and hugged him in turn. He quickly wriggled free and grasped his mother's legs once more. As if driven by pure instinct, Kate slowly dropped down to the ground and pulled the child against her chest. Though she didn't speak, she held him close and stroked his blond head.

Paul turned to Willa Dean. "How did he come to be here with you?"

"Kate, she found out that her boy wasn't of our Lord."

He understood what she meant. The child was a clone. It wasn't so inconceivable. Just unconscionable.

"At first she didn't mind. She loved him so much. Didn't matter how he came to be. Our children are our children however they may come to us. But then about two months ago she got sick." Willa Dean shook her head. "Bad problems."

Jill stood and moved closer, leaving Cody to her mother and sister. "What kind of problems?"

"Bad, bad headaches. Shaking in the limbs. Bad stuff. Very bad."

Jill looked at Paul then. "I noticed her right leg shaking in the hospital the other day. The nurse said it might be related to the seizure."

Paul took her hand and squeezed it. "As soon as it's safe we'll get her to the right kind of medical care."

Jill nodded, trying to find comfort in his words, visibly grappling to maintain her composure.

"Kate feared she might be dying but she feared her husband more," Willa Dean continued. "He was a demon, that one. He had some kind of big test planned for the child. Bad stuff, Kate said. Very bad stuff."

Jill trembled. Paul put his arm around her. "How long has Cody been with you?"

"She visited me some weeks ago and shared her fears. I told her to come back any time, I would take care of the boy. Last Sunday morning she brought me the boy. I've not seen her since."

Sunday…the day Karl Manning was murdered.

"She didn't tell you anything else," he asked, hoping for more. "She didn't bring any papers with her or other packages?"

Willa Dean shook her head. "She didn't even bring no clothes or toys for the boy. But we took good care of him."

"I have to go back to Paradise to finish this business," he told the old woman. "Can they stay here, where it's safe, until I get back?"

She nodded. "Good people is always welcome here."

Jill backed out of his hold. "I'm going with you." Fury snapped in her eyes. "Don't even think about trying to talk me out of it. If you go, I go."

Claire struggled to her feet. "Jill, please listen to him. Don't go back. Stay here. Please. I'm afraid for you."

For a moment Paul was certain Jill would be swayed by her mother's frantic plea. She looked torn.

"I can't let him face this alone," she argued. "Paradise is my hometown. The Ellingtons helped start this insanity…we have to help stop it."

Claire dropped her head. "I can't lose you."

Jill embraced her, held her tightly. "We're going to make it through this." She drew back then, pushed her lips into a shaky smile. "I love you."

Claire murmured the words right back to her daughter and pulled her close once more.

Like an out of control roller coaster plummeting toward disaster, Paul watched Jill say good-bye to her sister and then her nephew. She hugged her mother one last time then faced him. "I'm ready. We need those files. Every minute we waste is another they have to beat us to them."

If they hadn't already. He was very much aware that Kelly Neil could have been forced to tell her killers where the flash drive was hidden before her fatal crash. Paul had known their time was short, but getting Jill and her family to safety had taken priority.

For the good it had done him.

"I guess I have no choice," he said, conceding defeat.

Willa Dean reached out to him, placed one weathered hand on his arm. "Be careful, Paul Phillips, there is much evil where you be going."

He gave her a nod of thanks. As he and Jill made their way back to the Land Rover, he stalled and turned back to the village. Despite the dusk, in the distance he could just make out the silhouette of Willa Dean.

How the hell had she known his name?

A stillness settled inside him.

She knew his name the same way he knew the biggest challenge of his life awaited him back in Paradise.

He turned to the woman at his side.

Awaited both of them.

CHAPTER SIXTEEN

Paul stayed within the posted speed limits as they headed back to Paradise. The cover of darkness would be to their advantage. Still, as much as he wanted that evidence, he dreaded exposing Jill to the danger there. If someone else got to the town-house first, they might just lie in wait. Flashes of what he'd seen in Kelly Neil's eyes haunted him. The fear. Fear she'd seen in her sister's dead, unseeing eyes.

Things were going to hell in a hand basket for the chief and his pals. Desperation was making them sloppy. Kelly's death so soon after her sister's would attract attention. Of course it could be blamed on her grief. She was distracted and driving too fast. But if they'd made any mistakes, maybe even just one, the state police might notice. A trooper's cruiser had been among the official vehicles on the scene.

But Paul wanted more than a mere murder rap on these guys. Lots more. He wanted them, all of them, to pay for the untold evils he feared any half-assed investigation would find.

Dammit. After all this time he should be able to recognize a killer when he met one...to know evil when he saw it and be able to point it out. But it didn't happen that way. He only saw what the victim saw…pieces…fragments of horror.

"That's why she killed him," Jill suddenly said.

Paul glanced at her. She looked startled, as if an epiphany of her own had only just occurred to her.

"Karl tried to force her to tell him where she'd taken Cody. Kate knew what he would do if he found Cody so she killed him. Saving her child was the motive."

The image of the hypodermic flashed. *I'll use this…*

"That would be my guess." Paul checked his mirrors, noted the dark SUV or truck—too large for a sedan—in the distance behind them. Tension moved through him.

"The woman…Willa Dean," Jill went on, "she meant that Cody wasn't like other kids. Do you really think he's a clone of the child in Lynchburg or vice versa? Is that even possible?"

That kind of cloning wasn't supposed to be happening even now, much less more than three years ago. But Paul wasn't naive enough to think that everyone with the capability followed the rules.

"I think it's possible. We know Kate discovered something that terrified her enough to hide Cody and to kill her husband. She had access to MedTech files and to Karl's personal ones. She would certainly know better than either of us."

"That's why Connie behaved so strangely." Jill stared out at the darkness for a moment. "She was scared to death. She'd been helping Kate and after Karl's murder she probably had no idea what would happen next."

"It's all falling into place." One piece at a time, he mused. But it was coming.

Jill leaned back in the seat and exhaled a tired breath. "You watch things like this in the movies… read about them in books, but you never expect them to happen in your own family. There's so much controversy…where will this leave Cody? Is he human or is he something else? It doesn't change the way we love him, but will it change the way the world sees him?"

Her concerns were understandable. When the story broke…children like Cody, if there were more, would be caught in the crossfire.

"Something else, Willa Dean said," Jill said more to herself than to him, "Kate started having headaches and weakness in her limbs weeks ago. Do you think her coma-like condition could be a symptom of something more serious? Some kind of brain issue like a tumor?"

He could think of a number of troubles that started out with those same symptoms, but he wasn't about to give her more to worry about. "That's something a neurologist will have to determine." He glanced at the rearview mirror, noted the vehicle drawing closer. He readied to make an evasive maneuver.

"I still can't believe the people I've known all my life, the chief, the mayor, they were all in on it. How many others?" She laughed, a dry sound. "My own father."

She fell silent. No doubt considering that the man she'd loved and called daddy wasn't her biological father. In Paul's opinion, she was holding up well under the circumstances. While he clutched the steering wheel, his every muscle taut, ready to react as he watched from the corner of his eye as the vehicle moved up alongside them. SUV. The front passenger window was part way down. His breath stalled. Heart thudded to a near stop. Little arms thrust out, waving, and then a little girl's face appeared above the glass. He let go the breath he'd been holding.

Paranoia had definitely set in.

"We might be able to trust the senator," Jill offered, after a minute or so of quiet contemplation. "Mother couldn't directly connect him to anything. He has tried to be helpful, sympathetic even."

Paul was glad she hadn't noticed his moments of tension as the other vehicle passed. One of them on edge was enough. "But he could be in on it. His innocence could be a carefully developed facade. He is a politician."

"I wonder how many other people have been held hostage, like my mother, by this nightmare."

Paul had thought about that too. He'd also considered that the far-reaching effects might prove broader than either of them could imagine. "God only knows how far they've taken the experimental conceptions, genetic tampering, and cloning.

There could be hundreds of children involved." He glanced at Jill. "Adults too."

She nodded solemnly, then turned to stare out the window. He knew she was likely wondering what kind of experiments had been done on her and her sister. There may have been genetic tampering on one subject, her sister probably, while the other was monitored as the control.

The control. A chill thickened his blood. In Mengele's gruesome experiments with the twins, he'd used one for testing and one for *the control.*

They said they had to have a control specimen...

Claire's words rang in his ears. Jill was the control. And now the experimental procedures, whatever the hell they were, on Kate were failing...developing serious side effects.

"I should call Richard," Jill announced out of the blue. "The battery on my cell phone is low so stop at the next gas station or convenience store. Maybe we can find a pay phone."

Jealousy reared its ugly head, but Paul ruthlessly squashed it and forced a calm, even tone. "Why call Richard?"

"I think someone needs to know what's going on just in case we don't walk away from this able to talk ourselves."

As much as he hated to admit it, she had a point.

A few miles further down the road he stopped at a convenience store as she had requested, though he didn't exactly want to. He told himself that it wasn't jealousy, that he just didn't trust Richard. But that was a lie. He had no real reason not to trust the man. He'd always gotten concerned vibes from him. But that was before he learned the older man had a relationship with the woman Paul wanted for himself.

Waiting for Jill, he leaned against the hood of the Land Rover. He watched as she spoke on the pay telephone a few feet away. Like any good lawyer, she looked still and calm despite the information he knew her to be relaying. There was nothing calm about any of it.

He could watch her talk...move...just watch her, from now until eternity and never grow tired of looking at her. The wind lifted her blond hair, the silky tresses drifting in the air then falling back around her slender shoulders. She looked soft, fragile, but she had more steel and strength than any woman he had ever known. She made him want the normal life...the nuclear family. His chest tightened at the thought. Paul had never considered himself a sentimental person, not even before that day in that dark cave. But his emotions were on his sleeves now. He could no longer hold them back or pretend he cared about nothing.

He cared about this woman and somehow he had to protect her.

She hung up the telephone and started toward him, her expression grave...frightened. She was very afraid.

He was afraid.

"He's going to contact a friend in the Tennessee Bureau of Investigation and get us some backup."

She peered into Paul's eyes and said the rest, "He said we should be extremely careful."

Paul straightened from his casual stance. "He's right, you should—"

She held up a hand, ending his protest before he could actually launch it. "The answer is no. Where you go, I go. If we die trying to expose this nightmare…we'll do it together."

* * *

It was late when they got back to Paradise. Jill could feel the tension in the air as thick as the humidity and every bit as suffocating. It was as if the evil that waited knew she and Paul were coming.

The streets were quiet. There was very little traffic. She wondered as they passed house after house if those inside had any idea what was happening around them. They sat in their quiet little houses, the lights on, the television blaring, while some lab technician just a few miles away determined the genetic make-up of their future offspring. Did the conspiracy end with MedTech and LifeCycle? Or had it spread to the regular clinics, like the one in Tullahoma where Sarah Long had gone for female health care as she and Paul suspected? Hundreds, maybe even thousands of patients, completely unaware and trusting their physicians to serve them with compassion and integrity.

How would she ever be able to go to a physician or a hospital again and assume that all was as it should be? What did they do with the vials of blood they drained...what had been added to seemingly helpful medications?

Even if she and Paul survived this night and exposed the evil in Paradise, the nightmare would only be beginning for many. The innocence of all the unsuspecting ones shattered. Suddenly those nightmares she'd had as a kid made sense. Dark corridors with pipes snaking overhead. Whispers and moans. Jill shuddered and pushed the memories aside.

Paul rolled through town, taking his time, too smart to risk drawing attention. When they were two blocks from Connie's townhouse, he parked the Land Rover.

"We'll approach from the trees at the back of the houses. We don't want to be seen on the street."

She nodded. At this point, everyone was a suspect, even harmless neighbors.

Paul reached into the glove box and retrieved a small penlight, then set the vehicle's dome light to the off position. When he opened the driver's side door no telltale light blinked to life. Jill slid out into the moonlit night and hugged her arms around her middle to ward off the chill. It was a balmy night, ninety degrees according to the bank's thermometer they passed only a minute or so ago. But the chill had nothing to do with the climate. It was deep inside her. She surveyed the trees over the rooftops of the long row of townhouses up ahead. She prayed this would not be the last place she ever went with Paul.

"Stay close behind me," he said moving around to her side of the Land Rover.

It was too dark to see him clearly, but she could just make out the lines of his face. "Wait," she said, pleaded really. She needed one more moment with him before…before they plunged headlong into whatever waited inside.

He turned toward her, moved in closer, chasing away that awful chill. "I wish you'd stay out here."

She shook her head. "I'm not afraid to go with you, that's not why I asked you to wait."

He moved closer still, until his body brushed hers. She inhaled sharply and savored the essence of Paul Phillips one more time. How she wanted to get to know this man better. A few days would never be enough time.

And she wasn't about to risk death without telling him.

She'd made far too many similar mistakes in her life. She wouldn't make this one.

"I know you didn't want to take this case." She peered up at him in the moonlight, feeling his strong body all around her as he braced his powerful arms on the vehicle on either side of her. "I couldn't let you go. I needed you to help me with all this. But it's different now" big breath "I can't let you go because you mean a great deal to me—beyond all this insanity...I care about you." She shrugged and reached way down deep for her courage. "I wanted you to know."

The silence dragged on for several beats with him just looking at her, searching her eyes as if he feared she might retract her words.

When she could bear the tension no longer, she added, "I'm not asking for a commitment here and it's all right if you don't feel the same way about me. I just wanted you to know so if for some reason..."

"The feeling is mutual." He leaned down... almost in slow motion...and kissed her. It ended way too fast, but even in those fleeting moments she lost her breath, felt the truth in his words.

Then he let her go and disappeared into the darkness of the trees. She followed, praying that God would grant her just one more miracle.

The miracle of life.

When they reached the small patio size yard behind Connie's townhouse he stopped abruptly and leaned close to her. "Someone's in there," he whispered against her ear.

Her heart pounded so hard she couldn't possibly breathe. Jill followed as he eased closer, past the partition that divided the small patches of lawn. The bedroom window was raised, the screen torn away. Light spilled into the yard.

What if they came out the same way?

Fear stormed through her veins as she scanned the area for some place to hide. A patio table and two chairs were the only source of cover close by.

Paul flattened against the back of the house and eased closer to the window, Jill duplicated his movements. She could hear voices now. Two distinct male voices. They were arguing.

"There's no place else to look. The little bitch lied to us."

"Does that surprise you?" the other man growled. "She wants Jillian Ellington to get her hands on it first."

"We'll just have to make sure that doesn't happen."

Shivering at the menace in their voices, Jill eased closer to Paul.

"This is a waste of time," the first man groused. "Let's find out what he wants us to do now."

The second man said something agreeable.

Paul motioned for her to move back. They eased away from the window, not making a solitary sound. Where Connie's townhouse and plat of grass met the next one, he pushed her into a narrow gap between the two patio partitions. He squeezed in after her. She tried not to consider that spiders and other small critters loved places like this.

A moment later the men were climbing out through the bedroom window. Jill didn't dare breathe as the two moved past their position.

Long minutes later, when it was apparent they were gone, Paul eased out of their hiding place. He pushed her back when she would have followed. He moved in the direction the men had disappeared and she had to bite her lips together to keep from calling out to him.

Her heart thumped harder and harder in the darkness. She strained to hear any sound. The seconds ticked by like hours. If she moved, the sound might somehow give him away.

Finally, when the tension grew unbearable, she had to move. Thankfully, he appeared.

"Come on," he whispered.

Weak with relief, she obeyed. She swiped at her clothes, making sure she had no unwanted hangers-on. Paul hoisted her through the same window the two men had used. The interior of the townhouse was dark now. Her soul ached with the knowledge that Connie had died here.

God, she did not want to die here.

She didn't want to die at all, at least not anytime soon. She thought of the way Paul had made love to her when she so desperately needed him. She didn't want that to be the first and last time. She wanted to spend the rest of her life getting to know him.

Paul used the small shaft of light from his penlight to guide them. Kelly said the flash drive containing the files was sealed in plastic and then tucked between two slices of bread about midways in a loaf on the kitchen counter. Each week when Connie bought a fresh loaf, she'd transferred the files.

No one would ever think to look there.

Jill smiled at her old friend's ingenuity.

With Paul leading, they moved through the bedroom, into a short hallway and then into the living room. The narrow beam of light roved over a television set. The screen saver on her computer flickered, flashing a dim glow across the desk where it sat. Paul shifted right and the stream of light fell over a dinette table that separated the small kitchen from the living room. On the counter was an untouched loaf of bread.

Moments later he had the flash drive in his hand.

Her gaze met his in the faint glow of light, her heart thundering. "We can go now, right?"

"I have to do one thing first."

She didn't like the sound of that. "We should get out of here."

He inclined his head in the direction they'd come. "Keep watch at the window. I have to use her computer. It won't take long. I'll be right there."

Fear screaming inside her, she relented. What choice did she have? It wasn't like she could make him go. Arguing would only use up precious time. She moved into the dark bedroom and took up a position by the window. For courage, she clung to his promise. *I'll be right there.* He hadn't let her down yet.

A smile trembled across her lips. Richard had been right. Paul was very special. And he was most definitely the hero...the miracle she had needed.

A loud crash sounded at the front of the house.

Jill whirled toward the open bedroom doorway. Light spilled into the hall from the living room. Bright light.

Voices.

Male.

At least three.

Fear paralyzed her.

Paul's low voice.

The sound soothed her, she relaxed...started to move toward the door away from the window and any possibility of escape. She didn't care. She had to help Paul if he was in trouble.

An explosion.

The sound jarred her to a stop.

Another.

Then another.

She frowned.

Not explosions.

Gun shots.

She rushed down the hall...into the living room.

Paul lay on the floor. Her heart sank as the horror of what she was seeing assimilated in her brain.

Three wounds leaking blood. Chest. Abdomen. Shoulder.

Oh God.

"Grab her!"

Only then did Jill remember the other voices she'd heard.

The closest goon grabbed her. *Dark clothes...ski mask and gloves.*

A sob choked off all possibility of speech or sound. She reached for Paul. The bastard jerked her back.

"Get the flash drive and dump his body."

Jill fought the man's hold...stared at Paul. Willed his chest to rise.

He wasn't breathing.

The blood-curdling scream lodged in the back of her throat burst free.

A hand covered her mouth.

Something pricked the skin on her shoulder.

Darkness slowly closed in around her.

But she no longer cared.

Paul was dead.

If we die…we'll do it together.

She prayed for death.

CHAPTER SEVENTEEN

Blackness.

Pain.

Thick…thick layers.

A damp cloth swiped over dry, brittle lips.

A cool hand moved efficiently over bare skin.

Pungent, antiseptic smells.

Fatigue.

Blackness.

"Vitals have remained stable the last twenty-four hours?"

Male voice.

Push through the darkness…the pain. *Got to wake up.* One thick, heavy layer at a time.

"Steady improvement."

Female.

"Looks like John Doe is going to make it after all," the man said. "I guess miracles do happen."

Footsteps…fading.

Paul plunged upward, fighting his way through the cottony blackness…ignoring the steadily increasing pain.

His eyes opened.

Light. Too bright.

He clenched them shut again.

The rasp of rubber soles nearby. "Send the doctor back to 515, he's waking up." The female voice.

Pain.

Damn.

"Now that wasn't very polite," the woman scolded gently.

Had he spoken out loud?

Paul forced his eyes open.

He groaned.

"Welcome back, John." The nurse bending over him smiled.

"Not John," he muttered, his voice rusty, his throat dry.

She patted his shoulder. "We know your name isn't John, but you had no ID when you arrived and you were unconscious. So we've been calling you John Doe, our miracle man."

He blinked, a tear slipping from his left eye. There was something he needed to remember. "Where am I?"

"You're in Huntsville, Alabama. Don't you worry, we're taking very good care of you."

"He's awake?"

Male voice.

"Yes, Dr. Niemann. And he knows his name isn't John," the nurse proclaimed.

What the hell was he doing here?

"I don't understand," Paul muttered and tried to moisten his cracked lips.

The nurse prodded his lips with the tip of a straw. He drew deeply. The water was soothing.

"Tell us your name, young man." The doctor had gray hair. Sixty, maybe, but still full of piss and vinegar if his firm expression was any indication. He studied Paul closely. "We thought we'd be taking you out of here feet first. A fellow as determined to live as you, should certainly remember his name."

"Paul…Paul Phillips." It was easier to talk now. Not much, but a little. "How did I get here?" He glanced around the room, not inclined to move his head for fear or rousing the pain radiating just beneath the surface. Nothing looked familiar.

"A couple of teenagers found you in a ravine. They thought you were dead. And so did we when you first arrived. You'd been shot three times."

Three consecutive blasts echoed. He flinched at the memory. Felt the burn and the impact as the metal pierced his flesh. He went down. A scream. Then blackness.

Jill.

Paul sat straight up, pain roared through him, almost sending him back into the darkness. "I have to get outta here," he said through clenched teeth. The pain was fierce.

Screw the pain.

He had to get to Jill.

"I have to get out of here," he repeated. Why wasn't anyone paying attention? They just stared at him.

"You should lie back down, Mr. Phillips." The doctor was forcing him down onto the bed. "You can't be moving around. Not yet."

Paul grabbed him by the arm and stared straight into his startled gray eyes. "I have to get out of here, dammit. They'll kill her."

The doctor glanced across the bed, nodded.

Paul blinked looked to his left. The nurse injected something into his IV tube.

"No!"

Too late. He could feel the sear of the medication—tranquilizer probably—as it sped through his veins.

"Mr. Phillips, I know you're overwrought. As soon as you're well enough the police will be back to take your statement, but right now, you must rest. You've been on the brink of death for days."

Paul swallowed, grogginess already overtaking him, reducing the savage pain in his body. "How long...how long have I been here?"

"Five days," the doctor said. "Three of which we were certain you wouldn't live."

With the last vestiges of his strength, Paul clamped his fingers onto the man's arm once more when he would have walked away. "Please," he whispered, unable to speak any louder now. "You have to help me. Call Tom Cuddahy with the FBI. He'll know what to do. Please...call him...tell him I'm here..."

"Poor bastard."

Those two words followed Paul back into the blackness.

* * *

Jill lay on the small, thin cot, her thoughts wandering aimlessly. She relieved every moment she and Paul had spent together.

Tears welled instantly at the memory of those final moments. She'd watched two of those men carry him away. His body lifeless, blood darkening his shirt to a terrifying crimson color. Their orders had been to dump *his body*.

Jill prayed each day that the help Richard promised to send would figure out where she was. She no longer cared about freedom, she wanted revenge. She wanted the men who had killed Paul to die.

She wanted to kill them herself.

For six days she had waited and no help came.

But, she refused to give up. Richard would not fail her. And she would not fail Paul. Richard would insist the police keep looking.

She sobbed as she thought of what might have become of her sister. The ruthless sons of bitches who'd brought her here had turned her over to even more sinister people. A man and a woman. They assured Jill that, unlike their associates, they didn't use brute force to accomplish their goals, they used a much more civilized method. One shot of sodium pentothal and she'd told them exactly where to find the rest of her family.

She'd heard nothing about Kate or Cody or her mother since the interrogation. She prayed they were safe and in one of these rooms too. She had seen others. Mostly children. She shuddered at the concept of what they were doing with the children. She had to find a way to get out of here. To save those children and her family.

So far there hadn't been a single opportunity to escape except when she slept and even then those old nightmares from her childhood haunted her. Anytime she was allowed out of the cell she was escorted by two men to whatever place they wanted her. It was the same every day. A food and drink tray was brought to her morning, noon and evening, and at least once per day there was a trip to the lab. They drew blood or took a urine sample. They'd even taken spinal fluid again. Jill hoped they were working to help her sister, but that would imply these people were good in some way and they weren't.

Her cell was much like one in a prison, only cleaner and more modern. The wall that defined her space from the corridor beyond was transparent, but something much tougher than glass. She'd tried repeatedly to shatter it as she'd seen Paul do the day they were trapped in Kate's burning house. Men and women wearing white lab coats or all white uniforms walked the corridor all hours of the day and night. The cell was maybe nine by nine. There was a toilet and a sink, the rudimentary cot where she lay and nothing else. There had been a chair, but it was gone now. She'd thrown it at the glass-like wall too many times. No television, no magazines, no books. She wore a white gown and nothing else.

Something like the small eye of a camera peeked at her from the ceiling. She no longer cared if they watched her. Her only will to live came from anger and vengeance.

She hadn't seen anyone she recognized. Not the goons who'd brought her here and not the man and woman who'd interrogated her. No one spoke to her. Not even when she ranted at them or begged for help as they passed her cell. One of the children had glanced at her but the little girl's escort had quickly urged her away.

For all she knew she could be on a whole other planet. But she had a sneaking suspicion that she was in Paradise, somewhere at MedTech.

She closed her eyes and pushed away the awful reality. She lost herself in memories of making love with Paul. The feel of his hands on her body. The smell of his skin.

The sound of the door unlocking jerked her head up. A man, wearing the typical white garb, opened the door to her cell and stepped back for someone to enter. Her breath stalled in her lungs as anticipation roared through her.

Senator Wade.

Confusion dumbfounded her for a moment. Was she in some sort of hospital? A psych ward like Kate had been in only at some other hospital? That would explain several things. Including the senator's sudden appearance. She supposed her tantrums had lent credibility to her need to be here. If the senator had come to help her…

Hope welled in her chest. Maybe he was here to help.

Maybe Richard had sent him.

She sat up. "Senator Wade. Thank God you're here."

Whatever she'd thought she saw in his eyes turned immediately to fury. "Do you realize how close you came to destroying us?"

Her hopes plummeted. He was part of it. She shook her head and sagged against the wall, drawing her knees up to her chest. "Just go away. I don't want to hear anything you have to say."

"Due to no effort on your part Kate and Cody are fine, but because of you, because of all that you did, your mother is dead."

For days now, Jill was certain they could do nothing else to hurt her.

She'd been wrong.

Grief ravaged her. Like a wounded animal she cried out with the agony of it, rocked herself gently as she alternately sobbed and keened, her face pressed against her knees. She had done this. Oh, God. She had done this.

He waited for her bout of hysteria to subside and when she looked at him again, he said. "We're not going to kill you, at least not right away. You're far too important to our work."

She waved a shaky hand. "Just tell me," she said, her spirit broken. "Tell me what this all means.

Surely I deserve that much respect—if I'm so important to your work."

Like any politician given the floor, he became animated, took full benefit of the opportunity to revel in the sound of his own voice.

"Not that you deserve anything, but I'm feeling generous."

Jill got distracted for a moment with the many ways she'd like to watch him die.

"Forty years ago two brilliant medical minds came to this country looking for a place to further their research. After they arrived in America, they were joined by a third man. It took this team of combined genius two years to find the perfect place to begin."

"Paradise," she offered with a dry laugh.

He smiled that oily expression politicians had down to a science. "Oh, yes. Paradise, the perfect place, literally and figuratively. You have to understand that these men were far ahead of their time. They knew people would not be predisposed to their views. Motivation would be required."

"Benford Chemical," she guessed, stealing his thunder. She and Paul had figured that out days ago. Pain rippled through her at the thought of him. He was dead and that, too, was her fault.

Ignoring her, he went on, "I was the one they approached with the concept, I saw that it happened. But it was a slow process. Once Benford was seduced into producing the new chemicals, the side effects took time to take their toll."

She shook her head in resignation. How original. "And what did you get out of this?"

He smiled. "The promise of a senate seat."

Jill had to turn away. She couldn't bear to look into those selfish eyes any longer. He'd sold out his town for the mere price of a senatorial seat. She might have been able to generate some forgiveness if the action he'd taken had been on impulse in his youth and then he'd regretted it. But this plan had been in place for years before final implementation. He'd had plenty of time to rethink his actions. Thank God he didn't have any children. The last thing the planet needed was more of his kind of legacy.

"When the others, your father included, discovered what had happened, well let's just say that it made them much more receptive to our ultimate plan."

Jill barely listened during the next few minutes. She and Paul had already concluded the greater part of what he had to say. It was just as her mother had confirmed. Jill did learn that less than a dozen prominent citizens of Paradise knew the truth. Of those, with the passage of time, the number had dwindled to five. Four, he amended, when he recalled her mother was no longer with them.

She wanted so badly to hurt him. The desire was a palpable thing, breathing, growing inside her. Now she understood how her sister had been able to murder her husband. Anyone who had this low a regard for humanity deserved to die.

"You can't imagine the kind of money involved in this business. It continually amazes me what people will pay for the promise of a perfect child…a little gift that God has failed to provide. Our work is currently limited to the northeastern portion of the country, but we'll be branching out soon." He smiled. "If I make that happen, I'll be looking at a special advisory post in Washington in the very near future. No one will be able to stop us. It's the beginning of a new era." His laughter boomed in the confined space. "Really, what have we been waiting for? We can customize every other thing in our life, why not our children?"

Finally, a new reason to live. Jill wanted to make sure none of that happened. She wanted to bring all of MedTech down, starting with this man.

"What about the three original geniuses," she urged, suddenly feeling compelled to learn all she could. "Where do they fit into all this?"

"Unfortunately, one passed away," he said solemnly. "The other two oversee from a distance now. Karl actually ran the day-to-day operations. He has, as you can imagine, been replaced by another great mind. With our superior benefits packages we recruit the most brilliant in the field from all over the world."

"What kind of experiment or genetic tampering was performed on my sister…and me?" She was relieved to know that Kate and Cody were all right. She had sensed that Kate was, at the very least, since they continued to take blood and other samples from her. "I know Cody is a clone or has been cloned. I just don't know what you did to us."

The senator looked surprised that she'd figured out that much. "You have been a busy bee." He straightened his expensive suit jacket. "But I tell you what, I'll let your next visitor answer these questions for you." He started to leave but hesitated. "You know, you should thank me. Chief Dotson wanted to terminate you and Phillips right from the start and I wouldn't allow it. We needed you."

Jill clenched her teeth to hold back her response. If he wanted a show of gratitude he could just wait until hell froze over.

The guard who had remained nearby, unlocked the door again to allow the senator's departure. Jill sat up straighter, waiting to see who would walk through the door next.

Richard Lawton.

"Richard?" The name was barely a shadow of sound. Her heart rushed into her throat.

"I hope they're treating you well."

She scrambled off the cot and to her feet. This couldn't be. She surely heard him wrong. "How can you be a part of this? You're an attorney...a law professor. My friend."

"When the Manning brothers came to this country they were looking for someone who could keep them out of trouble with the law. Someone who knew the system. They didn't need another medical mind." He smiled and for the first time she realized how sinister that smile was. "They needed me. I've always been there, watching from a distance as Wade said."

She shook her head, refusing to believe. Her last hope was dashed.

"I made sure your application to Ole Miss was accepted. I agreed to oversee you there. Take you under my wing, so to speak." He laughed. "I must say, you threw them all for a loop. They expected you to stay in Paradise where they could monitor your progress. But you had plans of your own."

Suddenly it all made sense. He'd recommended a place for her to live. A doctor when she needed one. What a fool she'd been. Now she understood why every time she went into the doctor's office they always insisted on taking a blood sample. She'd been too busy to wonder back then. Between work and her studies, she'd barely kept her head above water. But Richard had always been there, supporting her in any way she needed.

Fury exploded inside her. "Did they tell you to seduce me too?"

His smile was tight, but there, just beyond the condescension she'd never noticed before. "No, that was a perk I opted to take advantage of on my own."

"You bastard. You killed my father and my mother."

He nodded. "We did kill the Judge. He became a liability. But your mother killed herself. She tried to prevent our men from bringing Kate and Cody back. Her death was unavoidable."

That agony welled inside her again. "What about the people in the village?"

He shook his head sadly. "There was a terrible fire. Several of the inhabitants died. The others escaped into the mountains."

Jill would bet Willa Dean was one of them who had escaped. There was something about her. Like Paul, she saw things...felt things.

"Did you come here to gloat?" she demanded, wishing she had a weapon—anything to cause injury.

"I chose to deliver certain news personally."

She stilled, her knees going weak. Fear constricted her throat. She wasn't sure she wanted to hear any news he had to pass on. But she had little choice.

"As you well know I encouraged you to seek out Paul."

The sound of his name was like a stab deep into her heart.

"I did that because he was one of ours as well and I wanted the two of you to join forces."

That revelation nearly floored her. "What?"

"He was an identical twin. His twin's life was terminated early during development in hopes of enhancing the surviving twin. There were a few other manipulations but I won't bore you with those." Richard folded his arms over his chest and rocked back on his heels. "The outcome was nothing short of spectacular. His advanced cognitive level and heightened sensory perceptions were unparalleled. He was very special. It wounds me deeply that he had to die."

Jill threw herself at him, pummeled his chest with her fists. She screamed at him, called him every despicable name she knew. He restrained her efforts easily, until she was too weak to fight anymore. Finally, she jerked free of him and curled up on the cot once more, her back against the wall.

"Get out of here," she demanded hoarsely. "I can't bear to look at you."

"You think you are the only one grieving?" he demanded sharply. He moved toward her and sat down on the cot. She scooted as far away as possible. "Paul was my son."

A sob tore from her throat. "No!" She refused to believe him. She and Paul hadn't spoken of his parents...but he'd certainly never claimed Richard.

"I was the sperm donor and a young law student I once knew intimately was the egg donor. She agreed to surrogate the pregnancy as well." He stroked his chin a moment. "You see the initial process of conception had to be performed repeatedly in the lab until the right genetic manipulation created the enhancements we hoped for. Once the split zygote had developed into embryos in her womb, the life of one twin was terminated." He shrugged. "Unfortunately the surrogate had to be terminated once the birth was accomplished since she started asking questions. Paul was adopted by a loving couple who served their purpose until he was old enough to survive on his own, and then they were disposed of."

Her heart ached for Paul. Now that she looked more closely at Richard, she did note vague similarities. Square, chiseled jaw. Dark hair and eyes. She shuddered. Paul deserved better than to be compared to this evil man.

She glared at him with complete hatred. "Weren't you worried that Paul would figure this all out once he delved into my sister's case? He could have exposed everything."

Richard laughed softly. "It was worth the risk. I needed him to fall for someone...to trust someone. The situation with Kate just presented the right opportunity that's all. You performed marvelously, by the way. He fell completely for you. Put your safety before all else which ultimately cost him his life."

When Jill would have ranted at him again, he stopped her with an uplifted palm. "But, not to worry." Richard smiled down at her. "All is not lost. My hopes were completely fulfilled. Your most recent blood test revealed that you're pregnant. I know my son was the father."

Startled, her arms wrapped protectively around her middle. Her body trembled so hard she could scarcely remain sitting upright. No matter how often she thought she'd cried herself out, she learned that she had not. *She was carrying Paul's child.* She shook with the force of her grief. If only he was here...just for one moment so he would know. But wait...

She drew in a deep breath, grabbed her wits with both hands. "That's impossible." She shook her head. "I've been on the Pill for years." She'd never missed a period. Not once.

Her old friend laughed at her, just as the senator had. "Dear, dear, Jillian. I've been keeping up with you for years." He gave her a pointed look. "I know everything there is to know about you. Those pills you take everyday are not for birth control. We took care of that little issue months ago. We'd already planned to get the two of you together, recent events simply made that happen sooner than we'd anticipated."

Her heart started to pound. Then it was true. She was pregnant and she was *here*. "I hope you rot in hell." She pressed her hand to her trembling lips, tried to hold back the sobs that rocked her once more.

Richard stood to go. "I'll check on you from time to time, Jillian. Please take good care of yourself. I'd like my grandson to come into this world as healthy as possible. I have enormous plans for him."

She scrubbed at her face with the back of her hand. She had to find a way to stop him…to get out of here before her baby was born. But first she had to know one thing. "Wait!"

He paused at the open door where the guard stood poised to lock it once more.

"Yes?"

"I need to know what you did to Kate and to me? What kind evil was imposed upon us?" She prayed it was nothing that would harm the new life she carried.

He smiled patiently. "I'm sorry. I thought you knew. You are merely as God intended. Until now you've served as nothing more than the control."

"And Kate?" her voice quaked, her stomach fisted in knots.

"As soon as we've equalized her neurotransmitters or some such malady, she's going to make history despite the annoying infertility problem. We can live with that minor defect." His smile widened to that sinister expression she now associated with the man. "Kate is our first human clone."

Shock rumbled through Jill like an earthquake, the tremors deep under the surface, the fault line across her heart.

Long moments after Richard had gone, the reality finally sank in. *She's going to make history.*

Jill's eyes closed and her breath caught on a sob. Paul's child was growing inside her. Whatever she did from this moment forward, she had to be very careful. She could do nothing that would risk this child.

She'd lost Paul. She would not lose his child.

* * *

He had to wake up.

As if coming from deep within the bowels of the ocean, Paul swam upward, through the murky water, the need to breathe a searing pain in his chest.

But he couldn't stop...had to swim harder... faster.

Jill needed him...he could feel it. She was waiting for him to come and rescue her.

He broke through the surface.

He gasped, sucking in all the air he could.

His eyes popped open.

Blinding light.

He blinked, tried to focus.

The hospital.

Alabama.

Shot.

He looked at the IV bottle hanging on the pole to his left and remembered the nurse had sedated him that way. Gritting his teeth he ripped the tape from his skin and jerked out the IV needle.

"Whoa there!"

Paul swiveled his head to the right.

Tom Cuddahy pushed out of a chair and rushed to his bedside. "I think you needed that thing, buddy."

Thank God.

"We have to get out of here." Paul pushed upward, pain spearing through him. He ignored it, swinging his legs over the side of the bed.

"Wait now. The doctor said—"

"I don't care what the doctor said!" he roared. "They've got her. I have to get back to Paradise."

"Okay, let's be calm a minute." Tom used both hands stop-sign fashion to make his point. "Just take a breath and bring me up to speed."

"You got the files?" The mere effort of holding himself upright took every ounce of strength Paul possessed. His breath was ragged from it. He'd sent a copy of Connie Neil's files to Cuddahy's email address before attempting to leave the townhouse. That was the reason he'd gone back into the living room while Jill waited at their escape route. Was probably the reason he'd gotten shot but it was a risk he'd had to take.

"Got'em," Tom confirmed. "Had a hell of a time figuring out what it all meant. But I got there."

"They've got Jill. We have to go after her."

"Here's the deal," Cuddahy said carefully, staying in front of Paul so that he wouldn't jump out of the bed. "I've got a team in Paradise already. They're keeping an eye on MedTech, LifeCycle and the local brass. But I haven't made a move. I was waiting on you." He shrugged. "The files are incriminating in themselves, but I had a hunch there was more and I didn't want to tip your hand if you had one." He exhaled a big breath. "I have to tell you, I did some sweating until I heard from that doctor yesterday. He said he almost didn't call…thought you were just delusional. Hell, I had no idea where you were, man. I had you figured for dead."

"So did I." Paul frowned, trying to recall how much time had passed. "How long have I been here?"

Cuddahy didn't answer right away. Paul glared at him.

"A week."

Paul swore. Jesus Christ she could already be… No! He refused to believe Jill was anything but alive and waiting for him. "How is that possible? I lost all concept of time."

"You were so combative they had to keep you sedated most of the time. And the doctor thinks you need to stay at least another week. He says you're lucky as hell to be alive. All three bullets nipped something vital. The staff around here's calling you the miracle man. You'd about bled out when they brought you in. The ER folks say you were living on sheer willpower."

"I'm leaving now." Paul readied to scoot off the bed. "Get out of my way, Cuddahy. I'm going after her."

He shook his head, empathy in those serious green eyes. "I understand how you feel, but the fact is she's probably dead already. I know you don't—"

"She's alive," he told him flatly. "I know it."

Cuddahy considered his statement, then backed up a step. "Well, I guess we're out of here then. I've got another team ready to scramble. We'll go at'em from all sides."

Tom was one of the few people who understood how Paul could sense things. And even he didn't know everything.

No one did…except Jill.

"I'll need some clothes," Paul said as he gingerly eased off the edge of the bed.

Cuddahy pointed to the bag sitting next to the chair. "I'm beginning to think I might be psychic too."

"And a gun."

The demand startled Paul almost as much as it did Cuddahy. He hadn't touched a gun in years. But he wanted one now.

"I can handle that," Cuddahy assured him.

"We have to hurry."

The nurses tried to stop them, but Cuddahy simply waved his badge and rolled Paul away in a wheelchair. He was weak as hell. He needed to conserve every ounce of strength he had for when they arrived in Paradise, which wasn't going to be soon enough for him.

The one thing that kept him going was the complete certainty that she was alive…waiting for him.

CHAPTER EIGHTEEN

It was late in the next day when Jill's cell door opened again. Though she had no clock, she'd learned to judge the time by the comings and goings in the corridor. She raised up as Richard stepped inside, he looked frazzled.

"Come with me," he ordered.

She shook her head. "Forget it." She moved to the corner of the cot, as far away as possible. How could she have let this man touch her? The thought made her sick at her stomach.

He manacled her arm. "I said come with me." He withdrew a revolver. "I didn't risk coming back in here for nothing. That child you're carrying is my retirement package."

Her heart lurched. *The baby*. Oh God. She couldn't do anything that would risk the baby. But if she fought him…"Okay, okay. Just be careful with that thing."

He dragged her from the cell, keeping one arm around her neck, effectively pinning her to him. They moved down the long white corridor until reaching a bank of elevators where he stabbed the call button. Jill looked at the numbers above the cars. There appeared to be eight stories above ground and four sublevels. She blinked, looked again. Four underground floors? She wondered if only those with the right clearance even knew these floors existed. Probably.

She swallowed tightly. She had to escape. But she couldn't do anything as long as she was a prisoner herself. She now knew with complete clarity how her mother had felt all those years. She'd done whatever necessary to protect her children. Now, Jill was sentenced to the same fate.

The elevator's floor indicator stopped on sublevel four. She shuddered, feeling as if she were in a missile silo. Her lungs were suddenly hungry for more air.

He punched the button for S1. The first underground floor. The claustrophobia that had gripped her eased as they moved upward. The doors glided open on S1.

This level looked vastly different from S4, where she'd been held prisoner. Looked like your typical basement storage area. Nothing but long, deserted hallways lined with doors.

"Where are we going?" she finally had the presence of mind to ask. Her legs felt wobbly it had been so long since she'd walked any distance.

"It seems we have uninvited company and I plan to make sure you and I are not discovered." His

BONE DEEP

fingers tangled in her hair and he jerked her around to face him. "Behave yourself and I might just let you live. As much as I want the grandchild you're carrying, I want to keep my freedom more."

She nodded obediently. His fingers loosened in her hair, the weapon lowered slightly. When he would have started forward again, she kneed him in the groin with all her might. He dropped like a rock. She ran like hell. She had no idea where she was going. She only knew that she had to get away from him...from this place.

She heard him swearing. He was probably getting to his feet already. He had the gun. She had to protect the baby.

The corridor ended abruptly. She rushed through the last door on the right.

Darkness greeted her. She felt her way along the wall. Another door on the right, she took that one. It closed with a thud behind her.

A long, creepy corridor lay before her. The low wattage security lighting kept it from being completely dark. The corridor, tunnel, she decided on closer inspection, stretched forward for as far as she could see. She ran, refusing to slow. He would be coming right behind her.

If she could just get away she could bring help. She didn't have the files, but she wouldn't stop until she found Paul's friend at the Federal Bureau of Investigation and then she would make him believe her one way or the other.

Footsteps echoed somewhere behind her.

317

Without daring to look back, she pressed her hand to her belly and ran faster.

* * *

"Look, man, I think you'd better sit down," Cuddahy suggested.

"Back off," Paul muttered. Yeah, the pain had him sweating profusely and he felt confident he was as white as a sheet, but he wasn't stopping until he found Jill. They'd been searching for hours. The afternoon was fading into evening. No one had been allowed to leave either of the facilities, MedTech or LifeCycle.

They'd found nothing. Yet, Paul knew she was here. He could feel her. The moment he walked into the building, he sensed her. She'd never left Paradise. *She was here.*

And she was alive.

Somehow those few days they'd spent together had created a bond that went deeper than any other he'd ever shared with another human being.

A crackle came over the two-way radio. "We've searched all eight floors. Nothing but labs, technicians, offices, and office personnel."

"The basement's clear too," came another report.

The LifeCycle Center was clear as well. The chief, the mayor and the senator, all of whom they had in custody at the moment, had taken the Fifth. Bastards.

Paul was ready to start his own kind of interrogation with one of them...preferably the chief.

"She's here," Paul insisted again.

"You give it a rest and I'll go through the steps with the acting CEO one more time."

Paul knew what he meant by that. Cuddahy was going to rattle the woman some more to see if she broke. She was slick, kept repeating that she knew nothing about their accusations. Paul doubted she would alter her statement but she might just let something slip.

His knees near the point of buckling, he rested his hip on a desk. Swiping his damp brow with the back of his hand, he studied the security monitors again. MedTech had a hell of a security system. Cameras everywhere. Even infrared heat tracking sensors that tagged body heat.

He thought of the basement in Karl Manning's house. Fireproof...sealed off except for that one necessary hidden entry.

What if...he straightened and moved toward the single security officer left behind to operate the systems. The rest had been taken to chat rooms—Cuddahy jargon for interrogation rooms. This guy, the youngest and most cooperative, was named Lee Partin and he'd casually advised Paul that he'd like to be an FBI agent one of these days. Why not capitalize on the opportunity to facilitate the lines of communication? Paul was a pro at playing the buddy-buddy role to get information. It was part of his training...part of his background in psychology. Hell, it was simply second nature.

"There are no other floors below the basement level?" Paul asked, instinct humming a familiar tune. He was on to something.

Lee shook his head. "If there are any, I'm not aware of them, sir. The elevators and stairwells only go down one sublevel to my knowledge. But—"

Something on one of the monitors snagged his attention.

"Holy crap."

"What?" Paul demanded hoarsely. Damn he'd be lucky to stay on his feet another twenty minutes.

"We got somebody in the tunnel."

He didn't remember hearing anything about a damned tunnel. "What the hell is the tunnel?"

"Escape tunnel in case of a fire or other emergency," Lee explained. "It should be in the main floor plans. You access it from the basement level. There's been no activity until now and the sensors don't lie."

Paul had a feeling the tunnel was about more than a fire escape. "How many?"

"Two hot bodies. One advancing on the other."

Paul leaned over the screen that had Lee's attention. He winced at the pain that accompanied his every move. "How do I get there?"

"Down to S1. Take a right off the elevator." Lee wheeled around and traced the path on the floor plan spread on a nearby table. "The last door on the right, then another immediate right and you're there."

"No pass codes or keys required?" Paul asked as he strode toward the elevator.

"Nope. As an emergency exit it's never locked from the inside. Just a mile and a half of tunnel and then a ladder straight up."

"Find Agent Cuddahy, tell him where I'm headed." Paul didn't wait for Lee's response. His senses were buzzing. He knew in his gut that Jill was down there.

Lee's instructions led him right to the tunnel door. Paul stepped inside and the door closed behind him. The dank smell assaulted him at once. Then his senses homed in on the mile and a half of near darkness before him.

Panic hit hard, paralyzing him with its intensity. Fear snaked around his chest, squeezing, making it impossible to draw in a deep enough breath, hindering the rhythm of his heart. He backed against the wall for support and focused on controlling his breathing.

Dammit. This couldn't happen now. He blinked, forced himself to focus. Not now. It took him another minute to pull it together enough to move.

Please help me!

Paul gritted his teeth and banished the voice of the little girl he hadn't been able to save. He would not hear it. *You're too late to save her.* He shook off that taunting voice too. He had to focus on here and now.

He pushed off the wall and started to move. Faster, pushing past the panic, tuning out the pain, the weakness from his still healing injuries. Jill needed him. Adrenaline flowed, lending him temporary strength. He'd promised her he'd be right there when she'd wanted to flee Connie's town-house. He'd let her down. He'd let that little girl down all those years ago.

But tonight he wasn't going to let anyone down.

A scream rent the gloomy silence.

Jill.

Paul ran faster. Ignored the pain searing through his body.

All his senses focused on one goal…protecting Jill.

The tunnel took a hard left. He skidded to a stop around the corner of that ninety-degree angle. Maybe twenty yards from where he stood, a ladder soared upward disappearing into the earth, leading to the escape hatch.

A man, his back turned to Paul, was forcing Jill up the ladder. Her blond hair swayed around her shoulders as she resisted.

Careful to keep his steps silent he moved as quickly as possible toward them.

"Don't make me have to use this!" the man warned her.

Paul slowed. *Richard?* The voice was Richard Lawton's.

Son of a…

The bastard had a weapon.

Paul's heart seemed to screech to a stop.

He eased a few steps closer and assumed a firing stance. "Drop it."

Richard jerked Jill down and against him and spun toward Paul.

She cried out, her arms stretching out to him. She called his name. His heart lurched back into a frantic rhythm. If Richard had hurt her. Right now Paul didn't give a damn about the hows or whys. He just wanted Jill away from that son of a bitch.

Richard's posture stiffened. Obviously, he hadn't expected to see Paul again.

"Let her go or I swear to God I'll kill you where you stand."

"Take one more step and I'll kill *her*," Richard threatened, pressing the muzzle to her temple.

A slash of blinding light seared through Paul's skull. The image of a little girl, being held exactly that way, the muzzle boring into her temple suddenly loomed before his eyes. He shook it off. This wasn't that child...this wasn't that cave.

This was Jill.

It would be different this time.

Had to be.

Paul stared down the barrel, zeroed in on his target. "Let her go."

Richard had the audacity to laugh. "Would you really kill your own father?" He nudged Jill with the weapon. "Tell him who I am."

She shook her head, refusing to speak.

He wound his fingers in her hair and jerked her head back, grinding the barrel into her flesh. She cried out in pain. Paul's whole body contracted.

"Tell him!" Richard demanded.

"He says he's your father," she sobbed. "He killed the people who raised you, Paul."

Renewed fury surged through Paul's veins. "You're dead."

Richard just shook his head. "I know all about what happened in that cave, Paul. You told me yourself. You haven't touched a weapon since you screwed up, have you?"

Paul blinked, but forced back the panic that threatened to climb up his back.

"You had a shot, but you were too afraid of hitting the child, so you didn't take it." Richard laughed again. "And that psychopath killed her any way. A very stupid mistake, don't you agree?"

Paul tightened his grip on his weapon. "I won't hesitate this time," he warned. "Now let her go."

"Are you sure?" Richard asked smugly. "You wouldn't want to risk hitting the woman who's carrying your child, now would you?"

Tension jerked through Paul. "You're lying?"

"Am I lying?"

Jill made a wounded sound as he twisted her hair again. "He's telling the truth," she cried.

Emotions battered him as if he'd gotten caught in a hurricane. Agony roared through him and he blocked it, forcing everything inside him to still. He had to focus. Sweat dripped off his brow. *Ignore every-thing else.*

"Now," Richard said, taking his silence for surrender. "You put your weapon down on the ground and allow us to leave as planned and I'll let her live. Give me any trouble and she dies."

"I love you, Paul," Jill cried.

Her words shook him. She loved him. She was having his child. Richard was going to take her away. Paul was going to lose again and it was his fault. He was a coward. Two steps behind when it counted. Now, the woman he loved and the child they had created together were at risk and he was helpless.

"Lower you weapon!" Richard shouted, impatient.

Something snapped inside Paul. The tension drained away...the fear...all emotion vanished, bringing that stillness once more. He stared directly at Richard. "Whatever you say."

That smug smile reappeared. "I knew you'd see reason. After all, we're from the same stock. Now, lower your weapon slowly."

Paul moved into a crouch, taking his time, then he lowered his weapon one fraction of an inch at a time. The muzzle of Richard's weapon moved away from Jill just a fraction.

Paul jerked his weapon into position and pulled the trigger. The explosion echoed through the tunnel.

Time stopped.

Shocked by the unexpected impact, the weapon dropped from Richard's hand and he grabbed his shoulder. He stared in horror at the blood oozing from beneath his palm.

Jill jerked away from him.

The next shot Paul fired shattered the bastard's right knee and he crumpled to the floor, screaming and writhing in pain.

"Get his weapon," Paul managed to shout before he dropped to his knees, no longer able to stand.

Jill grabbed the gun and rushed toward him. She fell to her knees and threw her arms around him. "They told me you were dead."

"They weren't off by much but I wasn't going anywhere without you." He pressed a kiss to her forehead, then surveyed her for any injuries. "You okay?"

Her lips trembled into a smile. "I am now."

Ignoring Lawton's screams of agony, they leaned on each other and walked away.

EPILOGUE

Jill peered down at her sleeping son and smiled. His dark hair was stark against the white ruffles of the bassinet. He was perfect. Fingers, toes and nose. Perfect and absolutely beautiful. Only three months old and already he owned the heart of every female they knew.

Like father, like son.

Speaking of father. She moved to the front window and watched Paul frolicking in the yard. He tossed the ball and Cody chased it, squealing in delight, the puppy right on his heels.

Skipper, the buff colored Labrador was barely five months old, Paul Junior's first gift from his father, and already he was huge. But he was wonderful with the children, affectionate and gentle.

Jill looked out over the lovely landscape of their new home. They'd moved to Maine eight months ago. Privacy was the first requirement. Rural Maine definitely provided that. The setting was small town, though a larger city wasn't so far away.

Best of all, no one from their old lives knew they were here. Well, no one except Tom Cuddahy. Paul stayed in touch with him to get updates on the MedTech and LifeCycle situation. The criminal investigations were drawing to a close and trials would begin soon. Both corporations had been dismantled. All files and financial assets, at least all those found, seized by the federal government.

With her mother's death there was no one left in Paradise. Home was here now. Though she did occasionally think of Willa Dean and the few villagers who had managed to survive the fire. Jill had sold her childhood home and donated the proceeds to helping the villagers rebuild. It was the least she could do after what they had sacrificed for her family.

She moved to another window and watched Kate digging in the flowerbeds. Her sister did love her flowers. It was good therapy and it made her feel a sense of accomplishment. Kate was doing fine now. Whatever they'd done to her during that week she and Jill were imprisoned at MedTech, it had worked, brought her almost all the way back to her old self.

The idea that it could happen again and that no one would know what to do still worried Jill, but she tried not to dwell on it. Every week there was more news about some failure with the cloned animals in different parts of the world. Shortened life spans, accelerated aging, rare diseases. Jill avoided those programs as often as possible. She didn't want to live dreading the future. She wanted to live each day God had blessed her with to its fullest with no fear of what tomorrow held. Kate felt the same way.

A closed session of Congress had decided it would be best not to reveal to the public the full extent of MedTech's and LifeCycle's work for the protection of the victims. Those like Kate and Cody, who were clones, would never be revealed as anything other than normal humans. The remains of dozens of failed experiments had been properly buried. Even now she shuddered to think of all the children who had been sacrificed in the name of an unholy science. Agent Cuddahy had ensured the remains Chief Dotson had attempted to pass off as Cody were recovered and given an appropriate burial as well.

For now, no one outside the investigation would know the evil done in Paradise. The world would continue to believe that those things only happened in the movies or in a book.

Cody, the ball clutched to his chest, ran toward his mother. Kate opened her arms to him. Paul knelt down and scratched Skipper behind the ears. He saw Jill in the window and waved, that charming smile that lingered about his mouth more often than not these days spanning the distance between them and warming her heart.

Their life was peaceful and good.

A frown tugged at her brow. The FBI had rounded up and was in the process of prosecuting to the fullest extent of the law those involved with

MedTech and LifeCycle. Senator Wade had turned state's evidence and ratted on all his pals. Unable to stand the pressure, Mayor Hammersly had committed suicide the night after Paul rescued Jill from that dark tunnel. Richard Lawton was claiming innocence and would, knowing his legal cunning, probably find a way to get off scot-free.

Everyone had been accounted for except one man.

Jill's mother had said there were three, one American, two Europeans, who came to Paradise all those years ago. At least she thought they were European, German or Austrian she believed. Richard was the American, of course, and had referred to the other two as the Manning brothers. One had died a few years back but the other one had simply vanished. Every time Jill thought of him, a chill skittered up her spine. Was he dead by now? If not, was he off in some other city, American or otherwise, working his gruesome creation experiments?

God, she hoped not.

She moved back to the bassinet and smiled down at her precious child...her *gift*.

Some things just weren't meant to be tampered with.

No man should try to play God.

And though her life was as perfect as human life could be with all its limitations and trials, until that last man was found, Jill would always be looking over her shoulder.

And waiting…
…for the other shoe to drop.

"There are no judges,
only avengers."
Josef Mengele
The Angel of Death

A NOTE FROM
THE AUTHOR

From 1982 – 1985 my husband and I were stationed with the United States military in Berlin, Germany. During that time I came to understand the horrors of all who suffered through the cruel reign of Adolf Hitler. Hitler's desire for brutal domination and the development of a master race is a heinous chapter in mankind's history. As ugly as that chapter is, we should never forget the evil that men can do lest we doom ourselves to repeat those same mistakes.

ABOUT THE AUTHOR

Debra Webb, born in Alabama, wrote her first story at age nine and her first romance at thirteen. It wasn't until she spent three years working for the military behind the Iron Curtain—and a five-year stint with NASA—that she realized her true calling. A collision course between suspense and romance was set. Since then she has penned more than 100 novels including her internationally bestselling Colby Agency series. Her debut novel, OBSESSION, in her romantic thriller series, the Faces of Evil, propelled Debra to the top of the bestselling charts for an unparalleled twenty-four weeks and garnered critical acclaim from reviewers and readers alike. Don't miss a single installment of this fascinating and chilling twelve-book series!

Visit Debra at www.thefacesofevil.com or at www.debrawebb.com. You can write to Debra at PO Box 10047, Huntsville, AL, 35801.

11487008R00202

Printed in Great Britain
by Amazon.co.uk, Ltd.,
Marston Gate.